A LIFE IN IV ACTS

CARA MADDY

authorHOUSE®

AuthorHouse™
1663 Liberty Drive
Bloomington, IN 47403
www.authorhouse.com
Phone: 1-800-839-8640

First published by AuthorHouse 8/17/2009

ISBN: 978-1-4490-1592-3 (e)
ISBN: 978-1-4490-1590-9 (sc)
ISBN: 978-1-4490-1591-6 (hc)

Printed in the United States of America
Bloomington, Indiana

This book is printed on acid-free paper.

In loving memory of Jim, Sara, and Darcy. I know we will be together again, but I still miss you today.

And for those who have given their lives to protect the freedom that I enjoy everyday. I have never taken that for granted. Thank you.

Cara Maddy

CONTENTS

JUST BEFORE THE CURTAIN OPENS: SANDIEGO CALIFORNIA

The sun is just coming up and the sand still feels cold between his toes. It's the last week of February so the wind that is beginning to pick up has a slight chill to it, but it's still early enough that the sun should burn if off before long and he should begin to feel it's warmth soon.

Jace sits alone this morning. Miles and miles of beach, eons of deep blue ocean before him, yet he is alone. Just the brooding young man and his sketch pad. It seemed a little odd to him that on a usually busy coast line there weren't more people milling about looking for sea shells, poking at dead jelly fish, or trying to find a quiet place to be romantic. He closed his eyes, turned his face towards the rising sun and smiled at his fortune that he was being allowed to be left here to discover the day by himself.

After a few moments of silent reflection, he stood, gathered his sketch pad and moved closer to the water. He could always find peace in the nature of things. The ocean was his playground, and the sea creatures his only family. For the life that he had left, he could live it here, in these quiet moments with his art and his nature and the rest of the world could just quietly slip away.

As he began to slide his pencils across the blank page, his perfect, alone moment was disrupted by a silhouette making it's way towards him from the north end of the beach. He tried not to notice and continued with his work, but considering that they were the only two souls on the long, deserted shore line, it became distracting the closer the figure moved towards him.

Soon, the figure took the shape of a young girl about his age he would have guessed. She still wasn't close enough to see her face, but long, brown, curly hair was blowing wildly about her shoulders. She had to be a tourist since she was wearing a sweater and jeans while he was wearing black cut off shorts and, well, nothing else. He continued with his art as she approached, ignoring her, assuming she would just pass him by. He didn't want to talk. He didn't necessary feel like being particularly rude either, but he would be.

She did not pass him by. She, in fact, came right for him. She stopped in front of him and waited for acknowledgement. Jacen didn't give time of day to his staff, he would not likely give it to a stranger. She sat down in the sand beside him. She would wait.

After a long while, Jacen looked down at her annoyed. He was young and full of himself but not in the way that other young men might be. He was demanding and angry most of the time. They would have been flattered at the attention. Jacen hatted attention. Who the...her eyes were a piercing blue color that he didn't think he even carried in his art collection. Her smile, although laced with braces, which made him wince a little as he remembered the awkward phase, was genuine. Her face, although that of a strangers, was small and familiar. Something about her told him to heed her even though it went against every thing that was normal to him. She stood, sensing he was ready to talk. Or perhaps at least let her talk.

"I don't think we know each other." He stated frankly. He didn't know how to talk any other way. She seemed unmoved.

"I think that I'm here to tell you that you will get what you need and I can give it to you."

Jacen felt confused. He came from money and power. She, although cute, seemed humble, simple.

"I'm not following." He told her. "I think you've got the wrong guy." He wanted to turn away from her and continue sketching, but she reached a small, tiny hand out to touch his own. His head told him to pull away from her, and somehow, he couldn't move. Why?

"Just give me a little time. I'm not sure why I'm here or what it all means yet."

Jacen stiffened.

"Time is something I don't have."

Jacen's voice became bitting and bitter. If he were any other man or living any other life, she might be able to change him. He almost feels sorry for this Angel of Mercy. Her soft voice would be waisted on him.

When his mother had died in childbirth, he was raised being told that she would have loved him very much but in the end it had all been for the best. Better place and so forth. His father, an extremely driven and wealthy man, died at the age of 40 from congenital cardiomyopathy. Not to worry. He left Jacen everything. Including a faulty heart.

Her small hand moved from his hand to his heart.

"There is peace that passes understanding and she will give it to you. You will get a new heart. Forgiveness will come with healing."

Jacen closed his eyes and laughed aloud. Yet, when he opened them again to retort, she was gone.

Suddenly, as if he was in some kind of time warp continuum, Jacen felt a pulling. Moment, by moment, frame by frame, everything around him began to disappear. It was like watching one of his paintings being erased. First, the ocean, then the sand slid out from beneath him. When the sun blinked out and he was standing in darkness, Jacen began to hear the beeping. A steady, rhythmic beeping of his heart monitors, respirators and the hospital chirping reality. Jacen's dark eyes fluttered open and he rubbed them to look around the hospital suite where he had been the whole time. She was gone.

"We are stronger where the strain had broken us.
And there is fight in us, I know,
That it will take more than a heavy rain to silence us.
When there's so much for us."
Dashboard Confessionals from their song
'The Widow's Peak'

ACT I: SEARCH ME AND KNOW ME

SCENE I: WASHINGTON STATE, STEWART HOUSE

Vickie thought about all of her children as her youngest disappeared into the last room on the left down the hallway. She had heard it said that even from the beginning of time, from Cain and Able, Mothers had a favorite child. She had three children, all of them as different from one another as they could possibly be.

David, the first born. The beginning and the end. Long hair, dark eyes, guitar wielding boy on the brink of man hood. He, who's walk radiated rage against a force she had no understanding of because she only lived a life of godliness and God was a god of love, power and sound mindedness so where David was going felt some days like madness. Sometimes, though, when they were alone talking, then, and only then could she see the little boy he used to be and the man he could become.

CJ. Beloved by all, CJ. She could run faster than the wind and no matter how angry she made you, it was only fleeting because her ability to punish herself was far more damaging than any discipline her parents could dish out. Her laugh was infectious, and her smile, well, once, the braces came off, it would be perfect. She was too thin, but healthy. Frankly she was rarely sick at all. At newly 18, she divided her time between track, theater and music. With more friends than she knew what to do with, her parents hardly ever saw her. She always checked in, and she always came home when she was told to. CJ the responsible.

Miss Catherine the Great then came to mind and Vickie again had to suppress a chuckle. It was unfortunate for Cath that she always came

1

last in the order of things but isn't that the way of life when you're the youngest? Cath looked nothing like her siblings and they had given her a hard time for that over the years. They favored their dad and she favored her mom and so they tried to convince her she was adopted or found under a rock or any number of other lies to make her feel like she did not belong because she was a striking blonde rather than a brunette like them. These were the times that Vickie would gather Cath up in her arms to take her over just the one mile away where her grandparents ranch was. There, they would sit down with all the photo albums of when she herself was just a little girl with the same blonde hair and round face. To her credit, Catherine, for all her struggles with allergies and poor immune system, was growing up strong and independent.

No, there weren't any favorites here. Vickie loved each child with every single beat of her heart.

At that exact moment the front door swung open and there was a gust of cold February winter that rushed in followed by a waifish, shivering figure that could only be her oldest daughter, CJ. She was wearing her Pullman High School letterman's jacket, gloves, a scarf, jeans, and boots, and still she shivered. Her dad always said it was because she needed more meat on her bones. Vickie thought it was kind of cute! She shook off the snow before she stepped into the house and then shut the door quickly behind her. Contentious CJ. As soon as she saw her mother sitting at the kitchen table finishing her morning coffee, she smiled.

"Hi, Mom, I just forgot my track bag. I'm gonna grab it and go."

And with that, she raced down the hall like a greyhound. Pullman High School Greyhounds. It Suits her, Vickie Though. She stood and put her cup in the sink and when she turned around again, she was startled to see CJ already standing beside her again kissing her cheek.

"gotta go!"

"Hey! Wait! Your sister left her coat in your car, can you get it for her please?"

It's funny how a pretty little face can go from happy to furry in .5 seconds.

"Mom, I gotta go!"

"You don't have a class until 3rd period. It will only take you a minute. I would have her get it herself, but in the time it would take her to get her socks and shoes on etc, you could have gotten it and been gone. Please do this for me." Dependable CJ.

"I'll be right back."

She's gone. Before Vickie can rinse and place her coffee mug in the dishwasher, on the back of the couch is Catherine's coat and CJ's little 1976 Datsun is puttering down the street. Not a moment later, Catherine came bounding down the hallway, saw the coat and Vickie cannot suppress the grin that creeps across her face as confusion clouds Cath's brow. Cath picked up the coat and inspected it for booby traps.

"I swear I left this in CJ's car. I swear I did!" she mumbles to herself.

"Well, put it on then and lets go. And don't swear. You know better." Vickie is still smiling as she herds her youngest out the door to school. It is Monday, February 25th. One day before David's 20th birthday.

SCENE II: PULLMAN HIGH SCHOOL GIRLS LOCKER ROOM

There she is again. Look at her. The long, mousy brown hair with the curls that cannot be controlled. Her mom had said over and over that people pay money to try and have hair that looked like hers. She hoped they got their money back. She got grounded for throwing a brush at the mirror one Sunday morning before church because her hair was so out of control. Her Mom said it was just hair. She wished it belonged to anyone else! Her teeth were strait. She had been wearing the braces for a year and a half now and they only hurt right after each visit. They assured her that there was a good chance that they would come off before she left for college in the fall. Now, about the flat chest. Nothing to be done about that except move away and start stuffing her braw. Thanks so much again to David who made sure that every one at summer camp and beyond called her "Wall". The stigma of some things just stay with you. It wasn't just her, he and his friends said it to her best friend Lynn also, however, by the eighth grade, Lynn had nice big breasts. No one had called Lynn "Wall" in a very long time.

She turned sideways and looked in the mirror again. Strait, thin stream line. It made her aerodynamically faster, but less girly. One of the guys.

"CJ, We've got weigh-ins, are you coming?"

"Yeah, Be right there. Gotta get my hair up." And with that she was gone.

In the gym, CJ fell in line next to Lynn.

"Are you OK?" CJ looked quizzically at her best friend as if she hadn't a clue whatever she could be talking about. Lynn and CJ had been friends since she had been 8 and Lynn, 7. Through thick and thin, good and bad. However, as well as you may know your best friend, sometimes, there are secrets you aren't willing to admit to yourself so how can you tell her? CJ was the keep it together girl and every bodies friend girl. She never saw all the things every one else saw in her. If they all really knew how ugly she felt or afraid of disappointing them all she was, would they still be her friends? Lynn would for sure, but what about the rest? CJ made her best smile. After all, she had won a few theater awards.

"I'm right as rain!"

"CJ, You're up! Let's get your weight. Step on the scale"

CJ stepped on the scale and it registered at 113 pounds. Her height was five feet five inches. She moved on to start her weight training maxes and as a force of sheer muscle and stamina she improved from her previous by 25 to 50 pounds in each category. She liked being an athlete. She had confidence in that.

Lynn watched a little enviously as CJ went from weight machine to weight machine pushing harder and farther than she ever had. She was stronger than any of the other girls in the class. Granted she was a senior, but she was also smaller than all of them, and was more competitive with a fire buried somewhere in those dark blue eyes. On the rare occasion CJ lost a race she was gracious towards her competitors, but very hard on herself. She would spend days following training harder. Lynn wondered sometimes if CJ thought that she only found value in her speed and strength. Did she not see that she had spiritual gifts as well? That she was kind? That she was a good friend? That she had a genuine heart?

When it was over, CJ came away with the top numbers in the class... again. She was happy and She and Lynn went to the showers and off to class, CJ to drama and Lynn to Math.

"I'll see you at lunch?" CJ's eyes twinkled and she smiled, looking back over her shoulder as she walked through the theater doors.

"Not if I see you first!" And she was gone.

SCENE III: DAVID'S GIRLFRIENDS HOUSE

"I'm leaving for work David. What time are you taking off?"

The sound is coming from the kitchen, but it still feels too loud in his head. He is vaguely aware that it is Monday morning and he needs to go and take a shower, but he might still be a little drunk. Sara peeks her head around the corner of the bedroom door.

"David, I have to go, I'm going to put Rae in the car, and then I'm leaving. When are you going to work?"

"Stop shouting. I'll get up soon. I have to work at noon, then I have to play at the pub at 11:30."

Sara was fuming. For the first matter, she was not shouting, he had another hangover. And for the second, it was a weeknight and if he was out playing, he was out drinking and that meant that he would just come home, pass out and Rae would miss out on seeing him and so would she .....again!

"Fine, since you get home so late and I don't want you to wake Rae, just go to your parents house tonight. I'll see you tomorrow night for your birthday party at your grandparents. If you can be bothered to make an appearance!" And with the slamming of the front door she is gone.

David rolls onto his back and covers his eyes with his pillow. Drama, drama, drama! Between Sara's ranting, his mother's religion, his father's hypocrisy, and his sister's perfectionism, it was no wonder he follows in his father's, and his grandfather's before his legacy and tries to numb things when he can with alcohol.

It's a small town where he's good at his job as a cook at a local grill and he's good in his band. So if people will pay a little to hear him play and if they'll give him a little beer and anything else while he plays, good for him. Just don't tell his mother or his grandmother and everyone will get along fine. Does his dad know? David's pretty sure he does. He doesn't care. As recovered as Dad is now, as much as he has forgotten, David has the very sober memory of child with a drunken father who took him and his little sister to the bar and plied them with orange soda and pizza for hours so he could stay there and drink his fill. How they managed to swivel the two miles down the road home in the truck every time with out someone ending up in the ditch or dead still amazed him. Somehow CJ seemed either not to remember or to have reached a level of forgiveness for their dad that David could not manage. Not yet anyway.

David pulls the pillow off his face and slowly lifts his body that feels like it weighs the size of Ol Bleu. Ol Bleu, the faded sky blue 1973 Ford pickup truck that his father had given to him recently. It had been in the family since the early 1980's and it was loved by all. Once in the shower the hot water washes over his body and he begins to feel the life starting to trickle back into his senses.

After the shower he dresses in his favorite Metallica T-Shirt, faded jeans and tennis shoes that he never laces because bending down just gives him a headache. Then he grabs his torn coat that he refuses to let his mother replace and heads out the door into the Washington State winter abyss to nowhere or anywhere but Sara's and her rules.

SCENE IV: PULLMAN HIGHSCHOOL TRACK

"On your mark....set....GO!" CJ stood for what felt like hours while she waited as the three other members of the 4x4 relay team took their turns passing the baton and running the long, monstrous, full length of the track. She was the anchor. The last leg and final hope of getting them to the state finals again. She slowly stepped onto the track as Mary took off at a mediocre run trying to pace herself so as not to get winded when she hit the 300 mark. CJ always thought people were a little nuts for pacing themselves for a 400 meter race. It was still a sprint and no matter how fast or slow you went, it was still going to hurt when you hit the 300 mark. Most people thought she was crazy for coming out of the blocks at a full sprint, but they were always a little sorry for thinking that when she always came across the finish line ahead of the pack.

She looked back behind her and pushed a strand of flyaway curls from her dark blue eyes. She popped a piece of gum in her mouth as she saw Mary rounding the last corner, hit the 300 wall and slow to a crawl. When Mary's right foot slammed against the first arrow on the track behind her, CJ crouched down a little and reached out her left hand behind her, palm open. As soon as Mary hit the second arrow, CJ started to advance forward just a little. With a fluid motion that was like a well practiced dace move, Mary reached her right hand out and passed the baton over to CJ's outstretched left hand and when it was secured there, CJ grabbed it and ran like the wind was carrying her. Her feet moved like a cheetah and her arms pumped as if pulled by a master puppeteer. She chewed the gum in rhythm to the pounding of the Astroturf beneath her, otherwise, she had learned, she would lock her jaw and her gums would bleed when the blood came rushing back into her mouth when she crossed the finish line.

When she rounded the corner at the 300 mark it was as if she had hit a brick wall. All of the sudden, things began to move in slow motion. She could hear all of her friends shouting on the football field cheering for her, and sometimes she swore she could hear the grass moving or the whooshing of the javelin as it went flying through the air. The last 100 meters were like being in Hell, or so CJ imagined, because she couldn't imagine any place worse than a world where things moved slowly and people were in pain.   Then it was over. She was across the finish line and everyone was rushing over and cheering ,...but, here was were the rubber would meet the road. Coach Taylor walked down the track with the ominous stop clock in his hands.

"4minutes, 9seconds. Not bad girls. But you'll have to do better. That pass between Mary and CJ was perfect and I need you all to be that smooth by the end of the season. 54 seconds CJ. Any faster and you'll go back in time!"

"Cute." CJ laughed with everyone else. She was a good faker. Lynn came up behind her and gently squeezed her shoulder.

"Still haven't gotten that big 52 seconds yet?"

"52 I got. I just can't get better. I feel slow." CJ sat down on the track and reached for her toes looking for a good stretch. Lynn sat next to her and made an exaggerated, obvious roll of her eyes.

"Didn't look slow to me!"

CJ rubbed her eyes and then rolled back onto her back and looked up at the sky. It was dark and she could hardly see anything blue but she could imagine it. She hated February. It was cold and bitter here in Washington and although she had never known anything else, she had big dreams of warmer places.

"There's always someone faster, right?"

"Of course there is." Lynn confirms this. CJ stood up then and pulled Lynn up beside her and started walking towards the locker rooms.

"Don't you ever think about the fact that someone out there has to be the fastest, or smartest, or best? Why not you, Lynn? Why not me?"

Lynn thinks about this simple question with deep possibilities for a second before she turns around to answer CJ. She is gone.

SCENE V: LOCAL RETAIL STORE

J.R. stands at the surplus counter looking at the different types of pocketknives and other hardware and frowns one his famous Stewart frowns. It's not a frown so much as a scowl. He needed to find a gift for his only son's 20th birthday, but what do get for the child who speaks to you only on a need to basis? He wouldn't call his relationship with David estranged exactly. More just strained. How do you tell him not to drink when you started drinking before the age he is now? How can you pass judgment on his bad decisions when you didn't take the time to show him how to make good ones?

J.R. hadn't had a drink or even eaten foods with alcohol in them since just before David turned twelve, but at that point, it may have been too little too late for father and son to have the kind of relationship that he wanted to. Now history was beginning to repeat itself.

His own father had been a heavy drinker and smoker and when his beloved mother had died of breast and lung cancer and the early age of 42, a bitter, sad, and lonely man was left to raise 3 boys alone in a harsh Montana big sky country in the early 1950's with only the bottom of a bottle to comfort him.

If alcohol could numb his father so easily, J.R. Thought he'd give it a try so at an early age he found that there were a few things that his hard working, hard drinking father could pass along for good measure. When he and his oldest brother, Doug joined the Navy together, there was more booze and more hard work and he was good at both so that suited him.

Then he met Vickie. Oh, he had known her since she was 11. After all, Doug had married her older sister Annie and they had started a family, but somewhere along the line Vickie had caught his eye in a new way.

She was different than other women. She was smart and yet she didn't make him feel stupid for not completing his education. She was pretty in a way that came from the deepest part of her heart and shone from her bright blue eyes. At the time they were married, He knew that he loved her more than just about anything or so he believed. Over time though, it turned out, his body became more and more dependent on the booze.

They had David a year after they were married and CJ came two years after that. Soon, they joined Doug, Annie and their brood in Montana. Finding work there was hard so J.R. took a job offer in Alaska where he would be working 4 months on and 1 month off. This was a hard schedule for the whole family especially when Catherine came along 6 years after CJ. It was a lot to ask of Vickie, but it did make the drinking go down smoother and the arguing less frequent. Life went for a long time as such. Vickie and the kids went to church every Sunday and the kids resented the spankings that J.R. gave them when they got home for being bad in church when he didn't even bother to go and J.R. went to the local saloon.

Sometimes, if it was his day to pick up the kids from school, he took them to the saloon too. If he forgot he had left them in the truck, they came in to remind him that they were waiting, so rather than leave, he bought them pizza and soda and they played pool for a little while then all went home happy. Right? If he was up in Alaska, then Vickie didn't have to watch the drinking and she was at peace. Right?

By the time David was eleven, CJ was nine, and Cath was 3, J.R. was spinning out of control. David was angry with him, CJ no longer believed him when he told her he would stop, and Cath was too little to understand. Vickie, for the sake of J.R. more than anyone, stepped in and took control. While he was working in Alaska, she sent him a letter. In the letter were divorce papers and a plane ticket.

"Either sign the divorce papers and go live your life how you want to. Or get on the plane tomorrow and I will meet you at the airport with an ambulance to take you to rehab. I will be at the airport tomorrow. You chose. All My Love, Vickie"

J.R. got on that plane and never looked back. Vickie saved his life. He loves her and all of those kids more than they could ever know, but here he stood at that counter trying to find a birthday gift to make up for lost time and trying to undo what cannot be undone.

He turned around and walked out the door. None of those things were good enough for David. David was too precious too him. He'd just lost the words and the right to tell him so.

SCENE VI:SANDIEGO CALIFORNIA

"Mr. Owen, I have some news to offer you, if you are feeling strong enough to hear it."

Jace lowers his eyes away from his hospital room window where he has been staring for a day and half now, looking for whom or what, he couldn't be sure since he didn't catch her name and he's not even sure if she was ever real in the first place. She sure seemed real though. It all FELT real! The early sun on his skin, the breeze, the sound of waves crashing on the shore. When he re-creates the scene in his mind he can almost reach out and touch her pale skin and feel how soft it is. He heard her voice! He still doesn't understand what it all meant, or why she was there, or why no one else was there on an otherwise normally crowded beach. He would chalk it up to a dream except for the fact that Jace Owen doesn't dream. Never has, never will.

"Mr. Owen? Can we talk now, or shall we come back later?"

Jace turned and acknowledge the team of physicians who had been standing in the door way.

"I'd like to hear what's going on. If I'm to die today, I'd sure like to be one of the first to know about it." He wasn't being particularly mean, or sarcastic, just matter of fact.

"May, I sit?"

The Chief Resident pointed to a chair beside the bed. It was in an effort to get closer to the patient and show greater care and concern. After all, Jacen Matthew Owen was worth more than the bank that funded the hospital so he thought he should get a little more touchy-feely. He thought wrong.

"No. just stand there and tell me what's going on. I am 19 today. Will I always be 19 or will I ever seen 20?"

Some of the residents looked away at the harshness of Jace's tone. The Chief's face turned a slight shade of pink and he clenched his jaw a little and then relaxed.

"Due to you're rapidly failing condition we are moving you up the donor list, but since your blood type is B negative, there are only 2% of the population who share your type so getting a match could take some time. We are looking and trying to be optimistic. Please don't loose hope, Jacen. Do you have any questions?"

Jace crossed his arms over his chest and let his gaze fall back over to the window.

As the residents began to shuffle back out the door, The Chief resident reached out his hand and touched Jace's arm.

"How are you really doing?" It seemed strange to him that a kid with all that money and all those looks should be so utterly bitter and alone at a time such as this. No one, no matter who you are, should die alone.

"Have I had any visitors?"

"Are you looking for someone in particular? Besides the usual paparazzi and gawkers?"

Jace shrugged his shoulders and then slinked down under his covers a little farther.

"Just a girl I saw once."

"I can leave a name at the nurses station to let her in if you want." The Chief felt some hopefulness at the prospect of someone coming to see him, especially a young girl. That might be the best medicine for him right now.

"Don't know her name. Probably never see her again." The Chief shrugged as he left the room and shut the door behind him, but as the door closed and a gust of air blew past Jace, he heard a voice. It wasn't just any voice, it was HER voice.

"Where there is hope, there is peace." Jace sat strait up in his bed and began to cough.

"What does that mean? I haven't got any hope! Didn't you hear? Losing battle, rare blood! No hope, no peace!!" With his shouting comes more coughing. Soon, the nurses rush in and try to calm him and still the cough. When the panic is over and every one has left the room, Jace sits up again.

"Please come back! I need to understand. I don't see the hope or the peace."

The room is still and quiet except for the steady rhythm of the monitors that are helping to keep the death monster at bay. She is gone again.

ACT II: THE SACRIFICES OF GOD ARE A BROKEN SPIRIT

SCENE 1: THE STEWART HOUSEHOLD

Vickie was finishing her devotional and morning prayer time when she hears a thundering "crack" in the bathroom. Next, CJ is storming down the hall into her room and there is a slamming of the door. Vickie, who does not allow tantrums of any kind to be thrown, but has never been a yeller, stands calmly from her chair, sets her coffee cup in the sink, walks back to CJ's door and knocks gently. When she opens the door without invitation, because, this is, after all, her house that her children are allowed to live in, CJ, her beautiful CJ, is sitting on her bed puffy eyed and crying.

Vickie sits down on the bed next to her. If it had been anyone but CJ, Vickie would have needed an apology for the fit, but CJ was rational and there was probably a good explanation for all these tears.

Vickie sits down on the bed next to her. If it had been anyone but CJ, Vickie would have needed an apology for the fit, but CJ was rational and there was probably a good explanation for all these tears.

"So?" Was all the her mother had to say before the whole sordid story about how she was going to straighten her hair first but curl the ends just so and then it had, POOF! come out frizzy. If that wasn't enough, next she then burned her fore head and now she can't find the shirt she was going to wear so she'll be late picking up Lynn and she's never late......

Vickie gathered CJ up in her arms. 18 meant nothing at moments like this because she was still her little girl for right now even though, after her mother found her a hair clip and she realized that what she really wanted to wear was the sweater that she borrowed from a friend, she would get into her little orange car and drive off to her life that didn't include Mom and Dad.

"Now, be quiet when you leave. Dave is sleeping downstairs. He came in late last night and I think that he's taking tonight off so we're planning on a big dinner at your grandparents' house for his birthday if I can convince him to make an appearance. So be quiet."

CJ grinned that silver straight grin from ear to ear. She hadn't seen Dave in weeks and she might get to see him tonight!

" I will be quiet as a mouse, and thanks, Mom. For everything." With a hug and a kiss, everything was right as can be.

SCENE II: PULLMAN HIGH SCHOOL

CJ sat on the landing after 1ˢᵗ period and chewed on a fingernail as the bell to start 2ⁿᵈ period rang. Jeff plopped his books down.

"Hey, CJ! What's cookin'?" He shouted as he slid his back down the concrete wall to sit beside her.

"I've got serious ants in my pants today, Jeff! It's killing me!"

Every guy at Pullman high school was a pervert just like every guy at every high school every where. So CJ having said that to Jeff was an open invitation for him to say something horrifying or disgusting, but not to CJ. There was just something about her that they all respected. She wasn't preachy, but she was pure. She wasn't goody too-shoes, but she was right. She was the one that drove them all home from the parties they weren't suppose to be drinking at, but she never drank a drop. She didn't tell you not to. She said she wouldn't ever do it, and it's not so much that they couldn't talk her into it, but they just didn't want to. You just don't mess with CJ. She's the girl you hang out with, but you don't date CJ. There's safety in CJ. These were the things Jeff was thinking about as she rambled on about how it was her brother's 20th birthday today and he was home and she was here but she wanted to talk to him.

"I know I never leave school, but I don't have another class till 3rd period, so I think I might just go home and hang out with David for a little bit. I'll be back in time for my next class. I'll check in with the office first."

Then she was gone.

"I'll see you in choir!" Jeff said to her mist as she left a trail of his papers flying on the landing.

SCENE III: THE STEWART HOUSEHOLD

A small trickle of light slowly filtered through a slit in the doorway as quiet voice whispered,

"David, are you awake?" Nothing. Again,

"David, are you awake? Wake up! I'm skipping school to see you on your birthday." Yeah, right. As if CJ would ever break a rule for anyone. Nothing.

The door shuts and the room is shrouded in utter darkness again. There is a tromping up the spiral staircase and footfall in the kitchen. Silence. Then it's coming back. The sliver of light again. Then phomp, pause, phomp. Pause....is that a grape? Is CJ throwing grapes at my head? That's it!

Before she can blink, the covers on the bed are flung back, the grapes that have been tossed into the bed are recovered and CJ is running up the stairs and squealing as David is hot on her heals pummeling grapes at her as he goes. They both collapse into chairs at the kitchen table laughing and argue a little about who is faster, but they both know that the only person locally who could out run CJ is David. So they spent the next hour talking and teasing before CJ had to go back to school and then David walked her back out to her car to see her off.

"So I'll see you tonight?" She asked as she got into her car and strapped on her seat belt. David rolled his eyes. Lately, the last thing that he wanted was to have a big family gathering.

It wasn't about his Mom, he loved her very much, and it certainly wasn't because of CJ. She was too perfect for her own good, but he would take a bullet for her in a heartbeat and he'd kill any body who every tried to hurt her. It wasn't even Dad. He knew the old man was trying, but sometimes, what felt to J.R. like trying felt to David like judging and a little of the Pot Calling the Kettle. He just wanted to find his own way without all of the redirecting that the elders in the family thought he should have. And lastly there were his grandparents. Facing the idea that he may have disappointed them was something he didn't want to know. He looked at CJ's small eager face waiting for an answer.

"Maybe."

"David. That's the best you can do?" Yep. He thought. It really is right now.

"I might have to work." CJ frowned. He thought she might even cry.

"I'll do my best."

"Ok. Thank you. I love you, David." And she was gone.

David watched her tiny little car sputter off into the winter cold and thought about his little sister. She was all of the things that he was not. She was forgiving, and full of hope. She had faith in a god she could neither see nor touch, yet she believed she could feel Him in a place that was in the very deepest part of herself. If only she knew the hardness of the world that he strived to protect her from. She didn't remember everything that they had grown up from. What she did remember she had overcome with grace, and he had grown bitter. She was the best part of him.

SCENE IV: PULLMAN/ALBION HIWAY

Although CJ had been in her car for over five minutes letting it warm up at the house before she took off, it was still really cold. She had left her letter man's coat in the back seat and if she was smart she would pull over and put it on, but it was only about seven miles or so back to the High School so she could just suck it up. It's not as though she were going to freeze to death. It would have been smarter if she had decided not to bring the stupid Diet Coke too!

The speed limit on the road was 50mph but with the snow and the ice, CJ took it a little slower. She grew up on these roads and she was a pretty safe driver, but as she was coming around the last corner, her Diet Coke slid onto the passenger seat and started to spill every where.

"Crap!" She shouted as she downshifted and reached over with her right hand to grab for it. When she couldn't quite reach it, she looked up, saw that everything seemed to be going pretty smoothly on the road, so, she unsnapped her seat belt and quickly reached down, retrieved the soda, and righted herself. That's the funny thing about black ice though. Everything can look on blacktop like smooth sailing, but be a death trap.

"Phew!" She sighed as she brushed a hair from her mouth. Suddenly, as she began her descent down the last hill, her car started to slide to the right. In a panic, CJ screamed and tuned the steering wheel to the left as hard as she could. It's moments like these, that you wish things were going in slow motion but for CJ, things were moving at the speed of light. The small Datsun, although not moving at the posted speed limit had enough momentum and under the severe Washington weather conditions, it slammed into the ditch on the right hand side with enough force to bounce the car back up on to the road and roll the car, drivers side first onto itself. CJ, having not taken the time to put her seat belt back on was flung mercilessly first over the gear shift, and then, when the car began to roll, the first time, caving in on the drivers side and smashing down on CJ's head.

When the car came up for the second tumble, the windshield buckled and CJ was flung free, shattering her right knee against the dashboard as she flew through the windshield and landed in the ditch on the other side of the road eight feet from her crumpled car.

At the bottom of the road a farmer in his truck was heading up the hill when he saw the small, mangled car reach it's final resting place. When he jumped out of his truck and saw CJ laying on her back, he ran to her car and fished around for a few minutes and found what he was looking for: id and a coat.

CJ Stewart

Brown Hair

Blue Eyes

02 14 73

Organ Donor

A moment later a car came puttering up the road and he flagged them down. The driver, who turned out to be a small, elderly woman, stopped.

"What seems to be the problem?"

Ice sickles began to form on his cheeks where the tears had been just moment before.

"Please," He pleaded, "This very young girl has just been in a terrible accident, please find a phone and call 911. I can't leave her or she'll freeze to death. I don't know that she's much alive as it is. Please!!!"

The elderly woman looked over at the car lying upside down in the ditch, and squinted. She gasped when she recognized the faded orange patchy paint.

"No! Not CJ! I will get help as fast as I can!" and with that she drove off. The farmer turned back to CJ, whom he had covered with her coat and a blanket that he had gotten out of his truck, but she was getting paler. He didn't know what to do. If she had a broken neck and he picked her up, he could kill her, but if he left her laying here waiting too long for help she would freeze to death. He took a chance and gently picked her up and put her in his truck to keep her warm.

The little grandma had come through for them because it wasn't long before there were multitudes of police and ambulances on the scene trying to asses how badly injured she was. It's funny, thought the farmer, other than her hair being a mess with blood that was pouring out of her ear, she looked like she was sleeping. Her face wasn't broken, her arms and legs weren't out of place. But something was very broken about that little girl, he knew. Because when he had tried to open her eyes to look in them, She was gone. Not dead, just not there.

SCENE V: WASHINGTON STATE UNIVERSITY FACILITIES PLANNING OFFICE

This was going to be one of those days, Vickie thought, where nothing is in it's place. Thankfully, Audrey was there to right it all. Vickie smiled at that. Audrey, her mother, who had been the office manager before her, although retired, often volunteered to come into the office and work as her secretary of sorts and it was always nice to have someone there who both knew the office inside and out…and her the same way. There was a gentle knock on the door and Audrey poked her head in.

"I have some copies to make and then I was thinking we could head for lunch. It's almost 11:00 now. So, maybe 11:30?" Vickie smiled. Then the phone rang. Vickie looked surprised. It was the private line.

"Vickie," Came her secretary Angie's voice,

"You need to take this."

"Mom stay here." Vickie said as she reached for the line. Call it a gut feeling, or mother's intuition or whatever you want, but something told her it was time. This was it. This was that call. He had finally done it. David had gone on a bender and was lying in a ditch somewhere or was in jail.

"Facilities Planning, This is Vickie."

"Vickie, My name is Tim and I'm the Whitman County chaplain. I'm sorry to be the one to have to make this call to you, but your daughter CJ has been in a car accident and is at Pullman Memorial Hospital. I can come and get you where you are if you need a ride."

Time stopped. The ticking of the clock was deafening and still there was silence all around her. Vickie's grip on the phone tightened and she felt as If all of the air was being sucked out of the room. Audrey reached across the desk, took the phone from her daughter and spoke into it.

"I'm sorry, but this is Audrey B. Cane, Vickie's mother, can I help you?"

Tim explained again who he was, what had happened and again offered to retrieve them for the trip to the hospital.

Peace that passes understanding. It was something Vickie had never known she would ever need and yet.... She never ever thought she would get this call and have CJ be on the other end of it, but here it was.

"No thank you. We will be there momentarily." Audrey hung up the phone and sat Vickie down in her chair before her legs turned to jello.

"Mom, CJ's been in an accident and she's at the hospital."

Audrey, with the rapid, mechanical motion that only a mother in a crisis can manage, gathered up purses, keys and her daughter and they were out the door without another word.

SCENE VI: PULLMAN MEMORIAL HOSPITAL

There was static, then a beeping and as Cathy walked by the front desk of the Emergency Room she caught the message coming in from one of their ambulances.

"Bus 11 to PMHER, can you hear me?" Cathy stood on her very tippy toes and reached over the counter top to grab the radio receiver and respond.

"Bus 11, this is PMHER, I read you loud and clear, what have you got?"

"SWF, 18, MVA, apparent BFT to head. We've intubated on the field, but her pulse is thready. ETA 4 minutes."

"We'll have a gurney standing by." She replaced the radio and ran down the hallway yelling for help and looking for a spare gurney.

When the ambulance pulled into the bay, Cathy had gathered a team of Dr's and medical staff to help the EMT's unload their patient and get her the help she needed. Cathy had been a nurse at this hospital for 20 years and had seen many things even for such a small town, but even she was not ready for what was coming.

As they opened up the back of the ambulance and gently but quickly lowered their patient down, things began to move in rapid succession. If you were an outsider looking in, it was like watching ballet. The EMT explaining what had been done to stabilize her in the field, the Dr's barked out orders while the nurses, Cathy included, took her vitals again, all while CJ was on the gurney moving into the building and in and out of Cat Scan machines and X-Rays. Moment by moment slipping deeper and deeper into her unconsciousness.

"Do we have a name?" One of the Dr's asked.

"It's CJ Stewart. Her mother works at the Facilities Planning office at the University just around the corner. I'll call her. I'm her doctor." Dr. Davies. He was just about every one's Dr in this town. At least all of the people that had lived here very long.

"It's been done. She's on her way." Tim Clancey, the County Chaplain stepped in and shook Dr. Davies hand.

"How's she looking?" Tim asked. It was always a shame to see kids in here like this.

"Like shit, frankly. What happened?"

"I just left the scene and it looks like she hit some black ice on the road. Can't tell much more right now until we get her car upright out of the ditch."

"I'm sending her to Spokane, Tim. I can't fix her here. I already called Heart Flight. I hope they get here in time."

Cathy smoothed CJ's blood soaked matted hair away from her small, pale face and the tears began to brim in her eyes. In the 20 years that she had been working at this hospital, she had been a part of many amazing things. She had participated in the delivery of many tiny little babies and heard their very first cries and saw their eyes opening for the very first time. CJ was one of those. This, however, she realized would be a first. It would be the first time ever that she might have to watch one of the babies that she so lovingly helped bring into this world, go out of it again.

Vickie and Audrey pulled into the ambulance bay of the hospital only to be greeted by police cars and a helicopter. As they ran out they were stopped short by a police officer.

"I'm sorry but you ladies can't go through here, we have an emergency."

"Is that emergency my daughter, CJ?"

Vickie was trying to hold it together, but the police and the helicopter? What did this all mean? How serious could it be? Where was CJ? Then it came again. Peace that passes all understanding. It was like a rain that washed over her. Everything was OK, because it was 1991 and CJ was strong and healthy. CJ was loved and she knew she was loved and God would make it right either way. Either she believed or she didn't. Faith was about trust not knowledge.

"This is the mother!" The officer shouter to someone, anyone. There may have been 10 people or 100 people there, it seemed like 100, but as far as Audrey was concerned there were far too many. Vickie grabbed Audrey's hand and forced her way closer to the door. She was stopped by another officer.

"Vickie, Hi, I'm Tim, the chaplain for the County, we talked on the phone." He held out his hand and she shook it merely on principle.

"I know this is a lot to take in, but they are transferring CJ to Sacred Heart in Spokane. They are bringing her out as soon as they get her loaded on the gurney and stabilize her."

Then, the doors swung open and a team of EMT'S came rushing out the ambulance bay doors with a gurney and a waif of a girl, pale as a sheet strapped down on it. They whizzed past Vickie and started loading her on the helicopter. Time moved in fast forward until Vickie shouted, "Stop!"

For a sliver of a second they all stopped, but then they continue. Tim stepped in.

"This is her mother, can she have a moment?" The helicopter pilot looked at Vickie with sympathy.

"I'm sorry but I can only give you about 10 seconds then we gotta go."

Vickie looked down at CJ and patted her hair and kissed her pale cheek. Nothing. This is not my daughter. She thought. My daughter laughs and cries and sings. She loves to sing.

"Can I go?" Vickie's voice is starting to fail her a little now. Peace please.

The Pilot shook his head.

"If she were a child you could, but she's an adult so there's not enough room. Ok, Here we go! Load her up, Dr Hernandez is waiting for her!" This is where Vickie's heart would have broken into tiny little pieces if she had been anyone else. If she were a child? What did that mean? She was her child! She was small and frail and breakable and unprotected up there without her. Audrey reached out and touched her shoulder and turned her.

"Vickie, It's time to gather every one else and go the hospital and wait for God to do His will."

Peace that passes understanding. There it is again. It's in the knowing the other people who have it too. Tim reaches out for Vickie and she does not crumble like the others in her situation before her have done.

"If you want, you can ride in my cruiser and I can probably get you up there faster." She stood there silently at first. They all did as they watched the helicopter shake and lift into the air carrying their very precious cargo up into the air and away from the mother who's heart was breaking.

"Thank you for the offer, officer, but I'm going to gather the rest of my family together, and her best friend and we'll all go as one. If this is the last time we're going to see CJ, we need to do it together." Tim sighed as he watched the two women walk back to their car and pull out of the ambulance bay. Sometimes, he thought, it takes a crisis of faith, to show you what you're really made of, and that woman, was a better testament than him.

Audrey and Vickie made their phone calls and separated into two cars and one by one they picked up J.R., Audrey's husband and Vickie's dad Clinton, David who had called Sara, Catherine, and Lynn and made the long trip up to Spokane to Sacred Heart Medical Center. It was a long quiet drive each one wondering some of the same things, and different things.

SCENE VII: HEART FLIGHT

"How much farther, She's crashing!!!"

Monitors began beeping wildly as CJ's blood pressure began to rise. Her heart started to race faster and faster and more blood started to pour out of her right ear and her nose faster than they could stop it, then just as fast as her pressure rose is began to drop and things began to spiral out of control.

"We're losing her!"

The monitors went monotone. Just that steady, high pitched, flat squeal of the flat line. CJ's heart had stopped.

"Charge the paddles and get ready to shock!"

Two minutes later CJ's heart is back in rhythm but the bleeding hasn't stopped as they are landing with a surgical team waiting on the roof of the hospital that already knew she had blood clots swelling on her brain that were killing her.

SCENE VIII: SANDIEGO CALIFORNIA

Jace opened his eyes and rubbed the fog from them as he realized that another few hours had come and gone and he was still here.

"Hi."

Jace nearly fell out of the narrow hospital bed as he turned in the direction of the soft voice that he was hearing again only this time it wasn't a whisper on the breeze of a door closing or a dream being swept away. It was ringing clear and crisp beside him and so was she.

It really was her! Sitting on the windowsill. Only this time, she, too was wearing a hospital gown. Her hair was matted with blood and she was paler than before. Jace had never cared about any one but himself before and lately he didn't even rank on his own list of 'to do's', but this girl with no name and a face he couldn't forget with her cryptic messages made him feel something. He couldn't have told you what it was because he had never felt feelings before. Anything. But he was feeling now. He almost wanted to live for curiosity's sake. It wasn't hope, but it was a step.

"Are you even real?" She was looking out the window and down to the street 12 stories down.

"Phew, that's quite a fall, don't you think?" And then back to Jace, "I feel real to me, but I don't know what's going on. I just know that I'm suppose to somehow find a way to show you how to accept all of this."

Jace sat up in bed and then swung his spindly legs over the side. In his pre teen years, he was tan and toned as he swam and surfed and painted on the beach. Now, He was pale and weak and his once spiked, well-groomed sun bleached hair had grown shaggy and dark. He looked brooding and old like his father. He took small tentative steps towards her and sat beside her at the windowsill.

"What is your name? Where did you come from? How do you show me to accept what I have already accepted? I know all about death. Everyone I ever loved has died before me and I will die soon too." Her smile. It's almost sweet with sincerity. He doesn't think she is mocking him, but the humor in any of this is lost on him.

"You never saw it did you? Death is always the beginning of something new. When your mother died, new life began. Yours. When your father died, it was an opportunity for you to find a new life and new meaning but you made other choices, now you are going to get another chance. With another death, you will see new life. Don't waste it on what you don't have or what you've lost. Use it to seek out where that life came from. Those are the people that can heal you. And you can heal them. Peace that passes understanding is only given to those who have the deepest faith. Those who are weaker need tangible proof of God's grace in a bad situation. Like you.

You say, 'God took' and, 'God made it that way'. Doesn't anyone ever account for simple human error anymore? Could it be that it's not so much that God causes these things to happen, but under the right situations with the right people, God could still use a simple accident to change lives? Oh, you people make me crazy! You make it so hard when it's just so easy!"

25

Now she had left the window and was pacing faster and faster around the four corners of the large room, her hands flying wildly and her expressions of exasperation getting more frantic as she talked. Then, after a moment, she came back and sat calmly again beside him.

"Find the heart donor's family. You need them to heal the broken spirit in you and some of them will need to see that even in death, life is renewed." She is gone.

SCENE IX: SACRED HEART MEDICAL CENTER, SPOKANE WA

As the Stewart family with Sara, Rea and Lynn in tow all filed into the lobby of the Sacred Heart Medical Center in Spokane, WA., things began to move in slow motion again. Vickie went to the counter and felt as if she was checking into a hotel.

"My name is Vickie Stewart and my daughter, CJ, was flown here from Pullman, and we were told to check in here at the front desk." At the mention of who they were, the front desk receptionist put down her pen and picked up her phone, dialed a four digit extension and then folded her hands while she averted her eyes so as not to make eye contact. Did she know something more than they did?

"Some one is coming." Was all that she said so they waited.

After what seemed like forever, as it always does when your child's life hangs in the balance, although, had it actually been timed it was probably only 7 minutes, a nun came and greeted them. Surprisingly, she didn't smile or say reassuring things, just ushered them to the family waiting area and asked if they wanted her to pray for them. Vickie, who was neither catholic nor lacking in observation skills, responded with,

"Have you heard anything about my daughter?"

"A doctor will be in to update as soon as they can."

"Then yes, I would like you to go and pray for her. We will pray here amongst ourselves. Thank you."

If it were a brush off, you never would have known it, because Vickie did everything, as always, with dignity and grace. Even if it was sending away non-family members. She just wasn't sure now was the time to introduce some one who wasn't a part of CJ's inner circle in, even for prayer. Oh, there would be praying. Of that, Vickie had no doubt. Even if you didn't believe, if you knew CJ, you knew she did and every one would be appealing to her God if not their own. She knew that where two or more were gathered together in His name, His will would be done. But what was His will in this? Did CJ complete all that He had asked of her? Was she strong enough to let CJ go? Was she strong enough to carry the burden of comforter for the rest of the family and friends who would feel the impact of this so deeply?

The nun left the room and each member of this small family found their places to wait for news, Vickie looked at each one in turn and tried to read their faces for what they might be feeling. Closest to her and the door was J.R.. Her rock, her fortress, her husband, CJ's buddy, was pensive and quiet.

Next to him was Audrey who was already in reverent head bowed position. A prayer warrior since always, she would not fail. When it was all said and done, it could not be said that Audrey Cane had not done battle on her knees before and for this one life she would fight the hardest.

Clinton Cane was the patriarch of the family. The quiet, steadfast glue that held them all in place in his own way. He had brought them all to Washington from Montana after the first world war and they would follow him anywhere, all of them. He wasn't one to believe in a god or a higher power, but, if it could save CJ, that little flint of a girl who came over three times a week just to sit in the corner by the heater and giggle or jabber about music, theater, track and boys, then he would give it a try.

Lynn and Sara sat in silence. Lynn looked cold so Vickie gave her a sweater. That was when Lynn's eyes began spilling over with tears.

"Shh." Vickie gathered Lynn up in her arms just like she had CJ that morning.

David sat, elbows on his knees, head hanging down with his fingers laced around the back of his head as he scanned the floor for crumbs or bugs or anything. The only thing he caught sight of was Cath's untied shoe so he reached down and began to fix it for her.

Vickie hadn't forgotten that it was David's birthday, but now was not the time. This was not the place. She would make it up to him. As if the thick air in the room pulled him on strings and he could read her mind, David finished tying Cath's shoe, hoisted her on his lap and then looked at his mother.

"I'm so sorry." She said in a whisper.

David, who hadn't cried since the day J.R. had hit him in a drunken rage so hard he left a grease mark on his face, felt his eyes getting wet. He shook his head and looked down to wipe his eyes before responding. He could not fall apart now. Not in front of them and not for CJ's sake.

"I'll get over it. I'll have other ones." The irony of that would not strike him until many years later.

Cath tried to sit still on David's lap, but she couldn't. So she got up and she began to pace. At 12 she was having very mixed feelings about all of this. She had never seen a gathering of every member of the family (aunts, uncles and cousins were apparently on the way) where there wasn't laughing and joking and food. Somber did not suit them and she felt out of place. These feelings of terror felt strangely out of order for her as well. Most of the time, she and CJ didn't get along. CJ was bossy, and had everything. She had a car and hated giving Cath a ride. CJ was the fastest runner, Cath had asthma. CJ didn't have a curfew, but Cath had to be in bed by 9pm. Where was the fairness?

They had screaming matches and she swore that CJ was everyone's favorite. Look at the way everyone gathered here for her now. CJ, every one's favorite shining star. Still, Catherine hated to admit that their bond was stronger than she knew because deep in her gut she was terrified that her only sister was slipping away.

So they all went on for several hours until a man came bursting through the doors wearing a surgical cap and scrubs.

"Are you Dr. Hernandez?" Vickie asked, remembering the name that the helicopter pilot had shouted as they loaded CJ.

"No, I'm Dr. Solomon. Dr Hernandez is the neurosurgeon who just finished working on CJ. Where we're at now is that she suffered such severe trauma to the frontal left lobe of her brain, that when Dr. Hernandez opened it up, the tissue had been without oxygen for so long with all the pressure that had built up and all of the swelling, he had to remove the part of her brain we call the left frontal lobe along with the two blood clots that started the problem. After we got her back into ICU, however, her pressure spiked again and we found that there was ricochet bleeding to the right side of her brain and we had to go in a second time. Dr. Hernandez removed two more clots from the right side. There is one smaller clot that is in the medial cortex that we cannot get to so we are going to cross our fingers and hope that it resolves itself.

Now we wait. CJ is young and strong, but she has a lot stacked against her. She was laying in the cold and had severe trauma. We have placed tubes where we did surgery for draining and there is another tube in her right side where we needed to repair her lung because it was also punctured. That she has survived to this point is saying a lot. I think it's good to be hopeful, but I want you all to be realistic. Take your time and think about what I've said. The next 48 hours are critical. If we see some real improvement in her condition then we'll talk about what to expect about the kind of recovery she may have. If we don't, then we need to talk about how and when to disconnect her from the machines and harvest her organs."

J.R., who up to this point had been waiting silently for further instructions or just to go quietly and claim his daughter in whatever state she was in and take her home stood to his feet.

"You will not cut my daughter into pieces and fish out her good parts to people who can't take care of their own!"

He was not shouting, but he was very firm and clear about his position. This was not the first loved one to protest organ donation and Dr Solomon, although not sympathetic, was in the business of saving the lives that he could, so he continued.

"CJ is 18 and that makes her an adult in the state of Washington and it also is her wishes to be an organ donor as stated on her driver's license.

Don't worry. We're not there yet. I also want you to be aware though, that the damage that I saw to her brain as Dr. Hernandez was working on her was very severe and she'll be lucky if she comes back at all to come back with an IQ higher than that of a 3rd grader."

Vickie had heard enough. The doctors had done what they could now it was time for faith, hope, and love to do what it could.

"You don't know her. She's either going to go or she'll come back. CJ doesn't do things ½ way. You'll see." And then,

" Can we see her?"

"Yes, but only 2 at a time. The ICU is small and open and she's still considered to be in critical condition. Take turns, but take all the time you need. Take the green elevators up to the 8th floor and take a right. A nurse will meet you at the door."

"Thank you Dr. Solomon." Clinton said as the Dr. walked out the door and Vickie turned and looked at the eager group.

"Who wants to go first?"

Suddenly, the small room with the small group was all buzzing with chatter as to who should go first. Before a decision had been made, Annie and Doug arrived from Montana and added more chatter until finally, Vickie had made a decision.

"Enough! Annie, will you please take Catherine up to see her sister? Then Lynn, you and I will go for a few minutes. after, perhaps, Annie, you and Doug could head back to Mom and Dad's with Catherine and Lynn. And we'll keep rotating as the night goes on as people want to. Does that work for everyone?" And everyone is at peace. Peace that passes understanding can be passed from one person to another if they are tied together with love, faith and understanding.

SCENE X: ICU

Catherine: There is beeping and whirring and there's a rhythm to it all as she sat beside CJ. She just looked at her. She couldn't do anything else. She couldn't touch her because there was still a part of her that thinks she's just sleeping and if she disturbs her, she'll wake up and hit her back. That would be a good thing, but she's also more afraid that she's wrong and that when she touches her she'll just lay there like she is now and she won't hit her back or yell at her or call her names. Just lay there. Get UP CJ! She wanted to shout at her. Catherine looked up and asked a passing nurse for a piece of paper and a pen. When the nurse returned, Cath jotted a note down and slipped it underneath CJ's pillow and kissed her on her road burned cheek. CJ's skin still felt warm. That was a good sign right?

Cath felt hopeful after all as she turned at took her aunt's hand and walked out of the ICU.

Annie: "Come on, kiddo, open your eyes and say something." She pleaded. Since CJ's birth she had never before now seen that girl in a state of stillness. If her feet weren't moving, her mouth was. There was so much life left in this small body before her and it was beyond her to believe that now it might cease to exist. She picked up CJ's hand and wrapped it in her own.

"Move CJ, please. Just show me some sign that you're still in there." She waited for a few a moments and when nothing happened, her heart began to sink. CJ stood beside her aunt and squeezed her shoulder. Annie couldn't have told you why at the time but she felt compelled to reach her right hand to left shoulder and pat.

"I'm trying, Aunt Ann. I'm trying." And just then her fingers fluttered. Annie jumped up and shouted,

"Her fingers moved!"

One of the nurses came over and checked her vital signs and monitors. Then she checked her pupils for dilation.

"Sometimes they have involuntary responses. I'm sorry."

Annie was still smiling. CJ was coming around. She was sure of it. It was working. Prayer was working!

Lynn: Best friends do anything for each other, but this was one she didn't know how to cover. CJ had carried her to her house when she was drunk instead of taking her home to face her own parents. CJ picked her up for school every day so she didn't have to take driver's ed. They were inseparable. How did she fix this for CJ? How could she make it better for her? She reached up and gently touched her bandaged head and broke down in tears again. CJ was going to be so mad when she found out they cut all of her hair off! She hated her curls, but she spent most of her life growing it down to her waist. When she woke up and found out what they did, there would be hell to pay for sure! She didn't remember CJ being this small either. They used to have their arguments about who was thinner sure, but CJ was always just a little taller and heavier than herself yet she didn't seem so now.

"How can I help you?" She cried into the white cotton blankets that covered CJ. CJ sat next to Lynn in the otherwise empty chair. She couldn't see her, but CJ had an essence that made you feel warm and loved and comforted all at once. Peace that passes understanding. Sometimes it flows from the faith of the mother to the faith of the daughter.

"Be OK. Remember what we always said. Together we are distance and speed. Take the best of both us and carry that for now. It will cover you while I'm here. I don't know the end."

Lynn stood and hugged Vickie who waited for her by the ICU door.

"Thank for all that you have made her to be." Vickie held Lynn for a moment.

"She's something else, isn't she?" Lynn wiped her eyes.

"She's the best in all of us I think. You know what's saddest, though, she drives herself to the limits and still thinks she fall short."

Vickie understood that about CJ. For CJ it was that she knew that her spiritual gift was that of mercy and compassion and sometimes that made it difficult for her to see her own greater worth. She worried that when God saw the deepest part of herself, He would not be pleased with what He saw and so she strived harder to be more worthy. Sometimes she forgot that she was just forgiven once and forever and love was enough. Her mother would tell her when she woke up all these things.

Clinton: It was moments like these that he wished that he had his banjo with him. CJ liked it. She also liked his mushroom gravy but he couldn't make that here now could he! He grinned at the thought of eight-year-old CJ at Thanksgiving salivating over by the stove as he made his secret gravy that she loved.

His favorite memories of CJ always went back to her sitting in the corner by the furnace. Any time of day, at any age that girl could be found in the same place in their house. She loved that old furnace right next to his chair. He looked down at her now with tubes poking out of her head and her face and he didn't even recognize this small frame before him. Her eyes, he thought. If she opens her eyes, then I'll know it's my girl.

He then looked across the bed to the woman sitting on the other side. His middle daughter, her mother. How can you protect them from something like this? Then he looked down and saw her feet. Her shoes were worn thin, and sad looking. Sure they may be comfortable, but no longer practical. He walked over and kissed her on her forehead.

"You're mother and I are going home, we'll see you tomorrow." Vickie smiled up at her father.

"Ok. Thank you for everything. I'll see you tomorrow."

As Clinton met Audrey at the doors to the ICU and they walked to the elevator she knew something was on his mind. She didn't ask though. She also knew after all these years that if he wanted to talk about it, he would. When they had reached the hospital lobby and were headed out the door, Clinton turned to his wife.

"Our daughter needs new shoes if she's going be pacing around this hospital keeping this family together." And they were gone.

David: From the time they were very young he had wrapping a cocoon around CJ trying to protect her from harm. Sometimes it worked for both and sometimes it came back and bit him square in the ass, but always it was for her greater good. She could never know how much he had done for her and he would never tell her. He also did not realize the bond that they had was stronger than he could imagined. He would know it now.

"David"

"CJ?" He looked down at her. Nothing moved. Nothing changed. But he knew he heard her. He stood and looked around. Nothing. He sat again and the tears came then.

"David. I'm still here. I think I'm OK. I don't know. Talk to me. I can hear you."

Trust. He just had to trust. His mother called it faith. He had lost faith in anything long ago, but he would try a little now.

"Are you hurt? Do you feel pain?"

"Yes I am hurt, No I'm not in pain."

"Are you getting better, is there any hope?"

"I don't know if I'm getting better, and David?"

"CJ?"

"There is always hope."

J.R.: His runner, his champion. She looked every bit like his mother, what he could remember of her anyway. He was only 9 when she had passed away, but the few pictures that he had carried with him, CJ could have been her. It was often said that she favored him and he was proud of that, but she was nothing like him. Well, maybe a little. Sometimes, as was true with him, if it wasn't perfect in that moment, it was all going to hell in a hand basket. She did have a flare for the dramatics! She was also so much of her mother. Charitable to a fault, and loving to everyone without prejudice. That was her mother in her. They both called it a gift from the Holy Spirit. Perhaps.

To look at her now, he wondered where she was. She had to be somewhere. All of that flare and personality doesn't just disappear into nothingness and nowhere at all! He resigned himself at that moment to the inclination that she had simply just shut down to heal. She was still in there, in the very quietest part of herself, (a place no one had ever seen or heard of!) biding her time while her very broken body got better. That's it and that's that. A father's decision had been made. He leaned down and gently kissed CJ's cheek and felt the warmth there.

Her organs were going to stay right where they were, he decided as well. She would need them when she woke up.

SCENE XI: PULLMAN HIGH SCHOOL

February 27th, 8am. Simon McMann sits at his desk with his fingers interlaced, bracing himself for this day. It is a day he wishes would end already before it has even begun. He looks at the clock. 8:02. In approximately 3 minutes, his receptionist is going to come bursting through the door and either she will be in tears because she knows something is wrong, or she will mill about the office as usual until he tells her something is wrong and then she will be in tears. This day has got to end already!

Just like a well-oiled machine, Judy Blanche runs through the door and barges into Simon's office without so much as a knock. This is not her usual routine of course for Judy is a receptionist with the utmost of skills and demeanor as does befit the duties of a high school office supervisor. Today was going to be different.

"CJ Stewart's been in an accident and they've flown her to Spokane." This is all spoken in broken words through tears. Simon stands to his feet and hands Judy a box of tissues and guides her to a chair in the corner of his office. As the acting principal of Pullman High School, Simon had made it a point to make his office a welcome place to be and so it was decorated with artwork that depicted ocean views and sea life rather than all of his credentials and he had comfy furniture. He wanted the kids to see him as a counselor rather than a disciplinarian. He was not above handing down a heavy sentence if the crime called for it mind you, but he wanted to be remembered for the lives that he could change with thoughts and words rather than harsh rules and disciplines. So far his methods seemed to be working.

"I spoke with her parents last night. She is in a coma right now, but her condition at this time is stable. I would like to hold an assembly today during second period since a lot of the seniors don't have a first period. Do you think you could arrange that for me?"

Judy bobbed her swollen eyes with the tissues and nodded her head that she could take care of that for him then stood to her feet and moved toward the door. At the doorway, she turned around again,

"Mr. McMann, What are we going to do?"

Simon looked down at the floor and shook his head. It was a tragedy. This hit him hard due to the fact that his own daughter, Emily, was in some of CJ's classes. They had only come to this town this year and they were new but CJ had been very kind to Emily and Emily had only nice things to say about her. He was still reeling from the thought of what if... What if it had been Emily?

"Now we wait." He said as she closed the door behind her.

At 9:30am, the gymnasium began to fill as students from all grades 9-12 began to filter in. Every one was curious why they were being summoned. There hadn't been a formal announcement during the morning opening in their home room like there usually was so the talk began to get louder and louder as more and more students filled the room and began to sit. Once everyone was inside, Mr. McMann closed the doors behind him and walked to the microphone stand in the middle of the gym. There was still quite a bit of chatter going on and laughter as students decided that they didn't care why they were here, they just didn't want to be in class. That was until Mr. McMann began to speak.

"Ladies and Gentlemen. Some of you may have heard already, but I needed to let you know that yesterday morning CJ Stewart was in a motor vehicle accident and she was injured very badly. The information that I have that I can give you so far is that she has had a couple of surgeries that appear to have been successful and she is now in a comatose state at Sacred Heart Medical Center up in Spokane. Her parents are asking that if you would like to go visit with her that you would give her another 48 hours of recovery time before you go, but after that time we should have more information to give you and where and how to find her. Thank you for your time and attention. You are dismissed."

Jeff sat in the bleachers and felt shock and awe. He was stunned to know that the girl he was sitting next to yesterday was not here today.

There was an ominous feeling deep in the pit of his stomach yesterday when he was eating his lunch out side and saw the Heart Flight helicopter flying over the high school and CJ wasn't in choir class. As Mr. McMann was dismissing everyone, Jeff jumped to his feet and ran down the bleachers to the microphone.

"Hey! Hello, every one, can you wait just one minute please?" He called into the mike. Some people kept going. Perhaps they didn't hear him, or perhaps they didn't care. Most everyone else, sat back down and waited. As the president of the senior class, Jeff was very popular and had quite a bit of clout with upper and lower class-men so most people respected him.

"I would like to ask just the seniors stay behind for a few minutes please. Everyone else is dismissed."

As everyone else filed out of the gym, the seniors filed in a little closer to the bottom of the bleachers and huddled in. This was a small town, and a small high school. Their class was 160 people strong and it was the biggest graduating class the high school had seen in a long time. They still had their clicks and not every one felt like they belonged with someone, except when it came to CJ.

"This is a big blow to all of us." Jeff began. He took the mike off the stand and moved in a little closer. Then he put the mike back and just came in to stand right in front of the entire senior class for a talk. He looked out at all of their faces. He didn't think that there ever been a time before that they had all sat in the same place and felt so unified before.

"We are less than 5 months from graduation and we are missing one of our own. What can we do? There has to be something more that we can do for CJ and her family than just sit and wait for her to get better. What if she doesn't?" It was a harsh question but the reality of it loomed in the air for all of them.

"What would CJ do if it was one of you?" He proposed.

"Is there anyone of us that can't think of time that CJ hasn't done something for us? Opened a door, encouraged you, laughed with you, cried with you? Sometimes, for me, she just stood there, and asked how

37

I was doing today. I want to do more than wait. I need help and I need ideas, people."

"Lets all go and visit together." Someone shouted from the back. Jeff thought about it.

"We need to remember to respect her families wishes to wait 48 hours, but that's a good start, anyone else?"

"The choir could put together a cassette of us singing for her to listen to."

"We could have a car wash to raise money to help with the hospital expenses."

Jeff started jumping up and down with excitement as more and more great ideas flooded in. At the back of the gym, Mr. McMann and Coach Taylor stood watching the display being put forth by the senior class.

"I'll be damned." Coach Taylor marveled as he crossed his arms over his chest and shook his head in disbelief.

"That is something else."

"So is she." Said Simon as he headed back towards his office to fend off all of the calls that would surely come flooding in today.

"So is she."

SCENE XII: SANDIEGO CALIFORNIA

"You look weaker today. I think it's going to happen soon."

Jace opened his eyes a slit to see her sitting in the bed beside him. She looked different. She was smaller and paler. Her hair was gone and it somehow made her eyes appear larger, more effective. He wasn't sure if the fact that they both fit on his small hospital bed was a reflection of how small she was or how small he had become.

"Are you always going to come here and be the voice of gloom and doom? Since you never have given me your name, I'd like to call you Grim." She frowned.

"Rude, much?"

Jace rolled his eyes. He used to enjoy her company, but he was tired and nothing she every said made any sense to him, so he was fine if she wanted to just go away. Maybe he could piss her off just enough to make that work.

"Sensitive much?"

"Touché. Any word on your heart?" She crossed one ankle over the other and he could see that her right knee was yellow and orange bumpy and her knee cap seemed out of place. It didn't seem to be bothering her though. Just for giggles, he reached over and tried to touch her. When his hand made contact it was a strange feeling. It was if he could actually FEEL her paleness. He tried again only this time he touched her right knee. He could FEEL the anterior crucial ligament tear even though he hadn't read a medical book in his life. One more thing. He touched her head. He began to shudder. He had never felt anything so broken in all of his sad, angry life. Her skull was in pieces and parts of the left side of her brain were actually gone. Jace leaned over the side of the bed and began to vomit.

"What the hell happened to you?" He asked once he had recovered himself. She looked down and her eyes welled with tears that did not actually come.

"I don't know. I can't remember. I feel OK though, so I'm pretty sure it's not that bad. I think we need to talk about you. You're fading away and I'm worried that if I can't convince you to see that there is more out there than what you've experienced, you'll get your new heart and turn it to stone rather than your new heart turning you into the man you're meant to be. Please change for the better. Love is not lost on you yet."

He wondered how someone so delusional about the state of her own life could care about him, a complete stranger. Why did it matter to her when it didn't matter to him?

"An organ cannot change my broken soul. Besides, this heart you're so sure I'm getting better get here quick because I'm out of time."

Then she did it. She reached out both of her arm and she hugged him. She held him so tight and even though he did not reciprocate, she did not let go.

"You will be loved, as she was loved."

Jace is afraid to ask whom, or where, or when. Her grip loosens and he realizes she is fading again. No!

"Please!" He begs.

"Tell me who you are!"

"I've been in and out of dreams for a while now. Some of you. Some of my family. I don't know what it all means, but I believe that God doesn't make mistakes and we're going to live through this one way or the other, you and I." She is gone. Real, but gone.

SCENE XIII: SACRED HEART MEDICAL CENTER/ICU

Vickie sat by her daughter's bed for a week and kept a vigil. People had come and gone, most of whom she had known. Coach Taylor brought a card signed by all the members of the track team. Lynn felt a little put out Vickie thought because she hadn't gotten to sign it, but that was only because every day after school, someone had brought her up to the hospital to wait for CJ to wake up. There was a basket from the senior class with an envelope bearing $2000.00 that they had raised with bake sales and a car wash. Vickie smiled at the thought of a car wash in February. Several members of the church had come by individually to sit by her side. Many of her close friends that she grew up with came and wept at the sight of her broken little body, but Vickie had yet to shed a single tear.

Peace that passes understanding. At this point it had become like a drug that blurred her vision and made her body numb. She felt immune from pain and suffering. It was as if she was being shrouded in a blanket of comfort. CJ had recorded a cassette tape of songs that she had sung as a demo to be sent to the college she was planning to attend in the fall and by pure coincidence they had not sent it off so Vickie placed headphones on CJ's bandaged covered ears and played the tape for her. They were a collection of her favorite hymnals and worship songs and Vickie hoped that by hearing her own voice it might inspire healing. While CJ listened, Vickie prayed.

It might have surprised people to know how she prayed. If she had be anyone else or even if the roles had been reversed and it had been her in that bed and CJ praying over her, there would have been begging and pleading. CJ had been studying the scriptures since she was a very young child and she knew that in her personal relationship with God she had known Him to be the Father, Creator, Teacher, Son, and if these rolls were reversed and CJ were the one praying it might sound something like this,

"Father, God, I call on You as the Great Physician to fix this! Make her better! She is needed here to further Your work and teach us all how to be more like You! I can't do any this without her and You know that I need her down here more than You do up there. Please!"

This was not the case. Vickie merely bowed her head and buried her hands in her daughter's covers and found CJ's own hand and held on tightly as she began to pray…again. She believed that when CJ had asked her at the age of five about heaven and earth and God and Jesus and what it all meant that the explanation that she had given her had been simple and to the point. From that moment on, whatever CJ did or did not believe she believed it with all of her heart. Here was when Vickie knew her faith was truly being tested. Did CJ belong to her or did CJ belong to God? Vickie's grip tightened on CJ as the idea that God might take her home to be with Him became a reality. Now the tears began to come.

Vickie didn't know how much time passed as she sat there and cried. She wasn't just crying for the week of crying she had missed out on. It was for those who knew CJ and were biting their nails waiting for word of what was to come one way or the other. Perhaps she also cried for all of the moments she worried she may never get to have again with CJ, like watching her fall over a hurdle on the track because she was being cocky and walking backwards after jumping over the first two without a problem and laughing about it, or hot chocolate and chili after Christmas Caroling around town. She loves that! Some of these tears were probably for the things she worried she might never get to do with CJ. Take her to college and drop her off and worry that she'll meet the man she'll marry there. See her really realize her dream of moving to Hollywood where it's warm most of the year.

Then, faintly, she could hear CJ's voice. It was coming from the headphones on CJ's ears, but Vickie was just close enough to hear part of the chorus from "HOW GREAT THOU ART" coming through loud and clear. It was back again. Peace that passes understanding. Did she mean it or didn't she when she had given her children over to God? Did she believe in Agape love coming only from God because it is a kind of love that runs far deeper and is much beyond the capacity of mankind's ability to understand it and that He had wrapped that around CJ or not?

"Hello, again." She began. " I am asking You to find a way to give me the understanding that I need to get the others and myself through this time. We miss her and I know that You're not finished with her in whatever capacity that You have for her. I need more power, more faith, and more of You. If You must take her, then please don't let it be in vain. Make her life a testimony of goodness and hope. Help me to share that. I'm going to need a blanket of comfort if that's what You do. Please don't take her from me, but help us heal if You do. Never my will, but Yours always be done. Amen."

As if the heavens burst and the skies opened, Vickie is shocked back to the moment when CJ's monitors start beeping in rapid succession and nurses come flying in and buzzing all around her and quickly shove Vickie out of the way. She is close enough that she can see CJ is moving. She is actually moving! Her arms are flailing about and she's coughing and gagging.

"She's chocking! Pull the tube!" Shouts a male nurses who had been taking care of her. As they pull the respirator tube out, CJ takes a few deep breaths and coughs some more and then she seems to settle down. They allow Vickie to sit by her side again and as Vickie runs a gentle hand across CJ's warm cheek, she notices CJ's eyes flutter open. CJ has opened her eyes! She blinks once, twice and then she slowly closes her eyes again as if in sleep, but breathing on her own.

Dr. Hernandez comes in and looks at all of the monitors and checks her chart and then he begins to look very carefully and closely at CJ. He checks the tubing in her head to make sure the drains were not dislodged during her thrashing and feels that everything is still secure.

"She just opened her eyes and blinked twice, Dr. Hernandez. That's good right?" Vickie knew her voice was a bit too eager, but after a week of nothing, she couldn't help it. Dr. Hernandez lifted each one of CJ's eye lids and flashed a small light into each eye and then pulled a chair up next to Vickie.

"She's breathing on her own which means that her lungs and her respiratory system have healed enough to start functioning on their own, and that's a sign that she's stronger than we thought. However, Vickie, her pupils are still fixed and dilated which means that she's still in a coma. Her brain is still badly in need of time to heal if it can."

He patted her on her shoulder and left the room. Vickie prayed some more.

Audrey: Of all of her grandchildren, CJ was the most talkative. She bubbled over like a teakettle waiting to spill. Even as a little girl she would prattle on about anything and everything that came into that little head of hers. Audrey never thought she would miss all that chatter so much as she did now.

As she came into the ICU she saw her own daughter sitting beside CJ's bed sleeping with her head next to CJ's own head and she gently roused her. With much coaxing, she had convinced her to go to the local Ronald McDonald house where they had a family room they were all sharing for a shower and a nap and she promised to stay with CJ until Vickie returned. She decided that it would be her turn to talk CJ's ears off for a change. She would tell her all about the things that were new. She even thought she would make some things up just to get a rise out of her.

"You know, Cath decided that since you weren't going to bother to be there, that she'd sleep in your room. If you don't like it, I suggest you get your lazy bones out of this bed and do something about it!"

That much was not a lie. Catherine had been sleeping in CJ's bed because she said it was the only place she felt she could get a decent night's sleep. No one was getting any sleep lately. Vickie said that she had found a note that Cath had left under CJ's pillow here in the ICU. She had moved it because she was worried that someone would take it, but she hadn't read it because she felt that they were Cath's private thoughts and she was entitled to them.

Just then, CJ's fingers began to twitch. Just a little at first, then, when Audrey squeezed her hand, she squeezed back. A moment later, her eyes were opened.

"I need a doctor!" Audrey screamed to no one in particular. The ICU was a fairly open space. The patients were only separated by curtains so everyone and their families heard her but she hoped they did so someone would come running. Sure enough, they did.

"I'm Dr. Bilson, what seems to be the problem?" A young man in a white lab coat said as he came running to CJ's bedside. All of her monitors were beeping at a steady rhythm.

"She's awake!" Audrey proclaimed. Dr. Bilson flashed his light in her eyes and CJ looked at him confused. She tried to speak, but couldn't find her voice.

"It's OK if you can't speak. Just nod your head yes or shake no to my questions." He told her. "Are you grandma?" He asked Audrey. Audrey nodded affirmatively still holding CJ's hand.

"Is this your grandma?" CJ looked over at Audrey. It took her a moment to focus and then she nodded.

"Is the president of the United States, President Carter?" CJ frowned and shook her head.

"Good! Are you in Washington?" CJ nodded.

"Is your name Carmen?" CJ nodded. Dr. Bilson looked at Audrey and smiled.

"I'll get Dr. Hernandez right away." And with that he was gone. CJ looked at Audrey and smiled. One of the nurses came over and rechecked her vitals and then smiled at them both.

"Good to see you, kiddo." She said. CJ did not look at her and did not respond. She just kept her eyes steady on her grandmother. Her gaze was not a question, but since she couldn't use her voice she used her eyes to plead with Audrey and she could only hope that her grandmother could understand her. Audrey touched CJ's cheek affectionately and CJ blinked. Then she blinked again. Again and again. Soon Audrey furrowed her brow in concentration as she watched CJ's face more closely.

"What is it CJ? Are you in pain?" shake.

"Do you need the Dr.?" Shake.

"Vickie?" Nod.

"Can someone call her mother over at the Ronald McDonald House, Please? It's very important!"

Vickie: The elevator is taking too long and the stairs are out the question. Vickie has had both knees repaired already and she's barely 40 so taking the stairs would hurt too much but a nurse from the ICU had called and told her that CJ was awake and she had to get down here right away. She had then called J.R. and David and they were on their way. J.R. would have to pick up Catherine from school but she felt that everyone should be here. Vickie fidgeted with her purse strap as she watched the elevator move slowly from one floor to the next.

"Screw it!" She said under her breath and headed for the stairs at a sprint. Once up on the eighth floor, although winded, she kept going until she got to the ICU and burst through the doors to see her mother sitting right where she had left her just a few hours before sitting diligently beside CJ who was what? Sleeping? But the nurse said she was awake! Vickie rushed to CJ's side and knelt down beside her daughter looking for the first signs of life in a light that was nearly blinked out.

"CJ, CJ, can you hear me? Baby, please answer me! Please open your eyes."

Nothing. Again, nothing. Audrey slid her motherly, tender, aging hand over and patted Vickie's fidgety, frustrated one.

"She's just resting now, Sweety. She'll wake again when she's ready."

Vickie looked up at her mother who eyes were patient and understanding. Peace again. It was there in the comfort that comes from being the child again and finding that place of home.

"Did she say anything?"

"It's not that she said something, Vic, but she understood the questions she was being asked and I found that hopeful. In her own way, I think she asked for you."

Vickie wanted to find comfort in these small things, but something in the pit of her stomach was looming. If things were looking up, why wasn't CJ waking up now? What was holding her back? Something seemed a bit off to Vickie, but she couldn't put her finger on it just yet.

SCENE XIV: SANDIEGO CALIFORNIA

"Jacen, I have fantastic news! We have a heart! It's being flown in tonight! You'll be prepped for surgery first thing in the morning. In order to insure that you do not reject the organ based on poor circumstances, such as a cold or fever, hypertension, or anything of that nature, we're going to run the gamut of tests on you today. We're going to check for any little bug that could fly into this heart and give it a hard time, know what I mean?"

Jace didn't like very many people, but he liked Dr. Alyster, his cardiologist and the closest thing to a friend that he had at this point. Kyle Alyster and Her. His nameless friend hadn't been by since the last time when he had touched her and felt her injuries from the inside out, but in the short time he had known her, he felt closer to her than anyone else he had ever known. She had known things about his past that he had never shared with anyone and she had glimpsed into his future in way that he had not dared. If he actually managed to live through this, he would somehow try to find her. Surely with all of his money and resources he could locate her. When they were both well, she could help him make sense of all these things and together they could help him find the heart donor's family the way she had said he should. All he had to go by was her description, but that was a start. He had all the money in the world, surely it could buy him the identity of just about anyone right?

"Dr. Kyle, there's just one thing I want to do before we start my day of testing, please."

Dr. Alyster leaned against the window frame, curiosity crossing his neat, well-mannered brow. In all of years that he had been treating Jacen Owen, he didn't think that he had ever heard a "please" or a, "thank you" or any other pleasantry, so this must be big.

"As long as it isn't going to compromise our big plans for extending your life, I'll do my best."

"I want to shave my head. It's for a friend who recently lost all her hair."

Although he knew that he was probably the closest thing Jacen had to a friend and confidant, Dr. Alyster did not hold Jacen in those regards for himself. He saw this weakened, frail body standing before him as a life wasted on art and surfing when his above average i.q. could have taken all of the money that had been left to him and served a far greater good and turned a far higher profit, weakened heart or not. He did feel a deeper bond these days than he used to, however. Something had changed in Jacen over the last week or so. He had developed softer edges and become more pleasant to be around according to the hospital staff. Kyle assumed, as anyone would, that these changes were a result of facing pending death, however, now, looking into his eyes, there was something else. Had he met another dying patient who had changed his life? Was that hope? He would not dare to believe that he was seeing actual peace in the once tormented eyes of this young man. No. Peace had not yet come, but it might.

SCENE XV: SACRED HEART MEDICAL CENTER/ICU

"Vic, Hon, wake up! CJ's awake! Vic!"

Vickie slowly opened her eyes and lifted her head off of CJ's bed and rubbed the blurriness from her eyes as she looked over at her daughter who was blinking slowly and looking around at the crowd of people who were staring at her. Vickie stood and moved in closer.

"CJ! Hey, Kiddo! It's good to finally see those blue eyes! You just don't know how good! Are you in pain? Can you understand me? Do you recognize me?...."

"Vic, I think she's a little overwhelmed. Dr. Hernandez is on his way. Just give her some time." J.R. gently placed a calloused hand over hers and smiled at her. The danger seemed to be over. CJ was coming back. David, Sara, Audrey, Clinton, Annie, Doug, and Catherine were all huddled around her small bed closed in by a curtain. They had been coming in and out of there in shifts keeping watch over their CJ for over a week now and they had their methods and motions down to an art so that they neither disrupted the nursing staff nor the other patients or their families as they came and went. Before long Dr. Hernandez arrived to check on his star patient.

Dr. Hernandez was not a betting man, but had he been, he would not have bet on this girl lasting through the first few hours after surgery. This one was one of the strong ones. He had also seen bigger families with more resources crumble sooner than the Stewart's. These folks were steadfast and strong! Somehow, in spite of bad news at every turn, they had managed to stand together and find the strength to be here every day and believe against every thing that was medically sound doctrine that she could pull out of this and here she was, eyes open, blinking.

Dr. Hernandez did not believe in God, but he knew he was not this skilled a surgeon. No one was.

"CJ, blink once for yes and twice for no. Is your first name Carmen?"

Once.

"Are you 18?"

Once.

"Is your Mom Vickie?"

Once.

"Dad J.R.?"

Once.

"Am I holding 4 fingers up?"

Twice. He was holding up 1 finger.

Dr. Hernandez sat down and looked at each family member in turn before he spoke.

"This is very promising, but we are far from out of the woods people. Let us not forget that just a little over a week ago, I had to remove a part of CJ's brain and her lung was so badly collapsed we are still keeping a tube in to keep it inflated. Her most recent CT shows that her internal bleeding in the retroperitoneal area near her pancreas has decreased but it's still a concern I have because her red blood cell count has been dropping a little at a time, which means she's still bleeding somewhere. I just want you to understand how critical she still is, but I'm hopeful. Ok? I'm hopeful." He stood again and turned to CJ.

"I'll see you soon, CJ." And with that he was gone.

All Vickie had heard were the words promising and hopeful. The group was a buzz with chatter and laughter at the prospects of CJ's speedy recovery and all of things that she could do when she got home and the letters that would have to be sent out to let everyone know how things were going and thank you cards and on and on they went.

David weeded his way through the crowd and seated himself next his sister and tilted her head so that she could see him and only him. By the look of utter confusion on her face, he could tell that this was all way too much for her to take.

"Head hurt?"

Once.

"Need me to get rid of everyone?"

Nothing.

"How about we keep Mom, Dad and Cath?"

Nothing.

"Mom and Dad?"

Nothing.

"Mom?"

Once.

"Want me to stay?"

Once.

"Ok." David stood to his feet to address everyone.

"Mom," No response, too much chatter.

"Uh hem, Mom, Mother, VICKIE!"

Everyone stopped and looked at David who again cleared his throat.

"CJ would like to rest now and she would like everyone to leave except Mom. Thank you."

Vickie looked down at CJ. Her pale, yet lovely daughter whose scratches on her face had long healed already and there were traces of freckles along her button nose.

"Do you?" She asked. It seemed strange to her that her usually bubbly girl who was always the middle of everything and could have 3 conversations all at once would want to be undisturbed at this time.

Once.

Everyone slowly filed quietly out of the ICU to a family waiting area just outside to await further instruction. Vickie sat on one side of CJ and David on the other.

After a few minutes, CJ cleared her throat and reached for her mothers hand with her own shaky one.

"Mom," Came a whisper. It was like hearing paper falling slowly to the floor. It was a sound that was there, but barely. Vickie leaned closer to hear. A tear began to brim her eyes at the prospect of being able to talk to CJ again.

"I need you to know I think that I did all that He asked of me. I would like to think that for every one that knows me well, they know that I knew He was love, and hope and mercy. I am proud of you and I hope that in some small way I was a little like you. That would be a great thing."

David looked over at one of CJ's monitors and noticed it was beeping at a steady rhythm but all the numbers kept flashing red. He didn't know if he should get a nurse, or stay by her side. Shouldn't they know if something's wrong? Don't they have monitors somewhere?

"Tell Cath that I love her." CJ begins to cough.

"CJ, rest now. Please don't exert yourself. Take it easy. Rest now, baby." Vickie pushes the call button for the nurse frantically. CJ turned to her older brother to meet his worried gaze.

"David, Find forgiveness in love and time. Remember to look up 'Has Any One Ever Written Anything For You.' Stevie Nicks"

"Please don't go, CJ!" David pleaded. But he knew what was coming. As her monitors started to beep more insistently, David held her hand tighter. Overhead he heard the emergency code to ICU and new it was just a matter of time.

"Don't cry. I'm going to be OK." Then she began to slip away.

Suddenly, a crash team was pulling David away from CJ and David was pulling Vickie away from CJ as there was a desperate attempt to revive her. For nearly thirty minutes three teams of 2 were rotating CPR. CJ was re-intubated in an effort to help her breathe again to no avail. After an exhausting and excruciating effort, CJ expired at 10:56am, March 10th, 1991.

There is no pain so great as that of the loss of child. There is no hole dug deeper than the pit of the stomach of the parent of a child who has left the world way too soon. With CJ's flat line Vickie's own heart broke into a thousand tiny little pieces and her cries could be heard through out the corridor.

JR burst through the ICU doors and gathered his little daughter's body in his arms and began to weep uncontrollably. This didn't just happen. She is strong, She was getting better. He had only left them just a few minutes ago. Dr Hernandez, who had returned when he heard the code being called, ordered a sedative to be given to Vickie and now she was just sitting beside him unmoving and fairly catatonic.

David just stood in the corner watching the whole scene as if he were a stage hand in a play that he had no real part in. He knew he should go to his mother and comfort her, but how could he find words of comfort when he felt so empty within himself? He had fully understood what CJ had meant by forgiveness and time and whom she had meant it for, however, he felt she couldn't possibly have meant it for right now. Where? Where is their beloved peace now?

Audrey came into the ICU then, Annie right on her heels and between the two of them, they managed to gather up first Vickie, then J.R., then David and heard them all back into the family waiting area with the rest of the family.

"Let them fix her up for us and tell us what the next step is going to be."

Audrey proclaimed. There it was. Peace. Mothering. It was the guidance that they all needed. To be sure there was not a dry eye among them, but Audrey, with Clinton standing by her side, brought a sense of gentle authority to the situation. A bit of calm during the chaos.

Within a few moments of all of them being together, Dr. Hernandez slowly entered the room and loomed in the doorway. He stood there with them and for a few moments no one said any thing. He made it a point not to get attached to his patients or their families, but she had been different. THEY were different. One by one he hugged each of them and found himself becoming weepy. Even he would feel this loss in a small way. She had reached out and touched him without having said a single word to him. She would stay with him for years to come.

"I am sorry to all of you." He began, " CJ fought hard and I fought for her. This is the part that I hate the most and if I could do it with anyone else I would, but in this matter time is of the essence. We need to harvest her organs quickly. Now. You...."

Before Dr. Hernandez could get in another word, J.R. flew in his face and was spitting distance. Dr. Hernandez stumbled back into the doorframe, but had nowhere to go from a father's rage.

"The hell you need to harvest anything! She will go back to God with the parts she got here with!"

"J.R." It was barely a whisper, but it was loud enough to be heard by everyone. From the back of the room, Vickie stood on week knees and looked her husband and the Dr. both in turn.

"It was her wishes to donate her organs. The laughter and smile and love that is CJ has gone home to heaven, but if her body here can save some other mother or father from feeling this pain and loss than I think it's the least that we and she can give them. What do we do?"

Peace that passes understanding. J.R. stood his ground, but Vickie held up her hand in protest and J.R. then closed his eyes and prayed for peace or comfort or understanding or SOMETHING! Then it came, even for him. It was like a blanket that covered them all.

"Dr. Hernandez, We need a moment to pray, please stay with us."

He didn't know what to say. He had never been asked to participate in a family prayer before. He didn't know what to do. He watched quietly as each member bowed his or her head and Vickie began to pray,

"Father, God," Between sobs, "Thank you for giving us CJ"

Then Audrey stepped in,

"Lord, Bless what's left of her body that is healthy that it could still be used as a vessel and a tool to save another life."

Vickie   again,

"May the lives saved by CJ be long and for Your glory, amen."

A unanimous amen resounded throughout the room through tears and hugs. How do they do it? Dr. Hernandez wondered. How are they pulling it together?

"Dr. Hernandez?"

"Yes, Mrs. Stewart?"

"Can we know? Can we find out where her organs have gone? Do we have a say?"

Dr Hernandez shrugged his shoulders and shook his head at the same time.

"It's sort of a two edged sword." He said.

"You see. Just as you, as the donor family have the right to remain anonymous, so does the receiver of the organ. Most folks are very grateful for the donation though so if you put your info out there, there's a good chance you'll get a thank you letter. And unfortunately, no, you don't get to pick and chose who gets the organs. CJ had a rare blood type and that means that perhaps not all her organs may be needed or can be used in a timely manner. Some can be stored for a while, some if not used right away are lost. So, if a death row inmate is on the list with her type, he gets it whether he's good enough or not."

Vickie smiled a little smile. It would do a death row inmate a turn of good to get a piece of CJ wouldn't it? They might get a change of heart.

ACT III: CREATE IN ME A PURE HEART, OH GOD, AND RENEW A STEADFAST SPIRIT WITHIN ME

SCENE I: A CELEBRATION OF THE LIFE OF CJ STEWART

Her funeral had been on a Sunday morning. It had seemed fitting considering most of them, including her would have been in church anyway. There wasn't enough room, it turned out, to house everyone in the small community church in their small town, so they moved the service up to the gravesite at the cemetery. Along the hillside, just halfway up, Audrey and Clinton had purchased plots for each of them overlooking their ranch house. Now, adjacent to the headstone that already had their names and the dates of their births, but their deaths still blank, was a large, deep, looming hole in the ground that was waiting to receive the body of their granddaughter.

It was still early morning and Easter would be early this year, so, as the snow was already beginning to melt away, the mass of friends and family huddled together to remember CJ and look upon her one last time.

The casket that they had chosen was a dark cedar because CJ had always loved the smell of cedar. It had cost them a little more, but what did that matter? How do you put a price on loss? How do you sum up the value of your child's final resting place?

What to dress her in? She hated dresses and frilly things. It had always been like pulling teeth to get her to wear a skirt to church on any given Sunday. When she had gotten old enough to argue the point she was sure that God was more interested in the state of her heart than her attire when she sat in the pew and she had been more interested in being on time than being proper. Now Vickie had a chance to forever encase her in a beautiful dress of her choosing, but as she searched through CJ's clothing looking for the last clothes she would ever wear, She did not want to remember the last thing she ever saw her in being something that was foreign to her. So CJ would be laid to rest in one of her favorite costumes from one of her favorite play productions. It would seem strange to some, but to those who know her well, it was perfect.

Vickie had almost put CJ's letterman's jacket in the casket with her, but thought better of it. She would keep that for herself. Perhaps when Catherine got to high school, she would like to wear it, or maybe Rea would if David and Sara stayed together. Maybe Vickie would just take it out of the closet from time to time and hold it close and remember what it had meant to CJ and how hard she had worked for each bar on the "P" that Vickie herself had sewn on by hand.

Catherine watched as more and more people made their way up the hill and filled the small cemetery. Their family was fairly small so they only took up the small space around the gravesite, but the rest of the cemetery was standing room only. Most of the people she had only seen in passing and many she didn't think she had ever seen at all. Where had they all come from? This was not a spectator sport!

There was a part of her that was feeling extremely protective of her sister and felt as if some of these people were vultures circling the dead and waiting for their opportunity to strike, and perhaps not even she realized that there was an even bigger part of her that was jealous that, even in death, CJ had more fans, more admirers, more of everything than she had ever imagined was possible for one person.

Through the eyes of a twelve year old, this was all bitter and sour. She had thought that she had loathed CJ for all that seemed to come so easy for her. Now, she would give anything just to have one more cat fight with her! Tears came then. Catherine's eyes brimmed and spilled over and the trauma of it all finally came crashing through so she collapsed in a heap on the ground beneath the raised coffin.

J.R., Vickie and Audrey all reached for her at the same time, but it was David who got there first. Before anyone had time to protest, David had Catherine swept up in his arms and moved like lightning. The crowd parted like the Red Sea for him as he made his way down the hill to the gate of the cemetery. When he was at the base of the hill, he plopped Catherine up on an old head stone and wiped her red, puffy eyes.

"Ok, kid. I get it. So do you want to stick around here or just wait for every body back at the church where the cake and ice cream will be?"

Catherine turned around and again looked up at the massive crowd, trying to make eye contact with her mother who seemed worlds away. If she left, would her mom be mad? Was it like sinning to send her sister into the ground without saying goodbye? The tears came again. David hugged her close.

"Cath, we can stay if you want, but it's OK if we come back later, all by ourselves when every one else is gone. She was our sister. Our goodbye should be a little more private, don't you think?" With that, Catherine jumped off the head stone, took her brother's hand and walked down the hill towards the waiting church.

Vickie stood at the top of the hill watching her 20-year-old son and her 12-year-old daughter shuffle down the dirt road away from the cemetery hand in hand. She wondered a little what David had said to Cath to ease her tender, broken heart at least for the moment. She felt a sadness and yet she smiled just a little. David was just the right person to rescue Cath this time. It was hard for her to relinquish her savior moment, but CJ needed her one more time and this time Cath needed an ally, not a mommy. Peace that passes all understanding came to rest on that hill at that moment again.

The message given by Pastor Mason was beautiful and rich in metaphors about the lost being found and CJ waiting for them all at the pearly gates. As She looked out at the large, looming crowd, Audrey could tell by the faces who was finding comfort and who was just overwhelmed with sadness. Faith and belief in something better than this life would make this day a celebration of the life of CJ for some. For those who believe in the day to day and fear there may be nothing more beyond that, had down cast eyes and seemed to Audrey to be the saddest of all. That's not to say that they are the ones who would miss her the most. Beyond her parents, no one would miss her more than her grandmother!

Annie, through tears and sniffles, sang a beautiful version of "How Great Thou Art," and then there was praying before a very, very long procession of people walked by to say their last good bye to CJ.

As Lynn stopped by the casket, she reached in and touched CJ's cheek. It was no longer the soft place it used to be. Lynn rose swollen, sad, deeply lost brown eyes to Vickie.

"Now what am I suppose to do?" She said barely above a whisper as the tears fell like a waterfall down her face and dripped from her chin. J.R. scooped her up in his fatherly bear hug embrace and she collapsed into his chest and began to heave with sobs.

"You do what the rest of us do, kid." He whispered in her ear as she cried and cried and cried some more while mourners walked bye and paid their respects and pretended not to notice.

"You do the best you can and you ask for help."

After about two hours, the last person left the cemetery while everyone started making their way towards the church for a reception. The only one left on the hill while CJ was being lowered into the ground was Clinton. He had dropped Audrey, Doug and Annie at the church and then drove back up to the cemetery for one last look. He just wasn't ready to let her go yet. As they started to shovel dirt over the grave, Clinton grabbed his chest and cried out. And yet he stayed. He waited while they buried his granddaughter. He cried like he never remembered doing so before. He stayed until he was missed and Audrey sent J.R. to find him and then they cried together for a little while before returning to everyone else.

SCENE II: ALBION COMMUNITY CHURCH

David and Catherine filed in through the front doors of small church; David burst through the swinging doors at the back, and then stopped at the first pew and looked down at what seemed like an endless row of more of the same down to the pulpit.

In reality, there were only 9 pews on either side, and the church, even for David, was a very warm and inviting place because it was small and traditional with it's pictures hangings of Jesus with the lambs at his feet or Jesus surrounded by children. Jesus wearing a halo. This wasn't a cathedral setting with massive stained glass or a pipe organ. It was simply their home church. The place where the community gathered to worship non-denominationally by faith alone. To feel loved and a part of something greater than themselves.

David had stopped coming here when he left home at 14, but it was still familiar and comforting, even today. He was still holding Catherine's hand and after only a brief pause in the atrium, he moved quickly through the middle of the pews to a door that led to the waiting and more modern annex where they would find the kitchen. Once there, David hoisted Catherine up on the counter and scrounged around under the counter tops looking for tissues or wash rags or anything that she could blot her still streaming tears with. Then he heaved his tired and sad body onto the counter across from her for a big brother/little sister heart to heart.

He wasn't sure he would be very good at this. CJ was good at this. Their deep talks had been very few and often ended with him shouting or walking out the door, but she had always found a way to make her point with out screaming or loosing her cool. She had been like Mom in that way.

"Talk to me Cath. What's all this about? This is more than just what happened to CJ. You were doing OK for a little while and now you're acting like this is your fault and you know better so spill it."

Catherine blotter her eyes for what felt like the hundredth time in that moment and then blew her nose…again. She looked over at David with red, puffy eyes and wondered how he could care so little. She figured he had some things that he should take back when it came to CJ also, but he was cool as a cucumber and it was driving her crazy! She talked anyway. CJ was always expressing herself about every little thought that came into her head and maybe that's what made every one think she was so special.

" What if," wipe the tears, blow the nose, "What if CJ doesn't know that I love her and they bury her with her thinking that I'm mad at her or that I hate her? I mean, she is always so bossy and yells at me when I borrow her stuff. She's always lecturing me about my friends and which ones are OK for me to hang out with and which ones are trouble. It's none of her business! She makes me insane most of the time and she knows it and now she's gone and I didn't take the time to tell her that it's OK that she's mean, I love her anyway!"

David caught most of that between sniffles and blubbering and blowing. He jumped down and moved a little closer but still kept some distance. The touchy-feely thing was just not for him. What CJ had in embracing people, David had in pushing them away. What David hadn't realized yet, was that people change, all people. Mom's, Dad's and even older brother's could if they would open their eyes and allow a little happiness in. Today would not be that day for David. Today he would observe and reserve. Today he would listen to Catherine the best way he knew how and wish that CJ were here.

" Why do you think that CJ did all of those things, Cath?"

"Because she was a bitch. I know every one else thought she was this sweet and perfect little princess who did everything right and never made mistakes but she wasn't so perfect!"

And now a step back! David had to turn his head a little and try to suppress a smile. He wanted to take some credit for his twelve-year-old sister using words that their parents would disprove of, but chances were it was her friends in school since he had been the absentee brother. He also liked that she was still talking about CJ in the present tense.

"Maybe. Or maybe she did all of those things because she knew that she wasn't perfect and that she wanted better for you. She wanted to see you achieve more than she did and your friends ARE shitty and you CAN do better. And you didn't borrow anything, you took without asking. There's a difference." Catherine was sitting at attention now. She had stopped crying and was left with just a few sniffles.

"Why are you taking her side?" She asked crossing her arms defensively over her chest. David could say one thing for his baby sister. She was the fire in this family. She was born with her fists in the air. He and CJ had been so much older than her that she probably had felt like she had to fight for any respect and she had managed.

"It's not about sides Cath. It's about where we go from here. You can chose to remember CJ as the bossy sister you hated, or you can remember her as the big sister who fought for the very best for you and loved you most of all. You make the choice. You have a long, long life to live. How will you decide to live with your memories of CJ?"

A moment later, Miss Jessup, one of the wives of the church elders came bursting through the annex door and headed strait for the open kitchen. She stopped for a half second when she saw David and Catherine on the counter and then regained her momentum. Once in the kitchen she began to open the refrigerator and take out pies and cakes and casseroles. Once one person had entered the annex, pretty soon more started coming in. They began to trickle in like ants. At first it was just a few who wanted to help set out all the food and there was a mountain of food! Then, as more and more people came, they had to open up the back door of the church so that people could file in and out and find space to breathe.

David stayed long enough to watch as people who didn't even know each other traded stories about their times with CJ. He hated it. He hated it all. They didn't really know her like he did. They hadn't been there through the bad times with them and watched her come out the better person for it. It made him sick to watch all of them smile and laugh and "remember when she…". They had no idea how special she really had been and now she would never be special again. Not like this anyway. So he left.

When J.R. and Vickie arrived at the church the crowd was huge! It was standing room only, but Vickie didn't care about any of that, all she wanted to know was where had her other children gone? She had stopped by the house first just make sure they hadn't huddled up there waiting for the madness to die down, but when they weren't there, she hoped that they had come here. She wasn't overly concerned since she knew they were together. David was 20 and so Cath was in good hands, but this was a day for family and they all needed each other and she needed all of her children on this day. As she looked above the heads of the crowd looking for long black hair, she began to panic a little when she was unsuccessful. Her sister came to her aid.

"What's the matter?" Annie asked, taking Vickie's coat from her shoulders and hanging it up.

"I can't see David anywhere and he and Catherine are together." Annie pointed to a crowd of preteens in the corner of the church playing cards and eating plates of food.

"Catherine is right there with her friends and I haven't seen David. Someone said that he left about 10 minutes ago when it started to get a little crowded in here."

J.R.'s face reddened with anger at the thought of David leaving again.

"That Damn kid has a lot of nerve..."

Vickie held up her hand to silence him. J.R. had a hot temper, but the respect and admiration that he held for his beloved wife ran very deep. He had turned his whole life around just for her and he would do it again in a nanosecond if she asked him to. Maybe someday David would find that kind of binding bond. He could only hope. Vickie looked at J.R. whose face was still hot with anger.

"David will grieve in his own way in his own time. You don't want to be here with these people you don't know any more than he does, so let him go. We are here because these people need to connect to her through us today. They need to say goodbye and since they can't tell her how they loved her, they need to tell us. We need to respect that and you can suck it up and get through it. Now please mingle and it's OK if you cry a little."

J.R. was left standing there wondering how he had gotten so lucky and how he was suppose to make it though this day without CJ.

As the crowd started to fade away and clean up began the few that lingered were not surprise guests. Lynn would probably be a permanent fixture in the Stewart household for at least a little while and that was fine. Coach Taylor and all of the members of the track team stayed for the whole day. They each wore nice pants or a skirt, but they put CJ's number 7 on their shirts somewhere in remembrance.

Mr. McMann had made it point to speak to just about every one there and get a clear idea of what and who CJ Stewart had been. She was exactly who he thought she was. She wasn't the perfect student, her grades were average, but she made an effort nonetheless. She wasn't preppy, but he saw the preppy rich students here paying their respects. Nor was she a stoner by any stretch of the imagination! Yet he remembered her buying breakfast one morning for one of them, so they all showed up today dressed in their best.

She was a jock of sorts with the track, cross country running and weight training, but she was soft and laughed easily. She played a large part in the theater department from all aspects, and so she fit in with that crowd too. He checked her records and she had never, until the day of the accident, missed a choir class. If you define popularity by the crowd you hang out with, then CJ Stewart was not popular at all. However, if you define popularity by the number of people who respect you, or just consider you a friend, then CJ Stewart was very popular indeed.

He saw Vickie Stewart standing by a doorway looking out at a crowd of teenagers. She seemed wistful. definitely sad. It seemed curious to him because she didn't seem to be falling apart the way that he would have been had their rolls been reversed. Had Emily been in that car rather than CJ, he could not have weathered this storm the way she was.

He approached her. He did notice out of the corner of his eye, her husband, a large, looming man standing close by.

"Mrs. Stewart?" Vickie turned to greet Simon and smiled. It was nice to see that he had stayed so long. She had seen a few principles come and go since the time that she herself had graduated for Pullman High School but she thought that she had respected him so far the most. His approach with these kids seemed to be working and there was a lot to be said for that.

"I'm glad to see you found us out here, Mr. McMann. CJ would have loved sharing this with you. Your daughter is lovely, by the way. She came over and introduced herself and asked if there was anything she could do to help. You have raised her well."

He smiled. Emily was a very a sweet kid and he was proud.

"Well, I don't know if that's so much a reflection of me or the fact that CJ was the first person to make Em feel welcome in a new school. She will be greatly missed." Tears came then. He couldn't stop them. As a parent he felt the pain that only one can. Vickie handed him a tissue and smiled a smile that only an understanding parent can.

"How are you OK?" He asked." I don't mean to pry, but I'm a basket case and she wasn't even mine. So how are managing to stay so strong?" Vickie guided him to a chair and they sat down. J.R. lingered in the background curious.

"Make no mistake, I'm far from OK, but I know CJ's heart. I believe that there is more to that girl that just that body on that hill." She said pointing towards the cemetery. "Her body parts have gone on to other people to give them life so she is still out there some where living for other people which is what she wanted and the parts that made CJ the person are all over this room today." At that they both scanned the room. It was mostly empty now but the spirit of the day still lingered.

"All the tears shed today, all of the memories and the laughing was all about that girl who is still here in my heart and yours and she's not going away. I also believe that God has a special place for that child and I will see her again when I die. I know that not every one believes that but she did and so do I so I have peace. I will miss her every day of my life, but I will find comfort in the knowing we'll be together again. That is how I am. How are you?"

And the peace that passes understanding passed from her to him in that moment and J.R. witnessed it.

SCENE III: SANDIEGO CALIFORNIA

Jacen sat in his hospital bed staring out his window for the fifth day in a row looking at nothing. His new heart seemed to be working fine and he felt better than he had in years except for the giant scar from the middle of his abdomen to his sternum, but he was feeling better. It was a good, strong heart that was for sure. He could feel it in a way that he had never felt his old heart.

She had not been to see him in a week. He assumed that meant that she had either gotten well, or well.... He furrowed his brow and threw his tray of food against the wall. It was frustrating not knowing what was going on with the girl who he only knew by the imprint she had made on his life. The last time he had seen her she had been pale and week and she had shaved all her long curls off but he still remembered them. If he closed his eyes she was in his windowsill again. If he was close to drifting off to sleep, they were on the beach walking together again, but when sleep came she'd be gone because she was no longer real. He hated that he cared at all. He liked it better when he was dying and he didn't have to know about her or care and what did all her messages mean? Who was going to bring him peace? If not HER, then who? Who was going to give him the answers? When he was strong enough, he would pull all of his resources and try to find her. What did he know? Her name is unknown to him for now, she must be about his age, and she lives somewhere where it's cold right now. It's not much to go on but it's at least something.

Just then the door opens and Dr. Alyster came into the room. He glanced around and saw the tray of food on the floor and his brooding patient propped up in bed.

"If you want take out, I can arrange for it, but no MSG." Not even a crack of a smile.

"What's bothering you today, Jace? You're new heart is doing great, it will still be another 8 weeks before we can be sure if your body won't reject it, but the first 48 hours are critical and after almost a week things are looking very promising. You even have a little color back in your cheeks. So what's the problem?"

Jacen shook his head from side to side and rolled his eyes as he flipped the covers back and swung his legs over the side of bed. He tried to stand and then, when his legs turned to jello and he began to sink to the floor, He grabbed the bedrail while Dr. Alystare rushed to his aid and helped to ease him back into bed.

"Not so fast, Sparky! New heart needs more time to rejuvenate the whole system that has been broken for a long time. Talk the talk without the walk."

"I just can't get that girl out of my head."

"The one you say came to visit you."

"I know it's absurd, but she knew me even though I had never seen her before in my life. You know how private I am about my personal life and yet she knew details about my past that you don't even know. How is that possible? It was practically supernatural."

Dr. Alyster walked over to the window and sat on the sill.

"Sit in the chair."

He hadn't meant to make that windowsill a shrine to her but it was one of the places he associated with her and he didn't want someone else's essence to linger there. As Dr. Alyster settled in the chair at the end of bed, he wondered what had gotten into his longtime friend and patient. Jacen Owen never cared about anyone else in his life. Sometimes he hadn't even cared if he lived or died and now he was obsessing about a girl that no one had seen except him. It's not that the average patient can't have visitors that come and go, but Jacen was not an ordinary patient. He was the owner of a multi-billion dollar corporation so people did not just come and go from his room unannounced or unescorted.

"May I purpose that perhaps in your heightened state of stress and the strain your heart was putting on your body that you created her to comfort you because you knew that you were dying?"

"GET OUT!" Jace shouted. If he still had food to throw he would. Dr. Alyster did not budge. Security guards rushed in, but Dr. Alyster shewed them out after showing them that every thing was fine. They had many arguments in the past and he was sure that was why Jace kept him around. He was not the pushover that everyone else was.

"I will leave after you sign this." He pulled out a piece of paper and handed it to Jacen on a clipboard. Jacen looked at it and then asked,

"What is this?"

"It's a donor statement. It's basically a thank you to the family for the donor heart." Jacen just stared at the document for a while. Then picked it up and cradled it closed to his heart before turning towards the window.

"Kyle?" Dr. Alyster opened the door and then turned back towards the room and looked at the quickly recovering, but still sad kid sitting on the bed on the other side of the large hospital suite.

"Yeah?"

"Where did my heart come from? I know since you were in on the surgery you had to know something about it."

"All I know is that it came from an 18 year old girl in Washington State who was in a car accident. She lingered in a coma for a little over a week, but I hear that most of her organs were viable. I'll check in later." Then he closed the door quickly and quietly behind him. Jacen sank under his covers and wished she would come so he could tell her about the girl who sacrificed her life to give him back his. He wanted her to know that when he was strong enough, he would find her so she could help him become the better person he needed to be and to understand about the peace. He needed peace because right now all he felt was confusion.

SCENE IV: SADIES PUB, PULLMAN WASHINGTON
6 MONTHS LATER

"THERE'S NO TIME FOR US......
THERE'S NO PLACE FOR US....."

Sara came in to the smoke filled bar to the sounds of Queen's Who Wants To Live Forever being played by David and his band. She filed in through the back of the crowd who were all standing and swaying and singing along as she tried to make eye contact with David whom she had hardly seen in the last week. He had become more and more reclusive since his sisters death. If she didn't know any better, she would say that he had died with her. He still came home every night and helped pay the bills, but he said very few words and if it weren't for the fact that Rea loved him and he loved her even though she wasn't his, she would boot him out on his ass. Yet as the music played on, and as she watched the way that he seemed to become one with his guitar, she knew she loved him too. She stayed in the back and waited as she always had for him to see her.

"WHAT IS THING THAT BUILDS OUR DREAMS YET SLIPS AWAY FROM US...."

David's fingers worked the guitar like a marionette putting on his best show. To the crowd who only came because they knew his work and liked the show, to look at him, and see the stream of black running from his eyes, they would think it was sweat. Here, and only here, on this stage, in these moments, with this guitar and these songs, would he take time to grieve. Love of music he and CJ had in common even if their flavors were different. She still came to hear him play from time to time while she was still alive. He could use some of that peace right now.

"WHO WANTS TO LIVE FOREVER? WHO WANTS TO LIVE FOREVER?"

Sara saw the tears. David would never confide in her, but she saw them none the less. "Let her go!" She pleaded in her heart. She thinks she even whispered the words a little out loud, but with this crowd and the booze and the smoke, no one could hear her.

His grief was too great for all of them and it overwhelming her. How could she help him find peace? " I need help!" She pleaded silently. And then her tears came.

"THERE'S NO CHANCE FOR US....

IT'S ALL DECIDED FOR US...

THE WORLD HAS ONLY ONE SWEET MOMENT SET ASIDE FOR US."

David often wondered in these moments up on the stage if CJ could still hear him. His mother believed that she had gone to heaven and that therefore she was not really gone, just not here anymore. If that were true, could she still hear him? He wasn't sure what he believed anymore. He believed in God and heaven when he was a child, but things were gray and blurry these days and he wasn't so sure what he believed but if there was a chance that CJ was anywhere, he could sure use a sign.

"WHO DARES TO LOVE FOREVER?"

Then David saw Sara. She didn't come to hear him play very often. Why was she here? And who was with her? David continued to sing and play on autopilot while he watched Sara. There was too much smoke around her and it was hard to see, but for a flash of a second he could swear he saw a flint of girl with long curly brown hair and blue eyes wearing a PHS letterman's jacket standing just behind Sara. Then, and only around Sara, the smoke began to clear. It was CJ! Clear and plane as anything he had ever seen, and he had not had anything to drink that night....yet! She said nothing, just keep her eyes focused on him as she moved and placed her arms around Sara. She just stood there holding Sara, but looking at David, her eyes pleaded with him to gain understanding. Then he looked at Sara again. He really looked at her, and he saw her tears. From clear across the room he saw beyond his own grief and could feel the pain he was causing her and he understood.

"WHO LIVES FOREVER ANYWAY?"

As the song ended and CJ disappeared, David put down the guitar and jumped from the stage. He moved through the crowd on a mission and found Sara at the back wondering what was wrong. He took a clumsy thumb and rubbed a tear from her eye.

"I get it."

Sara smiled a little.

"Who told you?" She teased. David put a protective arm around her and walked with her towards the door and towards home.

"You'd never believe me if I told you."

SCENE V: SAN DIEGO CALIFORNIA
DR KYLE ALYSTER'S OFFFICE

"Alicia, do I have any appointments left for today?"

Kyle buzzed into the intercom from his office phone to his receptionist in the other room. He had had a busy day and was hoping to duck out early so he was hoping the whatever he might have left could be rescheduled for another day. He was beat.

"You have one more today at 2:45 and then you are finished."

"What is that appointment for?"

"Just a follow up, Dr. Alyster."

Kyle started pulling off his tie and kicked his feet up on his desk then let out a long sigh.

"Alicia, please reschedule that for me. Tell them I apologize, but I will see them early next week."

"Um, I can try, but this patient's not very appreciative of that sort of thing." Kyle rubbed his eyes and put both feet back on the floor and sighed again.

"Jacen Owen?"

"Yep."

"Can you call him and ask if he could come earlier?"

"I can try."

"Thank you, Alicia. Oh, and I will owe you big time."

"Um, yes you will!"

"Thank you for calling Owen Medical Supplies and Pharmaceuticals. How may I help you?"

"Yes, this is Alicia from Dr. Alyster's office calling. Is Mr. Owen available?"

"I can check for you, please hold."

"Hello, my name is Meghan, Mr. Owen's assistant, may I help you?"

"Yes, Meghan, it's Alicia from Dr. Alyster's office, how are you?"

"Very well, thank you. Is there a problem with Mr. Owen's appointment today? He had mentioned that he had one."

"Well, Dr. Alyster wanted to know if there were any possibility of moving it up in the day at all, possibly at noon?"

"Let me check for you."

Alicia drummed her pencil on her desk and blew a hair out of her eyes while she waited for Meghan to return to the phone line. She had to give Mr. Owen's office credit for putting some interesting popular pop music on the line to listen to rather than the standard elevator or easy listening she was used to.

"Alicia?"

"Yes, I'm still here."

"12:00 will be fine. He will be there on time. Have a great day."

"Thank you. Good bye."

Alicia heaved a big sigh of relief before she buzzed her boss in the next room. She had been working for Dr. Alyster for 6 years now and most of his patients were very nice. Some not so much, but Jacen Owen was a force to be reckoned with. He was young, beautiful, angry and spiteful until he had got his new heart and then a new leaf? Maybe, but it was a little hard to swallow. She liked Dr. Alyster and if it weren't for the fact that she loved her own husband and children so much, she would be very much in love with her boss. He was very handsome and sweet. It was shocking he hadn't been scooped up yet. It probably had everything to do with being too devoted to his evil counterpart, she decided.

"He'll be here at noon."

"Thank you, Alicia."

"Can I get you something?"

"Coffee."

Alicia smiled. Maybe he had been out late last night on a date. There may be hope for him after all!

Kyle turned off the speaker phone and was thankful for the silence that surrounded him once again. He rubbed his eyes and then fingered carefully the file that sat on his desk in front of him. Give it to Jacen or shred it as his Dr's code dictated he should? This was the question before him. In that file lay all of the information on the donor of the heart that Jacen had received, Her name, date of birth and death, as well as her address and phone number. If he gave this information to Jacen without the family's written consent, it would be a direct violation of the rules and regulations that were set forth in the HIPA act. Not to mention that it was just unethical at it's core. If he didn't give Jacen the file, Jacen would find another way that would be unsupervised by him.

It was 10:30am. He would hope the file would go away on it's own.

SCENE VI:ALBION CEMETERY

Catherine sat on the grass that had begun to grow around CJ's grave and pick at the blades one at at time.

A few of them she placed between her thumbs and blew at them trying to get them to whistle.

It had been six months since they had laid her sister to rest here. At first, Cath thought that she would not be able to come back here by herself. She thought that she would find it creepy, or just too sad, and at first she did find it too sad, but after a while she found it got easier. Now she came several times a week. It was nice to sit and finally be able to talk to CJ and not be talked back to. To say anything that she wanted to about anything that felt like. Sometimes she imaged that CJ laughed with her. True, sometimes she did imagine CJ mocking or yelling at her because there was comfort in that too.

Today she brought paper lilies with her. She couldn't afford to buy real ones and they had always been CJ's favorites, so she made some out of paper and colored them in all of the colors of the rainbow.

"I don't know what you're favorite color is." She said as she spread the paper lilies across where she imagined CJ's head would be. "otherwise I would have made them just the color you like."

Cath had turned 13 a month after CJ had left them and with all of the grieving no one had noticed. Not even Catherine. Things had started to become routine again, but the pain still lingered. Decisions had been made. David was withdrawing from everyone. He checked in with Mom and herself, but he had even moved out of Sara's and was living downstairs again. Dad was working longer hours. If he worked he didn't have to be home where CJ wasn't either. Mom was keeping in touch. In touch with Aunt Annie and Uncle Doug in Montana, with Grandma Audrey and Grandpa Clinton, and as she received information from donor recipients, she began to correspond with them as well.

For Catherine, her decision was to stay out of all of it. To be invisible was what she wanted. She was not the healer that CJ had been. She didn't know how to comfort the way that her mother did, CJ had been given that gift and it had died with her. The tears came as she realized once again all of things that she missed about her sister. All of the things that they both took for granted while she had been alive and now could never have back.

At the gate of the cemetery looking up at the middle of the stretch of headstones, was David watching his baby sister fall apart again as he did a few times a week. He walked once again up to the familiar grave that he himself frequented when he was absolutely sure he was alone. He sat down next to Catherine and pulled her close. This was a dance they had done many times over the last few months.

"I love the flowers."

She laughed a little spewing snot on his shirt which she tried to wipe off with her sleeve that was too long.

"I wanted to make them one color, but I didn't know what color was her favorite."

David picked up a blue flower a twirled it in his callused fingers.

"Is that what all the water works is about? A color?"He asked. Catherine backed away from him and crossed her arms.

"If I don't her favorite color, what else am I missing? What will I forget? If I don't know, what are you going to forget? Do you know anything about her at all? Will they all forget her?" She was crying again and it pierced David to the core. He would never forget CJ. He saw her everyday. He could hear her last words like an echo. He still had not taken the time to listen to the song she was talking about because Stevie Nicks was not his style and he wasn't ready.

He hugged Cath again.

"Next time just bring yellow."

SCENE VII: SANDIEGO CALIFORNIA

Jacen stormed into his office, slammed the dark cherry oak door behind him and flung the contents of the file across the room. It was partly rage and partly desperation. Perhaps there was a very small part of him that knew deep in his heart of heart that there should be sadness as well.

He sat down on the couch near the bay window, heaved a heavy sigh of frustration and buried his head in his hands. There was a soft knock on the door, but he didn't answer. It was several minutes before he blew out a long breath and began to gather the scattered papers and right them again in the order that they came in. The pages were numbered in the bottom left hand corner and when he got them all stacked back as he had received them, he closed the file once again placing it in his top desk drawer and sat down in the large leather swivel chair that had once belonged to his father before him.

He picked up the phone and pressed the intercom.

"Meghan. I need to see you."

Meghan had been sitting at her desk, pensive and apprehensive. She had known Jacen for many years since she had been working for his father before him. He had left most of the business arrangements to herself and the board of trusties on a daily basis both before his illness and during. Since his transplant, however, he had become more hands on both in the physical and financial senses. It had been good to see the transformation from lost child to brilliant young man. However, this current display of fury or frustration or whatever it was, was something she had not seen in quite some time and she wasn't sure what to make of it. Still, as she entered the office of Jacen Owen, she saw before her a calm, mature young man who's face seemed tortured with both sadness and regret.

"What can I do for you, Jacen? Are you feeling alright?"

"Fine, Meghan. I need you to charter me a flight to Washington State. My final destination is going to be somewhere called Albion. I need to have a car and driver at my disposal the whole time I'm there."

He said all of this without making eye contact. Instead, he pulled out the file again and began leafing through the pages. Slowly he rubbed each page with his thumb longingly as if it might help connect them.

"I will make the arrangements today. When do you need to leave and when would you like to return?" Meghan wondered what was in the file, why it was so important and if it had anything to do with this recent storm or the coming impromptu trip. She knew better than to ask. Jacen would share when he wanted. Or not.

"I would like to go tomorrow and I will call from Washington when I am ready to return. I will stay in touch daily while I am there and I will have my pager and a cellular phone."

"Will you be taking an assistant?"

Jacen looked at Meghan for the first time in the conversation and smiled. He had a wonderful smile. It wasn't seen very often, but it was wonderful because it was rare and genuine.

"No. Not this time. I know everyone is going to freak out a little because the fragile boy is going somewhere alone, but I'm strong enough now and I need to go."

"Why? And why there? If you need a vacation, you could go lots of other places that don't require flying and you could take an assistant or a friend."

Meghan was only ten years older than Jacen so she felt like the older sister that he never had. He never treated her with anything other than professionalism, however, she felt that he needed a sense of family whether he wanted it or not.

"I was told before the transplant to go and meet the donor family. It seemed absurd at the time, but now I don't know what to think or do or feel and I wonder if it's because I haven't done what she said I should do. I'm changed in some way since the surgery and I can't explain why, but I think they can."

Meghan didn't know what to say. Jacen in all the years she had known him had never said more than two sentences in a day to her that wasn't about the business. She didn't know if she should feel special or scared. She sighed and left the office to go back to her desk and make the arrangements that Jacen had asked of her.

Jacen watched the door close and then looked down at the file again. He read the name again for what must have been the 1000th time.
Patient Name: Carmen Joselin Stewart
Date Of Birth: 02-14-73
Deceased: 03-10-91
Hair Color: Brown
Eye Color: Blue
Washington State Organ Donor
He pressed his fingers to his eyes to push back the tears that were trying to break through. Jace hadn't cried in a very long time. He couldn't remember the last time. Somewhere, somehow he needed reassurance. It was the only thing that made sense. People don't come to see you that you can touch and no one else can see unless....

"Jacen?"

Meghan on the intercom from the other room. He wiped his eyes quickly and pulled himself together.

"Yes."

"Your private jet is scheduled to leave a 9am tomorrow morning and will arrive at Sea Tac International Airport in Seattle at 11:15am and then you will fly first class on Alaska airlines at 11:50am and arrive in Spokane at 12:40am. There will be a driver and a car waiting for you there to take you to Pullman which is the closest hotel reservation I could get you to Albion. It turns out the Albion is only a residential community of about 750 people. They apparently have a post office and a church and I think that might be about it. Is there anything else?"

Jacen smiled a little. For the first time in his life he was going to leave California and he felt ready. He didn't know for how long and what he was going to say or do when he got there. He kind of hoped SHE might show up when he got there.

"No, Meghan that will be all. I'll call you when I get there. Thank you."

SCENE VIII: PULLMAN WASHINGTON

It was early, 7am, on a Tuesday, when Sara heard a knock on the front door of her small apartment. She was awake and had been for quite some time. She hurried to answer so as not awaken Rea before she absolutely had to. It being summer now in Washington and not having air conditioning in the apartment, Sara savored the morning coolness.

Vickie greeted her in the door way with some paper bags and a gentle smile as always.

"Good Morning, Sara, is it too early? I was on my way to work and just wanted to drop a few things by on my way. I didn't wake you did I?"

Sara opened the door wider to allow Vickie access and heaved a heavy sigh. Vickie made these rounds weekly even though Sara protested to no avail. It was a dance they did often, but on some level, they both found comfort in it. It kept Vickie close and it kept Sara in the loop.

"You don't have to do this, Vickie. Rea and I are doing fine."

Vickie headed for the kitchen and began to unload the bags of groceries and then moved towards what was to become the new baby's room to leave the newborn size bag of diapers, wipes, etc.. Then, she came back to the living room and the two women sat. Sara offered Vickie a cup of fresh brewed coffee, which she took and smiled a thank you, then she closed her eyes and breathed in the moment.

"How are you feeling Sara?" Sara, on instinct, reached a protective hand down and rubbed her increasing swelling belly and smiled.

"We are doing very well. The Dr. says that everything is on schedule. We should expect a normal delivery and recovery for both of us."

"And Rea is taking it all in well?"

Sara reflected on her little busy bee helper who would be just turning two after the baby came.

"Has David been by? I know it's none of my business and believe me, he has told me as much, so if you'd rather not talk about him I understand."

It's funny, when other people would ask her about David, it always felt as if they were poking around where they didn't belong. As if they were just curious for gossip's sake. When Vickie asked, it was because she loved them both so much and Sara could feel that love deep in a place she had not known before. Somehow, even though David was her son, Sara knew Vickie was not picking sides. They all mattered to her. When David and Sara had created that life inside of her, Sara had become a part of the Stewart's and that would never change.

"David has been by when we're not here to leave money and he leaves pictures and letters for Rea. I have been told by the day care that he has been by to spend some time with Rea there also."

Her eyes filled with tears.

"I think I made a mistake."

Vickie crossed the distance between them in seconds and wrapped her motherly arms around Sara. Since CJ had died, Sara had watched David mourn in silence. She had watched Rea greave for the aunt that she loved and lost too soon. And she had pushed David away when she needed him most because she had never taken the time to feel for herself or tell anyone what was going on within her because she didn't believe that she was entitled. This was not her family therefore it was not her pain to own. Was it?

"How? How is any of this your fault?"

"David was trying, he really was. He stayed home a little more and drank a little less, but I think it was too much. He withdrew more. He met some new people who wanted to play somewhere else that was open later and they moved around a lot so he started staying out later and longer and came home looking more lost. So I finally told him to spend more time at home or leave. The next day his stuff was gone. Didn't it ever cross his mind Rea and I miss her too?" Then the sobbing came. Vickie held her closer and wiped a tear from her own eyes.

"Sara, David and CJ were like fire and ice. David gave me daily heart attacks with his antics and CJ was always where she was suppose to be when she was suppose to be there.

However, they were somehow two halves of the same whole and I think his emptiness is different than the rest of us. I won't say it's greater. I'm her mother. I can't imagine anyone missing her more than I do. Just different. It's OK that you demand more of him than what he is giving in this time and space. He owes you more and you, Rea and that baby deserve better. He has his whole life to mourn his sister. CJ would expect better of him. I know I do. He'll come around."

Vickie stood and walked to the front door. Sara followed behind her and held the door for her. It was now close to 8am, the sun was high in the sky and Sara was beginning to feel it's warmth. She wondered if it might be a sign of better days to come. Vickie looked to the sun and closed her eyes and whispered a small simple prayer for Sara, for David, for hope.

SCENE IX: WASHINGTON STATE UNIVERSITY

Vickie entered the building a few minutes later than usual. Normally she would have called first and spent several minutes apologizing, however, the time spent with Sara that morning had been refreshing, reflective and much needed. She felt as though a large weight had been lifted. Not really sure what for, she thought, but she somehow felt better anyway. She would talk to David about things. What things, she wasn't sure, but things.

That settled in her mind, she walked through the Facilities Planning door and greeted Angie with her usual morning smile and hello before heading into her office where Angie followed her with a cup of coffee and her morning stack of papers that needed to be signed off on.

After flipping through the first few stacks of papers and making a few phone calls, Vickie leaned back in her chair and opened up her bottom left desk drawer and carefully removed the stack of envelopes that she had been saving there. There, all rubber banded together, she gently unraveled them and gingerly read though each one slowly as she had done hundreds of times before. They were form letters from the National Donor Recipients Group, but Vickie tried to imagine CJ parts as they were now helping each of these people live fuller, happier lives.

"Dear Stewart Family,

Thank you on behalf of (patients name here) for the generous donation of Anterior Crucial Ligament tissue from your daughter Carmen Jocelin Stewart..."

They all went on the same. One for the one good lung she had left, for the corneas in her eyes. Vickie had to blink back the tears as she thought about CJ's blue eyes fading from her memory. She hoped that they never would. Where was her heart? It had been eight months. Where was her heart?

It's an amazing thing the way that peace enters a room just when you need it the most. There was knock on the door and Angie entered the room. Vickie looked up and smiled. Vickie always smiled. Despite all that she had seen, heard and been through, Vickie smiled.

"There is someone here to see you. He says it's important and that you need to see him." Vickie stood up. She was a little puzzled. She wasn't an important person on campus particularly. Her job was essentially to let them know when and where they had enough money to build buildings on campus and when they could not. She could crunch numbers in her head faster than most people. Not bad for someone with a high school diploma. Who could be showing up at her office unannounced looking for her?

Just then a very young man with dark hair, dark brooding eyes, pail skin and a long, black coat came into her office behind Angie. He extended his hand to greet her across the desk and a baffled Vickie shook it.

"My name is Jacen Owen."

He turned to Angie and smiled dimples deep. Vickie watched the exchanged and thought she saw her secretary melt into a puddle of mush right before her eyes. He was charming that was for sure. Vickie herself felt a little week in the knees. It couldn't be possible could it? The one and only real Jacen Owen? Son of Multi-million dollar tycoon Walter Owen who had passed away leaving his fortune to a child, standing here in her office?

"Your name?" He asked, still looking at Angie. Angie's eyes darted to the floor and she smiled sheepishly.

"I'm Angie, Vickie's receptionist."

"Nice to meet you, Angie. I'm going to need to speak to Vickie privately. Thank you." With that he managed to manipulate Angie out the door and close it behind him. Then he sat himself down in one the chairs opposite Vickie's desk and motioned for her sit as well.

"How may I help you Mr. Owen?"

Jacen stood again to his feet. His eyes became fixed on something just above and to the left of Vickie's head on the shelf where she kept all of her pictures. He walked around her desk and picked up a photo, holding it close, inspecting the contents. With one hand he held the picture and with the other, his fingers traced the face, hair, arms, legs, and lips of the timeless figure trapped inside. Vickie watched as a young man transformed from businesslike, to eager, to deeply sad and regretful all in the passing of a moment.

"That's my daughter CJ. She died in a car accident last February."

It was a very long time before Jacen could speak. He was reliving every visit he had ever had from CJ. He closed his eyes and tried to re-feel her embrace and re-touch her hair. When he opened his eyes and found himself facing this stranger who had known her, the very deepest places of her and yet she was working and calm and …..peace. CJ had said peace.

"There is peace that passes understanding and she will give it to you." In that moment, he understood. If he could so deeply miss and regret a life he had only known so briefly and yet be touched by so deeply, how much more could he learn from this woman who was holding it together now?

Vickie still waited for an answer. What was this prominent young man doing here with her and why was he clinging so longingly to CJ's picture as if he had known her for years?

"I have CJ's heart."

ACT IV: MY FRAME WAS NOT HIDDEN FROM YOU WHEN I WAS MADE IN THE SECRET PLACE

SCENE I: ALBION CEMETERY

Jacen walked the long gravel road upward that led to the cemetery and stopped at the gate. There at the top he turned around and looked down at the small town of Albion, Washington. Population approximately 750 people located seven miles in either direction from anywhere that had greater substance of anything substantial such as groceries, gasoline, restaurants, movies. No, this was a town of residence only. People came to Albion just to live the quiet life and nothing more. Jacen thought that places like this were made up in books by Louie Lamore or seen in paintings. He hadn't ever thought that he'd ever live to see one. Frankly, he hadn't thought he'd ever live past nineteen and here he was on his twentieth birthday standing in a cemetery in the smallest town he'd ever dreamed there could be. Ironic.

He began to walk through the rows of head stones and read the inscriptions. The first sets that he came to were very old. Some of the dates on them were from the turn of the century or even earlier and what wording had not faded away completely were written in broken english with spelling based on how things sounded before there was an english dictionary. The cemetery was quaint and small. There wasn't any room for large family crypts however Jacen could see small stone wedges or little black iron fences that indicated family plots.

He touched through his light t-shirt and felt his fading scar that ran from the center of his abdomen to his sub-sternal notch. It had been a while since the surgery and he felt better than ever, which meant that CJ had been gone just as long. It was still strange to him how someone he knew so little of could impact his so deeply. He was still trying to piece together whether she had even been really there in California with him or not. He had felt her! He had touched her broken bones himself! Vickie had confirmed all that he had seen.

It took him about fifteen minutes and then he found it. How could he not. It was a beautifully marked grave that was well kept. There were hooks on either side of the headstone for flower pots and fresh flowers hung there regularly. Her picture had been imprinted on the front for all eternity. Her eyes, her smile, and her warmth. Jacen sat down on the bench that had been placed between her stone and that of her grandparents. He pulled out a journal and began to write in it.

He wrote of his past when he was younger and of his feeling of anger, of defeat and he asked her what he was to do to change those things. He drew her likeness the way that he had remembered her both on the beach and in the hospital. He wrote of his parents and he told her how lucky she had been to have had what she did and that he hoped she had never taken them for granted. Although he had yet to meet JR, he thought that any dad who was somewhat present was better than a dad who gave money in place of love and attention. He didn't realize how long he'd been there until a shadow cast across his paper.

"Who are you, and what are you doing here?"

Startled, Jacen stood, turned and was greeted by a young man, equally as tall as himself, but much thinner and paler with long brown hair and piercing blue eyes. Jacen had not been intimidated by many, and he was not much now, but something primitive and protective in this equal's warning tone gave him pause so he chose respect rather than conflict for the first time.

"My name is Jacen and I was just finishing."

David turned and watched Jacen's back as he headed down the hillside and wondered about the brooding young man walking away. He knew who he was. He had talked to his mother a couple of times in the week since his arrival, but why now? Where had he been? Why not just send a letter like the rest?

"Why is he so important CJ? No more lessons. I don't want to learn anymore."

SCENE 11:CANE RANCH HOUSE-ALBION WASHINGTON

Vickie passed the mailbox on the left hand side of the road the markings for the C/C Ranch hanging from it and turned into the long driveway on the left were the two story house, a small barn, the yard surrounding the house with two apple trees and about five and half acres of pasture behind the house. Looking from the right of the driveway was a small creek that emptied two miles away into the Snake River with a cattle corral and an additional seven acres before running into the fences of the next property. She always loved the long slow drive up to her parents house. She had been doing it since she had obtained a drivers license and it had never gotten old. She loved this town, these people and this place. Sure, she had dreams to travel and see the world, but home was were her heart had always been. Family was everything to her and there were no limits to the number of members a family could hold.

As they pulled up next to the house and stopped, they all began to pile out. They had come in two cars. J.R., Vickie, Catherine, and Lynn in one and David, Sara, and Rea in the other. David and Sara were talking again but he was still living at home. Vickie was hopeful, but time would tell all.

"Prayer is a powerful thing, Vic." Audrey had said to her when they had talked about the subject recently. Vickie watched as David aided an extremely pregnant Sara out of the car and then picked up Rea and walked into the house without her.

"We'll see." She thought closing the door to her own car and following the rest of the family in to what was to be a "welcome to the family, Jacen" dinner.

Stepping into the house, there was a warmth and the welcome smell of beef, turkey, gravy, potatoes, vegetables, salads, pies, cakes, cookies, coffee, tea and sodas everywhere. Vickie came in and greeted her mother and father with hugs and then was delighted to see both of her sisters sitting on the couch with their spouses.

"I didn't even see your cars outside! When did you get here?"

Betsy, her youngest sister whom she hadn't seen since CJ's funeral stood to greet her.

"Mom and Dad picked me up at the airport last night and we hid Doug and Annie's car in the garage to surprise you!" Betsy told her. Vickie hugged them each in turn and then grabbed a drink for each of them first and then her self before she sat down to catch up. First she wanted to know all the goings on in Alaska where Betsy and her family lived, and then she wanted to make sure that she and Annie were still on for their yearly Christmas shopping spree in Montana.

Everyone had been so busy catching up and not noticing the time passing when J.R. Finally pulled Vickie aside.

"It's getting a little late, don't you think? What time did you tell this guy to be here?" There was irritation in his tone, but then, there was often irritation in his tone lately. Vickie sighed and tried a little patience.

"I told him 4:00, but he may have gotten a little lost. Let's give him another half an hour and then we can go ahead and start. There will be plenty for him to catch up when he arrives." J.R. Grunted his disagreement but he retreated to the living room where the rest of the family was visiting.

David, who had been watching the display from the sidelines decided to take Rea outside to the tire swing that was still hanging from the large willow tree in the front yard. David wondered sometimes if it was still the original tire swing from his youth or if Gramps (which was what he had affectionately been calling Clinton since he was about

4) had replaced it several times over the years as each grandchild and great-grandchild had worn them down. It certainly looked like the same old half piece of hollowed out tire with smooth grooves from wear and tear. Rea laughed as David stood behind her and pushed her higher and higher and then asked to be spun around in circles like a top. David obliged as his mind began to wander back in time. It was easy looking around at that yard in autumn. He could remember so many things and every memory had pieces of CJ.

CJ being two years old and falling off of a big white mare that Gramps had. CJ cried and begged him not put her back up there behind David, but Gramps loving wiped away her tears, called the horse back and plopped her right back up there where she fell right back off again. She never did find her cowgirl stride. His gaze fell upon one of the lower tree branches and a small smile moved across his lips as he watched CJ fall off that branch again and again. For a smart girl, man could she be hard headed!

As Rea continued to spin and spin he looked at the small wood shed where he used to hide from his sister and wait to scare the daylights out of her. She hated that, but he loved to make her cry and then beg her not to tattle. What he wouldn't give for one more game of hide and go seek in the barn with CJ.

Audrey opened the sliding glass doors and called for them. Had so much time lapsed already? David checked his watch. It had been 45 minutes since they had agreed to wait the respectable half an hour. He sighed. He was kind of hoping the kid would have shown. For Vickie's sake if not for everyone else's. Maybe a little for CJ's too. He waited for Rea to get her barrings and then walked her inside where a smörgåsbord of fine foods were waiting for them.

While everyone sat down to eat, they were silently aware of the empty chair at the corner of the table. It wasn't necessarily the absence of the young man that had been promised to be there that was missed. Perhaps him a little. They were all looking forward to meeting the new member of the family as it were, but this was the first family gathering since the funeral and as nice as it was to gather together and catch up and spend this time, there was still an air of stillness that they all felt. There was a missing prattle amongst them.

A little buzzing was silenced and they could all hear it. It was different for each of them though. Or was it? Was she really gone? Vickie still felt a breeze of her whispering about her hair as she talked with Audrey. Audrey wondered what latest book she would have been reading as if she were sitting next to her telling her all about it. J.R. Felt only irritation as he and Doug expressed how disrespectful it had been for that young man to have keep them waiting and then not show up after all, and then as if blown by a gentle breeze there is peace between them and they begin anew with talk of new highways being built in the Big Sky country. Lynn watches and wonders when she will lose her place in the family. Clinton leans over to her and gives her a nudge and a wink. Lynn smiles shyly.

"How are you doing, Mr. Cane?" Clinton passed her some mashed potatoes. She took a small spoonful and then passed them on.

"There is nothing better than being surrounded by family. How goes the cross country season for you? You know that was always your strong game, not CJ's. She was fast, but you have the stamina. You're our distance girl."

Maybe CJ had meant it when she said once a Stewart always a Stewart. She had said that she, Lynn, would always be an honorary member of the Stewart family and maybe that was really true.

"The varsity team has a real chance at state this year, Sir." She replied, less sheepishly than she had been feeling just moments before.

Sara filled her plate with bite size portions of everything. She wanted to taste everything, but with this baby sitting so high, there wasn't enough room for her stomach to expand and the baby too, so she ate in theory only. It was such a privilege to be included in this family gathering once again. In spite of whatever differences she and David might be having at this time, this family always included her and Rea in their big moments. She was extremely peeved that this Jacen guy, whomever he was, had stood them up. Didn't he know who they were? Didn't he realize how much they had suffered already without the indignity of being stood up by some pricky hi-fa luting....and as her mind continued on it's tirade while she took her tiny bites, everyone's forks all dropped at once. Chairs around the table were all scooted back and every one of them stood and moved towards the window and watched as a large, black sedan with black tinted windows made it's way down the driveway and stopped at the front of the house.

It was very much out of place, this Roles Royce of a car compared to all of the standard family cars that the rest of them were driving. It had been stopped and the engine turned off for a good five minutes before the passenger front door opened and a young man with dark hair, dark glasses, and a dark coat that traveled all the way to his knees crept out onto the driveway and began looking around.

Jacen felt as if he were in the middle of a Norman Rockwell painting look outward as his driver pulled into the Cane residence and saw the ranch house and barn to the left and the cows to the right. And could that actually be a bull? Big, horns, testicles hanging down...yep, he wasn't an expert, but he was pretty sure those were the qualifications for a bull. When the car came to a complete stop and the driver had turned off the engine, Jace found himself frozen.

He had always been a loner. He had surfed alone, painted alone, He had even waited for death alone. That was until CJ had come along and now he didn't know how to be either alone or with people. He thought that for her sake he should try, but what was the first step?

"..Death is always the beginning of something new...." Had she meant it for before, when his mother or father had died, or now? Either way, he should go and find out. Even if they resented him for taking CJ's heart, he would try for her. He had to try. He opened the car door and got out.

As he looked around and took in the smell of fresh, clean air again and the sight of apple trees, the sliding glass door opened and Vickie emerged with a welcoming smile and outstretched arms. Following her was an older woman that she resembled that Jace could only assume was the grand-mother, a gentle man with a tattoo on his forearm who had his hand on the small of the older womans back, two women, one with dark hair, one with blond who also bore a remarkable liking to Vickie. Sisters perhaps, he figured.

Waiting at the door was a large, looming man with a full head of grey hair and a grey mustache. He neither smiled nor frowned exactly when Vickie introduced him as J.R. Her husband, CJ's dad. He shook hands firmly, and then Jace was herded into the dinning room where he was offered a seat.

He hadn't thought that he felt very hungry, however, as the mountain of food began to pass by his plate and each distinct smell began to permeate his senses, he began to partake and slowly, bite by bite, he began his first experience with a true home cooked meal made by loving hands that were not getting paid to serve him. He thought he might have just entered a new kind of heaven. Everyone else took their places again and continued their meal as if nothing had changed.

Vickie did the introductions around the table: J.R, her husband (CJ's father. Had they been close?), Audrey, her mother (that would make her CJ's grandmother, she seems o.k.), Clinton, her father (CJ's grandfather, he has a pleasant smile. And a bull!), Annie and Doug, family from Montana (If Annie looks just like Vickie and Doug looks just like J.R....), Betsy and Reggie, family from Alaska, Jamie and Patrick, family from Seattle (Annie and Doug's daughter and son in law. Apparently there were more cousins in Montana that were unable to be here right now, but they sent their regards.) Catherine, her daughter (CJ's sister who refused to make eye contact),

David, her son (they had met, sort of), Sara,(weren't they a little far away from a hospital for her right now?), Rea, Sara's daughter, her granddaughter, and lastly, CJ's best friend and always part of the family, Lynn.

Jace bowed to all of them respectfully and repeated each of their names in turn. They then began the business of including him in their day to day lives. As always, CJ became a topic of discussion at many points. It surprised him quite a bit to see her family talking about her as

90

if she were in the room with laughter and smiles, rather than somberly mourning her passing.

They asked him often how he had been feeling and how long his recovery had been. They asked about California and his hobbies. Clinton wanted to know about the tide and the naval base in San Diego. Lynn was curious about all the famous people.

J.R finished his food, pushed back his plate and leaned his elbows on the table staring down the young man at the other end of the table.

"What do you do?" He asked.

Jace didn't ask what he meant by the vague question because he knew what he had meant. His answer could go one of two ways. He could go with the tabloid playboy version, which would have been true a few years back, or he could just tell the truth.

"I get up 6 days a week, go into my company's headquarters and spend most of the day in meetings with either budget specialists, lab supervisors, chemists, etc., Then I meet with owners and manufacturers of other medical supply software and engineering tools and I try to buy them out to maximize my profit margins. One day a week however, I make time to go to the beech and sketch, swim, and surf again.

I used to be happiest when I was painting and drawing and when I was a punk teenager and thought that I was going to die, I just wanted to do so as an artist, but now I need to live a long and productive life and I need money to do that."

J.R found himself leaning back in his seat. He didn't know if he had been satisfied or put in his place. David simply smiled. CJ would be going to California after all and she would be rich too.

Audrey stood and began clearing the table of dishes. Vickie, Annie and Betsy quickly followed suit and then spread the deserts out on the counter top for display. Audrey grabbled some fancy china desert plates from the same glass china cabinet in the dining room that the dinner wear had come from.

"Who wants what?" Annie called out to the waiting group at the table. All at once people began to shout out their requests.

"Banana cream!"

"Chocolate cream!"

"Apple"

"2 cookies for me!"

"Make that 2 banana creams and a coffee!"

Jace felt like he was in the middle of an auction and was amazed at how well the four women could keep track of who was requesting what pie, cookie or drink and everyone else seemed to be enjoying the shouting game as if it were a regular sport.

"Jacen?"

Jacen looked up to see Vickie waiting for his order. He was a little at a loss. He had been so careful about his diet for so long that it was difficult for him to chose. He and Kyle had many conversations since the operation about how the new heart would be able to handle a new diet of rich foods and he should enjoy his new life, but he should also remember that if he indulges he should exercise and keep the heart healthy.

"May I?" He asked and gestured toward the counter where all of the deserts waited. Vickie smiled. Audrey walked over and handed him a plate.

"Of course. Please take your time. Have some of everything if you like!" She said and guided him over. It all looked so wonderful! He felt so full already from dinner, but he couldn't resist!

He didn't have much of a sweet tooth, but the banana cream pie seemed to be calling him. It wasn't just Vickie who made the mental note that, after much deliberation, he chose CJ's favorite.

After desert was done, everyone gathered outside into the front yard to visit. Jace sat on the wooden porch in a wooden chair beside Vickie and answered many questions as people came around to find out more about the mysterious keeper of one of the last pieces of their beloved lost girl. They wanted to know about his family. They were surprised to find that he didn't have any.

"Cousins? Aunts? Uncles?"

"Nope."

For Jace, the looks of pity on their faces were unexpected. He had known only isolation in his life but he had made that a choice. Hadn't he? Both of his parents had been only children and their parents had been long gone before his birth. He had neither wanted nor needed friends because he didn't think he could trust anyone to care about him for himself rather than where he could take them up the social ladder. He didn't run with the rich and famous. He didn't want to be on their radar. After his father died, he stayed out of the tabloids. His groceries and meals were brought in weekly and he had a different driver every two weeks. He didn't want to get personal. Not until now. He leaned over to Vickie.

"I'm going to go now. Thank your mom for dinner for me. Please remember what we talked about. I want three. I am going to be going back home in two days." Vickie scrunched her brow and frowned a little. She reached a hand over and touched his arm. He pulled back a little in reflex.

"Do you have to? I wish you would stay longer. Will you be back again any time soon?"

Jace leaned over and kissed her gently on the cheek. He had never met his own mother, but he hoped she had been a little like Vickie Stewart.

"We'll talk again before I go. I can send you e-mail at work, and I will write, I promise. I won't leave without saying goodbye. I have to go now and make some important phone calls."

He stood then and made his way to his car where his driver had been waiting. When he got in the passenger back seat of the car, he noticed an empty plastic plate of food, desert and two Styrofoam coffee cups in the passenger front seat.

"Vickie?" The driver smiled.

"Well, I saw her and one of the other nice ladies putting it together for me but the little squirt of a girl brought it out for me."

Jace smiled thinking about CJ's sister Catherine walking food out to his driver.

"Were you polite?"

The driver looked at Jace in the rear view mirror. Their eyes met. He assumed Jace had been kidding until he saw the straight jaw line and deep brown eyes waiting for an answer.

"Yes, sir."

"Let's go." They backed slowly and carefully out of the driveway and back into town to the hotel.

J.R watched the car pull away from the ranch and then sat down next to his wife in the chair where his daughter's heart had just been. He wasn't sure if he should speak first or if he should wait for her to say something. He didn't know what to say if he opened his mouth anyway. They were going to let this young man into their family but they didn't know anything about him! When did he get this company? What did they do? Does he smoke? Drink? Why did he show up now? Vickie smiled at him and patted his arm affectionately.

"He'll come around. He needs us. Somehow, I feel like we need pieces of him, too." She said reading his mind as she had been doing most of his adult life. And peace washed over him again despite his protest.

Vickie stood and began to gather the family around again to make an announcement.

"Jacen would like us as family to pick 3 charities that we feel would have been close to CJ to donate some funds to at this time. He feels like this is a big commitment so he encourages us not to rush to any decisions. I have some thoughts, but I would like to know what you all think first." It was the first time the entire evening besides the moment when Jacen had arrived that the group had been silent. After several minutes of no one talking they began chattering quietly amongst themselves. Vickie waited quite some time before she spoke again.

"Anything? How about the American Cancer Society? I know that most of you are aware that Dad has been battling prostate cancer for a little while now, but we are very optimistic at this point and even though we never told CJ I think this would have been something she would have wanted us to fight for. If you disagree or can come up with better ideas, please, I'm all ears." Everyone became reflective in that moment as they all gathered around Clinton. He looked amongst them and merely shrugged.

Soon, however, they were all back in the game and trying to get into CJ's head to figure out where she would have wanted the money to go. Shy, quiet Lynn was the next to speak.

"We desperately need a new track at the high school. I know that there are far more important things in the world and maybe that's selfish, but CJ loved that track and she loved our team. It wouldn't take much money. At least not coming from someone who has so much to give, right?" Her head flew around the yard looking for anyone to shake their head and disapprove. However, she was surprised to see everyone seeming to be in agreement and smiling at her. J.R swung an arm around her shoulder and gave her a squeeze and a smile.

"Good thinking, Lynn! I think that's the perfect charity for CJ! We need to hear some more, come on people! CJ had a big heart and it now belongs to a kid who hasn't known what it is to give or be loved until now." Suddenly, ideas were flying out of their heads and mouths like a geyser had sprung to life.

"How about the colleges AIDS foundation?"

"Or, WSU's veterinary school? She loved animals!"

"I know, their summer theater program!"

In the end, they all agreed to replace the high school track and football field, to donate whatever amount Jace saw fit to the American Cancer society, and to put what ever amount Jace felt was fair into a trust fund for a scholarship in CJ's name that a worthy student, chosen each year by Mr, McMann, Vickie and J.R from the high school would receive to the college of their choice.

That evening when Vickie crawled into bed next to J.R who had been asleep for quite some time, before she closed her eyes, she said a silent prayer. She asked for Jacen to have peace and feel a sense of family now. She asked for J.R and David to find common ground somewhere. For David and Sara to reconnect. She gave thanks for her mother and her sisters whom she could never make it though each day without. She gave thanks for Catherine and prayed for her to find the strength to confide in someone somewhere. She shed a little tear as she prayed for God's will in taking care of her father. The last time she had surrendered completely to God's will, she had lost CJ. Was her faith strong enough to do it again? She was reminded again of the meaning of faith. That it is the substance of the things she hoped for. The evidence of the things she could not see. She slept that night in a blanket of peace that passed all understanding again.

SCENE III: SANDIEGO CALIFORNIA

Jace walked into the office building still feeling the jet leg from previous evenings flight. Meghan greeted him at the door with a stack of papers and a cup of piping hot chai tea. He had never really developed a taste for coffee.

"Is everyone here?"

"They are in the boardroom waiting for you."

Jace checked his watch. He was even ten minutes ahead of schedule. He flashed Meghan a smashing smile and she found herself catching her breath. It wasn't so much that he was so shockingly handsome, that wasn't new. It was that he seemed genuinely happy for the first time. She had never seen him so relaxed and confident.

"Can I get you anything else?" She asked hot on his heals as he made his way to the board meeting that he asked her to arrange for him over their phone conversation yesterday at the Seattle Sea Tac Airport. He stopped and turned to her before opening the enormous oak door to the company board room.

"Yes, as a matter of fact. Could you please have breakfast delivered to the board room please? Something nice. Buffet style. Then, send flowers to all their spouses, regardless of male or female. As a thank you for their support and their hard work at the home front. Thank you, Meghan." And then he was gone.

"Whew....Whatever was is in the air in Washington, I think I need some!" She said to herself as she walked back to her desk to arrange breakfast for the board members.

Inside the boardroom, Jace made his way to the front,took off his jacket and set it on the back of his chair rather than the coat rack that had been provided in the back of the room. Jace had always attended board meetings after his father had passed away but they had all assumed that was because it was a stipulation in the the last will and testament of his predecessor not because he wanted to be there. He had always shown himself to be late, casually dressed, and uninterested in the topics being discussed until recently.

After his heart transplant surgery and recovery, Jacen Owen had come to every meeting for everything company wide and had shown up on time, dressed to impress, and had not only participated in the discussions, but had clearly done his homework and made a few changes that had propelled the profit margins forward by 2 million dollars in less than a year. So they would listen to this young man, and whatever tirade he wanted to have might make them all very rich indeed.

Jace sat down and greeted each board member casually and asked about their weekend. He was smiling. How odd, some of them thought. A few became frightened. Were they about to lose their jobs? After a half an hour of light conversation and laughter, the door opened and the smell of fresh fruits and warm eggs, bacon, croissants,and many other pastries as well as fresh coffee, and juices permeated their senses as tray after tray of food was brought in and placed at the back of the room with nice white Corningwhare dishes were also placed neatly and a server waited.

"Please," Jace stood and pointed to the back of the room.

"Go and get something to eat. There should be something for everyone. Even you vegetarians. Of course, now that I have a heart that can handle the fat from meat I don't know why anyone wouldn't love it, but it's a personal choice, so please, go and get some food and then bring it back to the table and we will eat while I tell you all why I have gathered you here this morning." He found it odd that no one stood and moved toward the food right away at his bidding. He hadn't realized that the new, kinder, softer Jacen was an oddity to these people. They had gotten used to the bully, the thrower of tantrums and his giant ego. Jace picked up the phone.

"Meghan, could you come in here please? Forward the phones to the answering service." A moment later, Meghan arrived looking puzzled.

Jace met her at the back of the room next to the food and handed her a plate and then took one for himself.

"please tell me you didn't eat breakfast yet." he whispered in her ear. She smiled.

"not so much." So they were served their breakfast and then sat in their seats, Jace at the head of the table where his father used to sit, and Meghan in one of the empty seats next to him with her note book.

Soon everyone else slowly gathered themselves up and started towards the food and the casual feeling was back in the room again. When they were all seated, Jace brought the meeting to order.

"Ladies and gentlemen. I took a trip recently, which you all know. I went to Washington State to visit the family of the girl who donated her heart to me. I'm sure that surprises a lot of you since prior to the surgery I didn't care about anyone else but myself and truth be told, towards the end there, I didn't care much about me either."

As he spoke, he began to pass around pictures that he had taken in Washington. If nothing else, Jace had always considered himself to be an artist. So he watched their faces as they teared up a little at the photos of CJ's beautifully cared for grave site with her likeness on it. Especially the one where he caught Catherine there placing yellow paper lilies. There were pictures of David pushing Rea on the swing at the Ranch house and Vickie. Vickie at her office with the many photos on the walls of her family, or Vickie out to lunch smiling when she remembered CJ singing in the shower. He had also walked around town and taken some images of the places and people that had matter to CJ. With the principle's permission, he had taken pictures at the high school inside and out. He took close ups of the broken down track and foot ball field before he left. He had walked where she had walked and secretly he felt like he missed her.

"I know that we have two major charities that we donate to. However, we give them one large donation, once a year at Christmas and lets be honest, is it because we're being charitable at that time or because we know it gives us a tax break? Look at these people! Think about your own families. They lost a daughter, a sister, a friend. At 18 she had apparently touched more lives by just being genuinely grateful and nice to everyone than most people strive for in a lifetime. I have her heart and I hope that I can do right by her and her family by giving back, so I offered to donate some money, I did not say how much, and believe me, the expense that this family has paid monetarily and in grief is far more than we can hope to give back, but I think it's the least that we can do since we have so much and I know I owe them something."

A tear came to his eye and this time he didn't hide it and he did not wipe it away. He would cry a little if it would get CJ's family what they asked for. Anything for her. He would do anything to see her again, to feel her again.

"I owe her my life. She said once that with death comes new life, and I shouldn't waste it on what I don't have or what I've lost. That peace that passes understanding only comes to those who have deep faith. I don't have that yet, but I saw it there." He pointed at a picture he took of Vickie with Audrey, Annie and Betsy. They were all standing together serving deserts smiling.

Joseph Olsen raised his hand then and spoke.

"Jace, son," He had worked for this company since he was 35 and now well past 60 and retired but an active member of the board, he had watched Jacen Owen grow up to be an angry tormented young man and was skeptical about these new changes, however he couldn't argue about the profit margins.

"did you know this girl? Did you meet with her before her untimely death? How do you know she said these things?"

Jace sighed. No one would ever believe that somehow while they were both dying, she had somehow teleported her body and mind to his hospital room and left him strange messages that he was still trying to sort through. Or that he had somehow connected with her in a way that didn't make any sense since he doesn't connect period.

Jace reached into his jacket pocked and pulled out a small, hardbound book with a lavender cover and a broken lock.

"Vickie, her mother, gave me her journal and told me to get to know her. She thought that it might do me some good to know the true thoughts of my heart."

The room fell silent. Suddenly, the pictures were like gold and the members began to look more deeply into them.

These were no longer pictures but family members to each and every one of them and Jace could read it on their faces, they were ready to hear what he needed to say.

Jace walked into his penthouse apartment, tossed his things on the plush brown leather couch and laid his keys on the table beside the door before checking his messages. He started with the first two from Kyle, wondering how things were going since he had been back and to check in first thing and then he deleted the rest without listening. He didn't want to hear from anyone unless they were a Stewart.

He picked up the phone and began to make the call to Washington and to the Stewart's Four rings and just about the time he was going to hang up and try again later,

"Stewart faucet repair, which drip do you want to talk to?"

"What?" Then giggling on the other end. Catherine?

"Is this the Stewart house?" Jace asked.

"That depends. Are you a telemarketer? My parents won't talk to you if you are."

Catherine! Jace felt relieved.

"No, Catherine, It's Jacen Owen calling from California. Remember me from last weekend?" Silence.

"Yeah. I remember. You have CJ's heart. Why are you calling? What do you want?"

Then Jace heard the phone crash on the counter and a distant,

"Mom, Dad, the phones not for me." Then more silence, until,

"Um, Hello?"

J.R. Jace cleared his throat and let out a slow deep breath.

"Hello Mr. Stewart. It's Jace."

"Who?"

"Jacen Owen, from California."

"Oh, yeah. How are you, boy? How was your trip home? Is the altitude difficult? You know after surgery and all."

He was trying to be polite. That was a step Jace thought. He had loved his daughter and Jace imagined that letting her go was one thing, but to see her heart walking around in a strangers body, was a different demon J.R would have to tackle all together.

"The flight was fine. Slept most of the way." Silence again.

" I'll put Vickie on the phone."

A little small talk was a small step in the right direction Jacen thought. It was a very small step, but a step none the less. Jace smiled at the realization that he had possibly shared more words now with J.R, than he ever had with his own father. Catherine's hostility had not been lost on him however.

"Hello? Jacen? How are you, dear? Was your trip alright? Did you fly first class? Of course you did! I've always wanted to fly first class. How are you feeling? A little jet lag I'm sure!"

Jacen laughed. She took a breath finally and waited for him to speak. She was all that he imagined his mother to be and so much more. He had pictured his mother being home everyday to send him to school and waiting when he got home, however as he got older, he saw her running to charity auctions and being in the spotlight instead of nurturing.

Vickie, however, took her personal time in the morning if only for a few minutes to pray, then sent her children to school before leaving for work. She worked hard and still made time to go grocery shopping, help with homework and get dinner on the table. Her hobbies were teaching cake decorating on Saturdays at the local Michael's Store, and he had been told that when she wasn't crunching numbers for the university, she could sew anything from wedding dresses to prom dresses or just cute little frilly toddler outfits if that's what the occasion called for. And yet here she was, just one remarkable woman in this small town that was hidden from the rest of the world.

"I'm doing really well, thank you. Really, for everything. I wanted to call and let you know that the board approved all of my requests to day. So, The high school will be getting a new track and football field during their Christmas break before the new seasons start. I will be back to oversee the project at that time."

Vickie smiled, turned to J.R and grabbed his hand.

"He's coming for Christmas!"

J.R smiled. He couldn't help himself. He had watched his wife crumble in a way no one should when CJ died and he was not the man he wished he had been to try and build her back up again. She had done that herself with her faith, her love and her belief that life is more than flesh and blood, it's heart and it's family. So if this boy could reconnect them all, then so be it.

"They will donate 1 million dollars to the American Cancer society in sums of a hundred thousand dollars a year over the next ten years. They will also set aside a scholarship fund in the amount of fifty thousand dollars in CJ's name to go to the student of your choice, however, they would like one board member to be involved in the choice as well. It can be me if you like or I can appoint a more senior member if you'd rather."

Silence again. When Vickie spoke again, her voice was soft, kind, motherly.

"I'd like to think about that a little bit and get back to you. Perhaps you would consider allowing me to meet the board members before we chose. It's a big decision. Thank you so much Jacen for the opportunities you have given us. I was so grateful to meet you and to share a few weeks with you and I look forward to your e-mails."

Jace wanted to keep her on the phone longer, to stay connected to all that he had experienced in Washington, but he knew that she was a busy woman with a busy house to run.

"Ok, I'll let you go, but one more thing. Do you think it would be alright if I wrote to Catherine? Like a pen pal maybe? She doesn't seem to like me and I'm hoping to change that."

"Don't take it personal Jacen. Catherine has been moody for a while now. It's been an emotional year for everyone, but she's also a 13 year old girl and there's a whole mess of goo you don't even want to know that goes into that! Wright if you like. I'll make sure she gets them. We'll talk again soon I hope."

"Count on it. Oh, and thanks for the journal. I'll bring it back at Christmas."

"Keep it. I've read it and I think she said to me all that she needed to through it. If I ever need to read it again, I know where it is. I feel that she has more to say to you right now. Good bye, Jacen."

"Good bye, Vickie."

After hanging up the phone, Jace took off his tie and threw it on the couch with his jacket and fished in the jacket pocket for the journal. He held it up and looked it over and ran his fingers over the binder that had been warn from the constant opening and closing. Then he held it close to his heart as he walked into the kitchen to get himself a bottle of water and moved out onto the patio where he had the most magnificent ocean view for some reading. He knew he should just go to bed, but he also knew sleep would never come without knowing a little more of her.

SCENE IV: PULLMAN WASHINGTON

Vickie pulled into her office parking space and waited while traffic went by before getting out of the car, locking it and entering the building. She was a few minutes earlier than usual today and as the early October chill filled the air she pulled her jacket a little tighter around her. It would warm up before the afternoon, but you could tell that it would be an early winter this year. She was greeted as usual by Angie at the front desk and then Audrey came around the corner with coffee and followed her into her office.

"Surprise!" She said and Vickie smiled at her and Angie. Angie shrugged her shoulders.

"She beat me to it." She said and handed Vickie her messages before returning to her desk.

"I didn't know you were volunteering today. That's great! We can have lunch together."

"Sounds good, but I have to go. Work to do. Enjoy your coffee. Let me know if you or Angie need anything else."

Audrey was gone as quickly as she had appeared. Vickie sighed. Jacen had been gone a month now and everyone was back into their routines. They exchanged e-mails bi-weekly and Catherine had received 2 letters from him so far. As far as she knew Cath had not written back. She had told Jacen not to be discouraged if she did not respond any time soon. He understood. He said that sometimes the writing was more for his own therapy than hers so Cath could do with the letters what she wished.

Vickie had only known him such a short time and yet she missed him terribly. Could you love someone you'd just met? She was a mother and he had CJ's heart, but it was more than that. It was that he had been motherless for so long and she had so much love to give. He was without a family and her family would make room for one more. They would make room for 20 more if there was a need. That's what family is for. They love, believe, hurt together and forgive.

Her thoughts wandered to J.R and David and then to David and Sara. Sara was a week past due to deliver the baby and they were all anxious. Yet David still wasn't talking. Not to anyone least of all Sara. Vickie believed he wanted to do the right thing, but he was somewhere still lost in his grief and he couldn't remember his beginning from his end anymore and the more they pushed the further he buried himself. Time is what David needed but it wouldn't wait for him to make up his mind. She hoped that soon, his memories of CJ would help him heal rather than run.

Vickie shook her head back to reality and began her days work. It was time. More than she knew for just then the phone rang on her private line.

"This is Vickie."

"Mom?"

"David? What's wrong?"

"It's Sara. She just called from the hospital. She's in labor. Can you come?" A tear of hope fell from her eye. This might be just what she was hoping for. With new life comes renewed hope. Peace that passes understanding swept over her once again.

"Your grandmother and I are on our way."

SCENE V: SANDIEGO CALIFORNIA: JACEN OWEN'S PENTHOUSE

"Natures first green is gold,
Her hardest hue to hold.
Her early leaf's a flower,
But only so an hour.
Then leaf subsides to leaf.
So Eden sank to grief.
So dawn goes down to day.
Nothing gold can stay.

By Robert Frost. Do I agree or disagree? That is the question I suppose. I would have to say that I disagree. Look at my mother for instance. She is timeless gold. She was a beautiful blond haired blue eyed girl who has the brains to run multimillion dollar corporations but yet she's happiest when the house is quiet after all the work is done and she can curl up under a blanket with a good book. She doesn't ask for fortune or fame, these are the things my heart desires. Did she ever have ambitions like I do? I don't know. If she did, she gave them up for the love of my dad and to raise up kids and be the best mom ever. If, in in my lifetime, I can become half of the person that she is, I will have done great things."

Jace closed the journal. He found irony in her choosing his favorite poet in her opening monolog. It had been dated May 16th 1989 when she was 16. He had flipped through the book and there were gaps of time several months apart over the two year span from when she had started the journal and her last entry dated February 9th, 1991. He read more about how much she admired her mother.

It was several pages and many months later before she wrote anything about other family members.

The time spent between was her expressing typical teenage grief about boys, her hair, her body. He found it strange that her mother was a whiz at math and yet she herself seemed to detest it. Then he came to an entry dated December 12th,1989.

"It's been 7 years now since Dad quit drinking and we moved from Montana back to Washington and I have been so proud of him. He has become the man that I always believed that he could be.

A little girl wants to believe that when her dad says he's never going to touch it again that he means it, but when she left her toy in the truck and finds his booze behind the seat or when they come home from the Christmas pageant and find a trail of blood to find out later that he cut his finger off and drove himself to the hospital, the disappointments become second nature. In seven years though, I have seen him rise to the challenge of true parenting. He has told me no and disciplined me when I needed it and I have enjoyed having my father. We laugh a lot and I think we're friends sometimes.

I feel sorry for the guy who ever wins my heart! He will have to prove himself very worthy to Dad to be included in this family. He cannot be a slacker or a loser. He will need to be respectful and respected. Polite and charming. Adorable will come in handy that's for sure! My Dad has my heart for now. I love him and respect the hard work he does every day to work through his demons. He loved us a lot to make some monumental changes and I will never forget.

I hope David realizes someday that we only have Dad for this short life time and he's wasting too much of it on his memories of what he feels he missed out on. Someday. Maybe when he's a dad, he'll get it."

Jace wondered who else besides Vickie had gotten a chance to read the journal. He hadn't ever really spoken to David, but CJ had been right. A father who had made mistakes and changed for the better, one who was present and loved you despite agreeing or disagreeing with you was better than one who allowed you to be raised by a series of nannies and never acknowledged you. One who died leaving you nothing but cold money and responsibilities. Let's not forget a deadly congenital heart defect! If David and his father were estranged, they needed to get their feelings resolved. Life slips away too quickly, hadn't they learned that yet?

SCENE VI:PULLMAN MEMORIAL HOSPITAL

"Ok, Sara, you've been here and done this before. Now, we can give you an epidural to ease the pain if you want."

Sara looked at Dr. Davies and bit down hard as another contraction came and went.

"I think I might brave this one out, thank you. I want the experience without the medicine this time around." Dr. Davies checked her again and made some chart notes.

"We could be here a while. Hang in there kid. Do you have anyone coming to be with you?"

"I called David. He said he was coming. I told him to call his mom. I know she'll want to be here."

Dr. Davies smiled.

"I imagine you're right about that. You know you need to retire when you start to deliver the babies of the babies you delivered." He turned to his nurse.

"She's at 4 now. Call me when she gets to 10 and we're ready to push. Also, call me when Vickie, the grandmother gets here." The nurse nodded and then turned to Sara and smiled as she checked her vital signs again. A moment later David entered and stood in the back of the room. When the nurse left, David pulled a chair up beside her and took her hand.

"How are you?" Sara pinched her face together and took in a deep breath and waited for another contraction to pass by. After it had come and gone, she relaxed her hand and released her breath.

"I'm in good hands. I'm glad you came."

David sat back a little.

"Did you think I wouldn't?"

Sara shrugged her shoulders and looked away.

"I wasn't sure. We haven't been seeing things eye to eye as of late. I want commitment and you want your freedom. I need to know you'll come home safe and provide a loving environment for our family and you want to be the rebel without a cause. We can't both have what we want."

David stood and walked over to the window. He thought for a long time before he spoke. He had been with Sara off and on since high school and he couldn't imagine being with anyone else. He knew that he was hurting her by holding her at arms length all of the time, but he also loved her, Rea and this new life waiting to emerge too much to go backwards.

"I don't know, Sara. Maybe we can. I love you and Rea. I'm excited about our new baby, but I'm still missing CJ, maybe I always will and the music is how I connect to her. I will agree to try harder to contribute more to our home and be home every night on weeknights if you will give me weekends with the band." Sara began to cry in between contractions.

"I think that's a good start. I'd hug you, but, ouch!" A wave of contractions began then a little bit faster and harder and David hit the nurse's call button in a panic. The contractions had subsided by the time the nurse arrived. David was pacing by now and wondering what was taking his mother so long. She was right around the corner when he had called her five minutes ago! The nurse checked Sara again.

"Only a 5 Sara, sorry. I can still call an anesthesiologist to give you an epidural if you've changed your mind."

"Thank God! Yes, she'd like that." Said David, still pacing and biting his nails.

Sara smiled and shook her head at the nurse.

"No thank you. I don't want any drugs." David stopped pacing for a minute and looked at her as if she had been struck in the head with a brick and came out stupid. He had never seen someone in so much pain before and he hated it. He couldn't stand to see someone he loved suffer. Watching CJ's final moments and have no control over any of it had torn him apart and Sara was choosing pain? Why? The nurse left and David sat down beside her again.

"Are you sure about the drugs? You think you can't love this child as much if it doesn't hurt to push it out?" She smiled and patted his arm, Then she grabbed with all her strength and squeezed as another contraction came over her. When it passed, she moved his hand onto her belly so he could feel the life they had created together squiggling around inside.

"David, I want to know that I was strong enough to do this without the drugs. I know it will hurt, but only for a little while. The reward will be worth it."

Just then, the baby rolled around and David pulled his hand back by instinct.

"Oh my god! That was awesome!"

He put his hand back where it had been on Sara's belly and waited for more. He smiled and leaned in to kiss her. He did love her. He just had some demons that were personal to work through and he didn't want to drag her through them with him.

Vickie and Audrey arrived then and everyone gave hugs. The nurse came in and saw them and went to page Dr. Davies who arrived a few moments later. He checked Sara again and agreed that she was only at 5 centimeters dilated and they should settle in for a long wait.

"Vickie, coffee?"

"Sure." She followed him out of Sara's hospital room and down the hall towards the cafeteria. As they entered, she was taken back the large cafeteria at Sacred Heart Medical Center where she had many meals and many cups of coffee. So, as they sat down at a small table, Vickie found herself feeling sentimental and uncomfortable all at once.

"So how are you really doing, Vic?" Dr. Davies asked. He hadn't seen her since CJ's passing and he thought about her and her family often. She smiled and reached across the table and touched his arm.

"I'm alright. I really am. I believe that when one door closes, God opens another." He sat back in his seat and wondered what new door had opened for her lately. She spoke again.

"I've received some letters from people who have gotten some of CJ's organs, but the recipient of the heart came and spent some time here with us."

"Wow! So, tell me about this person. Man, woman?"

"He's a young man from California without a family of his own."

Dr. Davies sat up in his chair and leaned his elbows on the table.

"Is he some punk kid that's going to do something stupid that might destroy CJ's heart?"

Vickie smiled a little yet she jumped quickly to Jacen's defense.

"Oh, no. He's a fine boy in his early 20's with a great job and lots of responsibilities. We agreed to stay in contact and he's even writing to Cath. Hopefully that will get her out of the funk she's been in."

"Is Catherine alright?"

Vickie shrugged and fumbled her coffee around in her fingers.

"Who knows. She's not talking to anyone but CJ. She goes to the cemetery several times a week. She's moody and irritable. I'm hoping that being back in school with her friends around will help but I haven't seen much of a change yet."

"Maybe you should bring her in for a visit. If she's depressed maybe we can prescribe something for her." Vickie shrugged her shoulders and sipped her coffee.

"Maybe. Physically she seems fine, I mean for Cath."

Just then, Dr. Davies got a page.

"Excuse me." He stood and went to a nearby phone. Soon he was back grabbing both of their coffees and dumping them in the trash.

"It's time, lets go have a baby." He said and Vickie followed him as he rushed out the cafeteria door and down the hall.

At 12:04pm with David holding Sara's hand and Dr. Davies coaxing, Sara gave birth to a beautiful baby girl. Dr. Davies cut the cord, ran an immediate APGAR test on her in which she scored a 7 out of 9, cleaned her up a little, and then placed her in her mothers arms before allowing her grandmother and her great grandmother to return to the room. Everyone cooed and coddled the baby and when the nurse ran a second APGAR test, she scored 9 out of 9. A perfect score for a perfect little girl. As they passed her around, David took her, held her close and then made his way to a rocking chair in a corner of the room.

" What's her name?" Audrey asked. Sara smiled. She had known she was having a girl since her last ultrasound but she had decided to keep the information to herself. She had picked out a name a long time ago and had been calling her by her name since she found out.

"Her name is Christine." Everyone smiled. David looked at her for a long time. She did look Christine-ish.

"It's perfect." Vickie said.

Many of the family members and friends had come by throughout the day to see the new member and bring gifts, but by seven o'clock, Sara was exhausted, so David had asked everyone to leave and for the nurse to make sure that they were undisturbed for the remainder of the night. David stood from the rocking chair he had been sitting in and turned off the T.V..

He walked over to where Sara lay sleeping and gently touched her cheek. From there he moved over to the bassinet where Christine was also sleeping. At his presence, she awoke and began fussing.

Quickly he scooped her up, walked back over to the rocking chair and began singing her a lullaby that his mother used to sing to him, CJ and Catherine while sitting in a rocking chair so they would fall asleep.

As he sang his gaze fell to Sara sleeping and he noticed a silhouette beside her bed. He rubbed his eyes and the vision became clearer. CJ. It wasn't the first time he had seen her since her death. He knew it wasn't real, couldn't be real, but it brought him comfort anyway. She came around the bed and moved closer to him. This time she was wearing her hospital gown just the way he had seen her last, but her long curls were back. Her braces were gone and her teeth were straight and beautiful. When she smiled, it was still his CJ, full of life and fun. She leaned down over Christine and blew her a breathless kiss.

"Forgive, David. It's past time. She brings life and responsibilities and you cannot judge what you know nothing of."

"I don't know what you mean."

"Let go of the past. She is the future. You cannot have peace with anger."

111

"When did you become so wise?"

There it is, her smile. God, how he missed her! He knew this wasn't real. It couldn't be. Even his mother believed she had gone to heaven, where-ever that was.

"I watch over my family, all of you. Even the members to come."

She began to fade then, and David reached a free hand out to grab her.

"Forgive." She said before she disappeared completely. David stood and placed the sleeping Christine back in her bassinet and then sat himself back into the rocking chair. He hummed the lullaby to himself and he tried desperately to hold onto the new memory of CJ while he drifted off to much needed sleep.

SCENE VII: PULLMAN HIGH SCHOOL

It was one year ago today that he had been given a new heart and they had lost a precious member of their community. This was Jace's third trip here to Washington and he felt he should be here today to walk on the new track that CJ had inspired and his renewed life and deep pockets had payed for. So he sat on the bleachers and watched as each member of the track team came out from their respective locker rooms and onto the track. He would watch them practice and when they were done and all their equipment had been put away, he would walk the steps she had once ran.

A tall man in a brown suit came and sat beside him.

"I haven't seen you here before. May I help you?"

Jacen extended his hand and the man took it.

"I'm Jacen Owen. I'm in town visiting the Stewart's. If I'm disturbing practice I can leave." The tall man smiled and patted Jace on the shoulder.

"Mr. McMann, the principal. I've seen your name on the check. Thank you for the new track and field. Our students appreciate the donation, however, may I ask, why the anonymity? Surely a young man such as yourself would like to be recognized where ever he can be."

"Please don't presume to know anything about me. I may have acquired CJ's heart, but I do not have her spirit or her love for the people. I'm only trying to get through the lessons she wanted me learn one at a time."

Simon sighed. It was sad to see so much bitterness in such a young man, but if what he said was true, and CJ had her way in his life, he would find a bit of the love of the people in spite of himself.

"That's all any of us can do, Jacen. One lesson at a time." With that, Simon stood and walked down to the field to meet with some of the students and the coaches.

Jace had gotten a private education through tutors so his exposure to peers and socialization skills were limited at best. He watched silently as the team did their warm up laps and then stretches. He spotted Lynn sitting separate from everyone else on the field.

Everyone was laughing and jumping around, trying to keep the blood circulating against the cold March wind, while Lynn did slow long stretches and kept to herself.

Then he saw it. Had she just wiped a tear away from her eyes. He pulled a monogramed tissue out of his coat pocket and walked down the bleachers to the track. He didn't want to cross the track and disturb their practice but he had never before been one to care what people thought of what he did or when so he paused for only a half a moment before walking over to Lynn and drawing all eyes.

He kneeled down beside her and handed her the tissue. She took it, noticed the personalized monogram and then looked up startled to see him. Quickly she stood to her feet, glad that she was wearing leggings and not shorts since she hadn't bothered to shave her legs that morning.

"What are you doing here? I don't mean that in a rude way. I'm just very surprised."

Jace shrugged and then began to notice the eyes watching them. Coach Taylor looked up from his clip board and noticed the young man who was a little too old to be on the team and not a student talking to Lynn and walked towards them.

"Can we talk? I was mostly just checking on how the track and field had turned out, but I noticed you were upset. I know what today is, Lynn, and I'm sorry."

"Young man, may I help you?" Coach Taylor addressed Jace. Lynn intervened on Jace's behalf.

"Are you ready?" and then,

"Coach Taylor, Everyone, I would like you all to meet the benefactor of our new track and field, Jacen Owen. He was the recipient of CJ Stewart's heart and his family has made some large donations in CJ's honor and he wanted to come down and make sure that we were satisfied with what we have received." She started clapping and the others followed suite. Coach Taylor shook his hand and wiped a tears from his eyes.

"Make a speech." Lynn whispered. Jace's face turned a shade of pink.

"I had asked," he started turning to Lynn and then back to everyone,

"that no one ever know where the money for your track and field came from, but just that it was done to honor CJ's memory. Thank you." More clapping and shaking of hands before Coach Taylor sent them off to work. Lynn watched while all the girls huddled in groups to talk about the gorgeous guy with the dark eyes and dark hair that Lynn knew.

"Do you think they're dating?" "Do you think he's seeing her?" "Where's he from?" Lynn had to laugh a little. She and Jacen began to walk around the track.

"Thank you. I haven't been the talk of good gossip since junior high. This will be fun for me."

"You mean since the 'wall' incidence at summer camp when you were 12 and CJ was 13?" Lynn stopped walking and stared at him shocked at how he could possibly know about that. It wasn't a big secret, but why would he know about that?

"Vickie gave me CJ's journal. I think that she felt I might learn how to be a better me if I could learn more about her. I hope she's right."

They began walking again.

"What's wrong with the you that you already are?" How bad could he be. Handsome, money, single. She was still waiting for his downside.

Lynn had her crushes that came and went, but since CJ left her alone without anyone to confide in, she had been preoccupied with her own settling of life and feelings to move on to dating these days. She would graduate this year and she still didn't have any plans for her future. She didn't know where to go from here.

"I'm not a nice guy, Lynn. I'm rude and selfish. Until the day I got a new heart, I knew only of hate and nothing of love. Before the Stewart's I had never seen family or forgiveness.

I still have a long way to go in my healing process. I have a good heart now, but I don't know that I'll ever be the man worthy of it."

"Lynn, are you going to work out this afternoon, or not?" Coach Taylor yelled to her from across the field. She reached out a hand and touch Jace's arm.

"I think that CJ would have chosen you to keep her heart. She always believed in everyone else but herself. She gave, but never asked for anything in return. It's a double edged sword, love and hate."

Jace watched as Lynn began a slow steady jog down the track. He reached down and picked up a handful of sand out of the long jump pit. He tried to picture CJ running down the short runway towards the board which had been replaced by a perfect solid white line that she would plant her foot and propel herself forward into the air as far she could go and land in the sand all crumple of arms and legs and hair. He would go now and leave them to their practice. He would be back though. Many times probably, he would return to this place.

SCENE VIII: PULLMAN WASHINGTON

J.R sat at the bar with his diet soda and cheese burger waiting. He didn't know why he had been called here or why this would be the place chosen for meeting, but he had been called and he was here waiting regardless. It was a beautiful day out and just a week before his own birthday, but as was true of most bars, it was dimly lit so he felt he was sitting in darkness. It was sad that he would always have to associate the week before his birthday as the anniversary of his daughter's death. David would be haunted every birthday also with the remembering of CJ wrecking her car. He shook his head. So much pain and loss, and yet, he smiled at the thought of that new baby grand daughter of his. She was a peach! He did adore and dote on her. He loved Rea too. David had done well and he couldn't be more proud of his son. He would tell him someday when David was ready to forgive him and let him into his life.

He and David hadn't spoken except in polite passing without eye contact since CJ's funeral, but these were David's terms and had been since he was 14. He had grown increasingly angrier and distant since J.R had become more focused and present. It was a vicious revolving door that monkey see monkey do mentality wasn't it? Yet, here he was, waiting. Waiting for his son to remember that he had a father who loved him. Waiting for the hole in his heart that had been left by his beloved daughter to stop hurting so much. Waiting for his youngest daughter to start talking to him again. Waiting for his wife to need him as much as he needed her. Waiting for peace.

"Hey, Dad."

J.R turned in the stool beside him to find David seated there. There was a feeling of awkwardness mixed with relief at seeing his son calling a meeting with him. He was slightly apprehensive, however, he would move heaven and earth for any of his children, so if David needed something, he would be here to make it happen.

"Are you hungry? Can I get you a burger? A soda?"

It was not lost on David that his dad did not offer him a beer and since they were seven miles from the Idaho state border where the drinking age was 19 rather than Washington's 21, he just ordered a burger and ginger ale.

"How are the girls?" Usual casual talk. Before long they would fall into wether or not there would be enough snow for snowmobiling this year. There always was, but it made for conversation among strangers. David sighed.

"Dad, I have some things I need to say. I just need to find a way to get this out so I don't want to have a discussion, I just want you to listen this time." J.R turned back in his seat and faced the bar again and waited for David to begin.

"While CJ and I were little, we waited a long time for you to be someone that you weren't. When we wanted to talk, you passed out on us. When we wanted to play, you got aggressive and locked us out of the house if one of us got hurt and cried. You were a liar and disconnected and I hated you because I needed more from you than that. CJ forgave more easily, but she was like that. She had a way of seeing past the past and leaving it there. For me it was too little too late. I know this is going to sound very odd and I'm surprised that it's you that I would chose to share this with, but I've been seeing CJ here and there."

J.R looked at David with his face screwed up in a look of confusion and wonderment. David continued.

"I know it's crazy and maybe I am, I don't know, but since she's been gone I've become acutely aware of most of my own shortcomings. Of which I might have a few."

J.R smiled, so did David.

"What I mean is that CJ says that it's time to forgive. I know she's right. I think that door swings both ways, Dad. I'm truly sorry for the time that we've lost for my bitterness and anger. I have to move on. I owe you, Mom and Sara that much. God knows I owe CJ at least that."

J.R took in a slow, deep breath. He had been waiting so long for this moment. Now that it was here, he knew he wanted to hug his son close, but he couldn't. Too many years of living in the same house and yet being isolated from one another had taught them to keep to their own battle lines.

"I can never take away the things that I have done that have hurt you, David. What I put all of you through was inexcusable and I will never pretend otherwise. Part of me wishes I could remember everything as part of my penance, but most of those years of my life are just a blur. Every day I live with my regret, but if I have accomplished anything, I have learned that every day is new. That if someone like your mother can forgive me and stay through all that I have put her through, there must be something in me worth while and I need to strive to see it. I love all of you wether you forgive me now or never. I am proud of you every day. When I look at all you have done in spite of me, I am proud. So, thank you. Thank you for getting here. I'd like to think we'd have worked our way here with or without CJ."

David smiled as the memories of a tiny little CJ with flimsy hair, crooked teeth and octagon shaped glasses on the rim of her nose jumping rope and crumpling to the ground laughing as she missed a step flooded his mind. He finished his burger and threw a twenty dollar bill on the bar. His dad stood and shoved the twenty back in David's pocket before David could protest and waved him off. David shrugged. He knew he couldn't win that one. As they walked out the door together into the sunlight and parted ways, David got into his car and turned the engine over and watched as his dad drove out of the parking lot and down the street back towards home.

"No, Dad, I don't think I would have worked my way here without her." He fumbled through his sun visor for the senior picture of CJ that he kept there. He looked at her for a few minutes and placed it carefully back in it's place for safe keeping before driving back to Sara and the girls.

SCENE IX: ALBION CEMETERY

"Can you believe this guy! 'I think you would like it here in California, Catherine. You would be very popular.' Where does he get off?" Cath read a few more excerpts from one of Jacen's latest letters to her to CJ's headstone and rolled her eyes some more while she paced. She had been receiving them for over a year now twice a month. She had never responded, yet she read ever single one. Truth be told, her angst was felt least severely against him than everyone else in the world at this point in her life.

Since CJ's passing, things had declined from Catherine's point of view from every angle. No one at school other than a few teachers had even acknowledged that she had lost her sister and she thought that should have been significant. She resented her friends for being ignorant about her loss. They talked about her behind her back as if she didn't know that her sister died. They tried to be very hushed about it, but hushed is not the same as sensitive or understanding.

Her mother asked periodically how things were going, but she knew that, even though she really did care, she had so much of her own things going on and so many other people leaning on her that she didn't need to hear from Cath as well so Cath blew her off. Someday her mother would thank her. Right?

Dad. Yes, well, her dad just wanted to be buddies. That seemed as much as he could handle these days. He and David were getting along like a well oiled clock, which didn't leave much time for her. She didn't ask him for anything, but he didn't offer, other than the occasional ride to school or sometimes asked her to go with him to the store or to pick out a movie.

Her grandfather seemed to be getting weaker and weaker daily. Grandma Audrey had stopped volunteering at Mom's office and was staying home full time with Gramps. She had hired a hospice nurse to come in a few times a week to help with the things that she couldn't do for him. She visited him often, but it was breaking her heart to watch him losing weight even though he was eating fine and to not be able to go for walks in the pastures with her like he used to.

Jace, as they all now called him, came to visit a couple of times a year. The more often he came, the less she hated him. At first, she felt as if an alien had landed in their family with an attitude and a lie. So he said he had CJ's heart, but where was the proof? Where was the paper? Then she found it.

Two Christmas' ago when he came to oversee the laying of ground of the new track for the high school. That was when she made her move. She snuck into his hotel room by forging a letter from him, after all, she forged letters from her parents at school all the time, that said she was a family member stopping by to pick up a change of clothing that she gave to the desk clerk who let her into his room where she rummaged around through his belongings and found what she was looking for. The donor letter. The letter he had never taken the time to send to thank their family for their donation of the heart. He had signed it, just never sent it. She had taken it and now she kept it under her bed. It still made her angry to think about it, but less so more and more with each visit. He was less and less the bad guy since he seemed to make her mom happy.

His letters were nice and as far as she knew he wasn't writing to anyone else. Her not writing back yet was only her way of trying to have some kind of control of something. At 15, she wasn't entitled to much.

SCENE X: PULLMAN WASHINGTON

It was a warm evening for early May when David and the band began their set at the bar Saturday night. As they were just warming up the crowd was light hearted and laughing and seemed to be having a good time. It was just before 9pm so there weren't very many people there yet, but the night would pick up before midnight. Closing would be at 2am, but as he had promised, David and the band would wrap it up a half hour before and he would be on his way home to Sara and girls before then.

Tonight they were playing some their heavy metal selections. David enjoyed the release he got from playing the hard and fast riffs that came from that style of music. They even tried out a few original songs that David had written. They were well received. So well received, in fact, that the owner gave the band a free pitcher of beer rather than their usual limit of two free glasses. David watched as people sang along to the songs that they knew and stomped and cheered for the songs they were hearing for the first time.

How could anyone not see what a rush this was? The adrenalin he was feeling from the crowd's energy as they began to fill the room to capacity was like a drug that he couldn't get a fast or high enough fix from.

At about 11:30, the band took a fifteen minute break and David sat down at the bar and drank another glass of beer. In a small town, everyone's your friend, everyone's your brother, even the people that you've never seen before.

"great stuff, man!"

A giant man in a plaid shirt with a mustache said, patting him on the shoulder so firmly that David had to catch his breath, before sitting down on the stool next to him.

David offered his hand to shake and the man firmly gripped it and shook it with abandon.

The man was well beyond drunk, David knew, but he wasn't judging anyone. It was Saturday night and everyone was just looking for a good time. The large, burly man turned away from David and began to give his attention to a middle aged woman at the end of the bar. It was not a large place, but most everyone knew someone who knew everyone else who was there and it was jam packed with people and sweat.

The volume of voices was rising faster and louder moment by moment however as David found himself sitting there at the bar for the last few minutes of his break, one voice began to rise above the rest and grabbed his attention. The women sitting at the end was become more and more agitated by the moment. David had always been one to keep to himself and mind his own business, but he had been raised to respect women and this one seemed to be in a state of being presently disrespected.

"Thank you anyway, but I already said no." Said the woman. The giant man in the plaid shirt moved in closer to her.

"See, I still think that you want to. Is this a no means yes thing that I hear all you women do?" He said. David leaned back in his seat and shook his head.

"Jack-ass" David said under his breath to himself. The woman stood and backed up away from the ominous man who was leering at her. The more she protested, the more it fueled his ego. He stumbled forward again and reached for her. She slapped his hand away and protested more firmly.

David stood and moved forward toward the woman to help.

"Excuse me, Dude," David said patting Plaid man on the shoulder. The man turned to David and gave him a great big drool smirk and leaned heavily on him.

"Hey! It's the Leader of the Band Guy! Hi Guy! I love this guy! She won't go to my car with me, but I'd bet she'd do it for you, will you make her go out with me? Come on, Man!"

David smiled at him, patted him on the back and tried to prop him up on the bar again. He looked at the woman who's eyes were wide with terror and smiled. His face was calm and the deep blue of his eyes carried a reassurance that everything was going to be o.k. Somedays, he had CJ's eyes.

"Are you alright?" He asked her. She nodded that she was getting there. Suddenly, Plaid Man realized even amidst his drunken stupidity what was really going on and he flew into a rage. It's interesting how alcohol can influence the body's chemistry to either cause you to make decisions you wouldn't other wise normally make, or to perhaps strive you to do the things that you were already motivated to do just that much faster and with more fury.

"What is this? She's fine! Back off, Man! We're leaving now, Band Man. Come on, Beth." Plaid Man grabbed for the woman he called Beth's hand and she moved into the corner, cowered and began to shake.

"My name is Grace and I SAID NO!" She screamed at him. The rest all happened in slow motion. It is amazing how fast a drunk man can move. In one fluid motion, Plaid Man reached out his fist and connected it with her face. David only had seconds to react. His instinct was to strike back, but he moved his body between them instead and crouched down to check on the crumpled Grace who was in a disheveled heap on the floor. The rest of the band who had already began to gather again on the stage for the next set jumped down and tried to make their way through the growing crowd that had gathered in the south corner of the bar.

David reached out and moved Grace's hand away from her swelling left eye.

"Jake, I need some ice, Dude." He called to the bar tender. Jake and David had been friends since high school. He couldn't see it, but he could hear Jake gathering the ice together for him and putting it in a table rag.

"I think we should get you to the ER." He told her before standing to get the ice from Jake. As he stood and turned, he found himself face to face again with Plaid Man.

"You're out of here. BRETT!!" David told him before raising his eyes to signal Brett at the front door who was still checking ID's and had missed the whole incident.

"You wanna bet!" Plaid Man said before placing one hand on David's chest and jabbing the other hand into his right side. David was a third the size of Plaid, but he reached up with both hands and shoved the massive hulk of a man back into the bar and at Giganto's level of inebriation, he stumbled and fell without much effort. Within seconds, there was a dog pile on top of the man in plaid and he was subdued.

"He has a knife!"Someone shouted. There was shouting and screaming while Brett, Jake and the band tried to clear some space around David and Grace. Three Washington State University football players kept Plaid Man down on the floor. He was still raging, and no one was even sure he knew who or what he was angry about.

Only moments later, police arrived and began taking statements. Grace's lips and left eye had swollen so much that she couldn't speak well enough to give anything other than yes or no answers and David did as he always had. He stood back and watched and waited for his turn.

As he stood waiting and drinking more beer, he began to feel the effects. He began to feel a little unsteady. Before long, David, who had been standing against the far wall next to where Grace had been attacked, began a slow slump to the floor as his eyes rolled to the back of his head and his legs gave out from underneath him.

"David? What the hell?" Jake jumped the bar and rushed over to David and shook his friend who was passed out cold. A police officer followed and checked his pulse.

"He has a pulse, but barely. How much has he had to drink?" Jake shook his head.

"Not as much as he can take, believe me. A couple of beers maybe." The officer looked him over briefly and then he saw it. There It was. David was seeping dark burgundy blood from his right abdomen. The officer lifted his shirt and inspected him from front to back. He knew from the witnesses what had essentially transpired here tonight. He looked up at one of the other officers trying to do crowd control near the front door.

"Jim, I need a bus and fast. We have a stab wound here."

SCENE XI: ALBION CEMETERY

The grass had grown up nicely around CJ's grave site and her grandmother always did such a nice job bringing fresh flowers by weekly even now three and half years later. The plush green tapestry made for a soft cushion for her prostrate position this day. So many moments of slow release with loss, grief and learning to cope with both and now this. It was all happening again. Tears of fear and frustration rolled down from her sleep deprived swollen eyes. She sighed as she began to talk.

"I can't do this again, CJ. I can't give another. I'm not that strong, I'm really not. I have been blessed in this life more times over than I can begin to count, but I just miss you so much. I only have so much pain, suffering and loss that I can take before I will truly break!"

CJ stood beside her with a soft light radiating like a halo around her whole being, silently watching this lament. CJ had never seen this one in a state of pain or weakness before. This was the first time CJ had witnessed her crumbling in exhaustion and defeat.

Slowly, CJ folded up her costume gown around her legs and crouched down first into a seated position beside her and then she lay down beside her, wrapping her arms around her to hold onto her while the other woman wept for a long time.

Before long, without understanding why because she was lying on the ground, she began to feel a sense of warmth and comfort as if she were being wrapped in a blanket. She couldn't explain why, but she felt compelled to pray quietly to herself and just breathe in deeply. CJ stayed close and held her and they laid there for a long time.

"Shh" CJ cooed as she rested a glowing head on the other's heart. "I will always be with you, Mom."

SCENE XII: SANDIEGO CALIFORNIA

"Hello?"

"Kyle. I need you to change your schedule and go to Washington with me today."

Jacen. When had he given him his private number again? Oh, yes, when he was on his death bed and it wasn't going to matter anymore. Sometimes Dr's do make mistakes!

Kyle got out of bed and made his way toward his modest kitchen and to the freezer where he kept the coffee beans so they would stay fresh longer. This conversation was going to need coffee. If he was going to start his day with a phone call from Jacen Owen, he was going to need a lot of coffee.

"If I was going to reschedule my appointments for the day or a couple of days, and I'm not saying that I am, because I am not, why, friend, would I be doing this to my other very important, yes, as equally important as Jacen Owen, however not as rich as, but important none the less as, patients?"

He could almost feel the eyes rolling with impatience on the other side of the line. He sensed Jace pacing back and forth wearing a small pattern in a single floor space despite the massive penthouse he occupied.

"When I tried to check in with the Stewart's this morning like I do every Sunday, no one answered, so I called the Cane's who are the grandparents and Clinton answered . He told me that David was in the hospital. There was some kind of incident at the bar where his band plays and he got stabbed. I am officially hiring you as his physician."

Kyle sat down at his kitchen table and waited for his coffee to brew. Now he needed it for sure.

"Jace, I'm a cardiologist. Yes, I went to medical school, but my specialty is the heart. Unless he was stabbed in the heart or a major artery, I'm not going to be anything but in the way." There was a frustrated sigh on the other end of the phone.

"This is my family, Kyle. I know that I ask a lot of you, but I need this. If for nothing else, be another set of eyes and ears from the big city for these small town doctors. Please, I will beg."

Kyle rubbed the back of his neck as he felt a head ache coming on fast. Over the years he had made more exceptions and broken through more ethical red tape than should be allowed for Jacen Owen and it was getting out of control.

"I'm sorry Jace, I just don't know how it would be possible to move a weeks worth of patients around on such short notice."

SCENE XIII: SPOKANE WASHINGTON'S SACRED HEART MEDICAL CENTER

The limousine pulled up to the front entrance of the hospital where the driver got out and opened the back door for two gentlemen, one young man who could have been in his mid 20's and another man easily in his late 30's or early 40's. Both were sharply dressed. This is what those who saw the limousine pull up would say for a long time to come. It wasn't every day that mode of transportation made it's way through the hospital parking. People were eager to see who, why and what was the special occasion.

Jacen and Kyle made their way to the front lobby reception desk.

"May I help you?" Asked the small woman behind the desk from behind her thick rimmed glasses.

"We are looking for David Stewart. He was brought here two days ago from Pullman I believe." Jacen informed her.

"Are you family?" She asked. Jacen didn't know how to respond to that. Legally? Technically? No. More or less he was, though. His heart was. He paused so long that she spoke again.

"If you are not a member of the family, then I'm sorry I cannot allow you to enter the ICU."

"Excuse me," Kyle stepped up to the counter. Thankfully, she hadn't noticed him standing there at all. He reached inside his bag and pulled out his hospital badge and medical license.

"I'm Dr. Kyle Alyster, cardiologist up from San Diego California to consult on some cases in the ICU." She beamed brightly at him and her eyes followed his left arm down to his hand to see if there was a wedding ring.

"I'd be happy to take you there." She said pouring on as much charm as she could muster together, having forgotten all about Jace already. Kyle smiled back and played along with the flirting.

"Thank you, but you seem busy down here with these phones ringing, so if you could just tell me what floor, I'm sure it's well marked. I can find my way from there."

She was a little disappointed, however, more people were looking for assistance and the other receptionists were equally as busy. Jacen had since disappeared around a corner out of her line of sight.

"O.k," she said, pointing to a set of elevators. "Take the green elevators to the eighth floor and then go left down the hall a ways and the ICU will be on the right hand side of hall way. Have a nice day Dr."

Kyle winked at her just for good measure and thanked her before he heading for the green elevators. Jace slipped onto the elevator with Kyle just before it closed. Surprisingly, they were the only ones on the elevator at that moment. Jace couldn't help but smile at his friend for his creativity and humor under pressure.

"You're a sly dog, Dr. Alyster. I didn't know you had it in you." He said patting Kyle on the shoulder. "Does this mean you're not mad at me any more?" He asked, still smiling. The elevator stopped on the eighth floor and the doors opened. Kyle walked straight ahead.

" Not even a little bit." He replied without a glance towards Jacen.

Once at the ICU, Jacen waited, while once again, Kyle worked his physicians charm to inquire into the whereabouts of David. A moment later, J.R arrived with Kyle to gather Jacen and bring him to where everyone else was keeping watch over David.

Inside David's small room, some of the family had gathered. Sara was sleeping in a chair in the corner with nearly two year old Christine on her lap. Rea was reading in another corner. Vickie kept a close vigil over her son as she had done her daughter years before. David was not in a coma the way CJ had been, however, they were keeping him heavily sedated as his injuries were very severe and too much movement could be detrimental.

Kyle kindly introduced himself to everyone careful not wake Sara. Vickie stood and hugged him and thanked him for taking such great care with CJ's heart and being so wonderful with Jace all these years. Kyle inquired as to what information they had been given and how he might be able to help. He explained the limitations of his experience but assured them that he would offer any assistance that he could.

Jace heard all of these things transpire in the back ground. He stood in the door way and couldn't take his eyes away from the windowsill. It was as if he were being drawn into the past and still standing right there with everyone else at the same time. Standing at the window, looking outside, with her back to them and her long dirty blond hair cascading down her back, was Catherine. She was a few inches taller than CJ had been, but she was thin and her jaw line was similar enough, that Jace felt as if he were being pulled back to another hospital and another room where another girl had stood at his windowsill broken, fragile and full of wisdom.

He walked over to her and waited for her to see him. He had continued the letters to her. She still had yet to write back. She was talking to him now during his visits, and that had taken over a year. For the most part, at this point, the writing had become for his own edification rather than for correspondence.

"Hey," He said, barely above a whisper. Catherine smiled without looking at him.

"Want to take a break and go find a snack or something?" He asked. His hands were in his pockets as he waited for her to answer. She turned quickly and hugged him briefly.

It had only been two months since his last visit, so he wasn't sure if this was a 'good to see you again' hug or the 'thank God you're finally here' kind of hug, but he'd take either at this point to avoid all of the medical talk going on behind him.

"I thought no one would ever ask." Cath responded taking his hand and heading for the door.

"I'm taking Cath to the cafeteria for a drink if you need us. Rea, do you want to come along?" Jace offered. Rea looked up from her book and smiled, but then she looked over at David, who at this point in her life, had become the only dad she had ever known and shook her head. She wasn't going anywhere without him.

Jace looked at Kyle to see if he would like go with them, but he was very busy listening intently to what J.R and Vickie were telling him about what they had been told so far regarding David's condition. If it weren't for his incredible ethical integrity, Jace would have thought Kyle would have already gone and checked David's chart himself. However, Kyle, being the good Dr. that he was, would wait for an invitation from David's current physicians if one was offered. So Jacen and Catherine left everyone in the capable hands of Dr. Kyle Alyster who intended to do nothing for now but be a sounding board which was the best medicine for all of them right now.

Catherine navigated them to the cafeteria as if she were an employee and worked her way through the line finding things exactly where she knew them to be. Jace watched her and felt a mix of wonder and sadness knowing full well how her level of expertise had come into existence. It had been a few years, but a child's memory is vivid. It was as if she even had a favorite table because she knew just where she wanted to sit after he had paid for their drinks.

She was a window girl, like her sister, he thought as she picked a table that overlooked the front of the hospital and a street below. She was quieter than he remembered CJ being. From his few conversations with CJ and her journals, she had said so much. Cath, well, she was nice and quiet most of the time. They had talked in polite passing conversation some, but mostly, he watched her growing up from afar. As his memories of CJ's face faded, Catherine's bore a remarkable resemblance to her sister he thought.

"Cath?"

"Yep." She didn't look at him. Just stared out the window. She didn't seem scared or even worried. She wasn't portraying a sense of boredom either. It was as if she were just waiting for whatever was coming next. A been here, done this before sort of fixation.

"Tell me about CJ." He said to her. He wanted to reach across the table and take one of her hands to reassure her that he wasn't trying to pry or interview her, but he cared about CJ and wanted to know more about her. Catherine looked down at her hands and then back out the window again.

"No." She said flatly.

"Why?" He pressed, leaning back in his seat defensively.

"I can't. Not here. Not in this place. CJ was never CJ here."

Jace let out a slow long breath. That was like a sucker punch to his abdomen. This was where she had said goodbye to CJ and he was a jackass for asking her to relive it.

"Have they given you any idea how soon David gets to go home?" He asked trying to sound optimistic. Tears began to fill her eyes then. She reached a hand up and pulled a some stray hairs back behind her ear and wiped her eyes with a sleeve that was too long. She rolled her eyes in frustration and shook her head.

"As soon as they find a kidney donor."

When Jacen returned Catherine to David's room, Kyle was not there. Vickie informed them that he had been invited to review David's chart by the attending physician and that he would be back shortly. Cath resumed her place by the windowsill and Jace pulled up a seat beside David and watched his steady breathing and wondered how things had gone so wrong.

Vickie looked over at Jacen, the once brooding angry young man turned power of the people. Keeper of her daughter's heart. His head bowed as if in prayer, his shoulders shaking. When she called his name and he looked up, he wiped his deep dark eyes. She reached over and took his hand in her own.

"I don't belong here." He said barely above a whisper. She smiled at him and shook her head.

"Where else would you be? Family belongs here. If you didn't want to be family by now, you never should have walked into my office three years ago." He squeezed her hand then stood and propped himself against the wall watching David's monitors and their steady rhythm.

"Why does he need a kidney?" Jacen asked after a few minutes. Vickie sighed. She was glad that J.R had taken Sara, Christine and, with much coaxing, Rea out to get something to eat. Sara did not have the stomach for all of this. Vickie began to explain as much as she understood.

"Apparently, The stab wound punctured the right kidney and part of his liver. They have already removed that kidney and the liver appears to be repairing itself, however, he lost so much blood initially, and the stabbing caused an infection that they have since gotten mostly under control, but it did irreparable damage to the remaining kidney and he needs another one."

Jacen was very familiar with transplants and how they worked. He had needed an organ that had to come from a cadaver, but his own research had taught him that the best donors were family members. He rubbed his face with his hands, the day already starting to wear on him and he had only been there for a few hours at that point. He couldn't imagine what it had been like for all of them during those precarious hours keeping a vigil over CJ and now David.

"So, have you all been tested? Family members are the best candidates, right? Surely at least one of you is a good candidate. Especially Cath! Siblings are usually the best ones! I've heard of people actually having more children just so they can use them to be donors of bone marrow.

It doesn't mean that I agree or disagree mind you, but one of you must be a match."

Vickie urged him to sit back down. Neither of them noticed Catherine's silent tears in the corner.

"I wish any one of us were. Unfortunately, Cath is the wrong blood type. None of us are a match. You see, David has a rare blood type he inherited from J.R's mother. CJ also had it, but her kidney's have already been donated to other people. So we have to wait and pray for another match."

Kyle and another physician entered the room looking very serious in a comradeship sort of way with David's chart in hand. The other physician thanked Kyle for his suggestions, checked David's monitors which had not changed, and then shook Kyle's hand again and said that they would talk again later before leaving the room.

"So," Kyle said as he checked David's monitors himself.

"Anything new happen while I was gone?"

Jace looked over at him with his eyes bright and renewed with a sense of hope.

"Yes." Jacen said before he pushed the nurses call button on David's bed.

"I think I'm a match for David. I want to give him a kidney."

———

Kyle and Vickie sat in the cafeteria while Jacen went through a barrage of tests that would take hours. In most other hospitals, it would take weeks to get all of the results back to find out if David and Jacen were a match for a new kidney, but Sacred Heart had a transplant team on stand by with all the testing information and equipment at their disposal so they would have their results within 48 hours or less.

"Do you think it's dangerous for him? To donate I mean. He's already been through so much with the heart surgery." Vickie asked. Kyle waited a while and weighed his answer carefully before he answered. He had only just met this woman, but he had been curious about her for quite some time. Who was the driving force behind all of the changes in his once moody, selfish patient? Here was her son needing a kidney desperately, would she wait for another if surgery would put Jacen at risk even if he was a match? Kyle gave her a reassuring smile.

"Mrs. Stewart, it has been over 3 years since we did the heart transplant and Jacen has always been careful about his body. He has never been a smoker or drinker of excess. He takes his anti-rejection medications without fail. He's young and resilient. I think that if he's a match for David which may not be as much of a stretch as people might think. If CJ would have been the best candidate, then Jace might be too.

Most transplant patients will show signs of weakening before they get stronger after surgery, but not Jacen. Within a week of receiving CJ's heart, he was demanding his release from the hospital and setting up hospice care at home of whom he then fired four days later when he felt he didn't need that either. I would be a little more hesitant about Jace being the recipient again because I would worry that the heart was failing, but I don't see the harm in his donating. It's a rough surgery I won't kid you about that. It will be hard on both of them and they will have equal recovery time. However, Jace has the money in his pocket to see to it that they both get the best of care and the best team available in the country. If he's not a match, I promise you, he'll reach deep in those pockets and find you one today if he can."

Vickie smiled at the thought. Jacen had become a better man since she had met him three years ago. He had grown from a brooding quiet young man with the weight of the world on his shoulders to now, an often smiling guy who visited them a couple of times a year, usually on the holidays, during family times, and seemed to be enjoying his life a little more. They never talked about his money. They did talk about family and work. He would ask her budget questions since that was her area of expertise and she would give him advise on ways to cut costs and share space between companies in exchange for just spending time together and discussing how many times now he had read CJ's journal. He had become a part of her family in all the ways that count and if he decided to give David a kidney, then they would be intertwined that much more.

"I will not ask Jacen for anything but his support right now and I am thankful for him everyday."

Sincerity that is genuine is a rare thing in todays time and Kyle found himself staring at it. He knew at that moment why Jacen would disappear and miss appointments randomly throughout the year. He had a family now and they were all here. He would have half expected Jacen to try and convince them to relocate to San Diego, but why? Why move them to all of the reminders of what he had hated about his life before CJ and her life changing heart when he could just leave it all behind whenever it bothered him and come here to them and their love and understanding? It was a good life for Jacen Kyle figured and he would stop fighting him on it. It wasn't doing him any good anyway. For all of Jacen's changes, he was still a stubborn ass!

"How are you feeling now?"

Jacen looked around and was surprised to find himself standing on the beach in San Diego again. It was morning again, but this time the sun was high in the sky and the breeze was so light it was barely moving. Still, alone on the beach, just he and CJ, Jacen knew he was dreaming, but he would stay here as long as he could this time. She was standing before him so close this time he could smell her as if she were fresh out of the shower. Her long, beautiful curls were back, her braces were gone, and her body appeared whole and healed.

"I have missed you, CJ. I know it's crazy because you died and I've only ever dreamed of you, but I believe with everything I am that I know you and have always known you. I wish you had stayed or that I could have had another heart so that you could have lived."

She reached her arms out and wrapped him in them. He held her close and took in the feel of her, the smell of her, the weightlessness of her.

"That could never be, Jacen. Another heart would never have led you to the healing that you needed. Anyone else's might not have given you a chance to forgive the past and live the life you needed to. You have so much to offer in love and you were going to waste it on hate and bitterness, but my heart was an opportunity to heal you and them."

Jacen smiled as he thought about Vickie, Audrey, J.R., David, Catherine, and even the very ill Clinton who was still hanging on after all this time. Jacen had been paying for his care even though Audrey had insisted that it wasn't necessary. It was the least that he could do for them. He was very fond of them all.

"I think they would have healed each other without me."

"Some of them, yes. But, some of them still have a ways to go. Some of them still feel me and find healing in that and some of them are still hurting after all this time and are lost. Find a way to help her. Remind her that she was not left behind."

Jace wasn't sure which she CJ was talking about because in the Stewart family there was an overwhelming she to he ratio. He would figure it out though. For her, he would move a mountain just to have this moment last.

"And what of your grandfather? How can I save him?" CJ pulled back and smiled. Her deep blue eyes glistened and he wanted to swim away in them forever. God, how he had missed her!

"Save him from what? From no longer being in pain? You are doing well by my grandfather, but his time is almost up. He's ready and I'm anxious to be with him again. Please don't try extreme measures to prolong his life. It's not what he wants and it will only extend the pain for him. They will grieve his passing as they did mine, but they will take hope in knowing he's with me and we'll all be together someday."

She reached out and touched his face with her soft hand. All at once he was overcome with an overwhelming sense of her. Everything about her, Her name that had haunted him all these years, her being here with him unbroken in body and spirit, and he couldn't take it anymore.

He gathered her up in his arms, hair, face, blazing blue eyes and kissed her slowly, deeply, passionately for all the things that he had missed about her and had missed out on himself when she had left him. He half expected to float right through her, but his hands connected with her face and her hair. His lips melted into hers. He took his time and before long she was kissing him back. It felt between them as if that moment would last forever and Jacen knew that he would remember it that long.

When she pulled back she was smiling at first and then she giggled a little. He wasn't sure if it was a good sign or bad. His tanned cheeks turned amber.

"What's so funny?" He demanded. He was still holding her. He intended to for as long as he could make this dream last, yet he could feel himself being pulled back. The beach was fading little by little so he held her tighter. She was laughing now.

"It's David." She said.

"He's throwing ice at you. It's a game we use to play to wake each other up. I have to go."

"No. Please stay. I want more."

CJ smiled and ran a finger over his lips.

"I can't stay. I died remember? You will love another, but I will always be in your hearts. You can't move on if you won't try. Don't look for me anymore, Jacen, look for her. She needs you now. Wake up." She was gone.

Jacen's eyes began to flutter open. He felt a wetness on them and rubbed his face. There was another splash of wetness and he turned in the direction of the offending sprinkling. He blinked his eyes opened again to find David in another bed across from him flinging ice cubes from a plastic cup at him.

"Good afternoon, Mr. Funshine!" David said when Jacen finally opened his eyes all the way and sat up.

He leaned forward, but the pain in his left flank reminded him to think better of that. He was about to push the nurses call button and start a riot which had been his habit in his private suite at the hospital in California, but before he did, David reminded him that he had a pain pump right next to his thumb and it would give him instant relief.

Once the pain had subsided, and he was able to relax, he looked over at David again who was strumming a few bars on his acoustic guitar.

It was just the two of them in the room at the moment. He and David had never really talked much. David had never been unpleasant, just kept to himself mostly. Perhaps that was why Jace respected him. He understood that CJ had been very close to her brother and that David had never really talked about her so he vowed never to bring her up.

"How long was I out?"

"Bout two days I'd say, give or take. Of course I can't say for sure how long I was out for myself, so don't count on me, man!" David answered still playing a slow melody.

"I woke up two days ago, though, and hey, thanks for the kidney. You really didn't have to do that. I hope you're going to be alright. I mean that's two major surgeries for you."

Jacen smiled. He thought about reaching over to shake David's hand, but it was too far a reach and he knew the pain would kill him if the fall out of bed didn't so he stayed put for now.

"My heart surgeon assured me that to be an organ donor would be o.k and I was a match so it made sense. I would do anything for this family. I hope you all know that by now." There was another long silence between them as David slowly, painfully placed his guitar down along side of the bed before turning to Jacen again.

"I'm glad you said that. I want to talk to you about something."

Jacen braced himself. This was the most David had ever said to him and he sounded fairly serious. Jacen was waiting for a bomb to drop. He was afraid he was going to be asked to leave to the family by the son of the Don. It felt that ominous in that moment.

"Summer vacation is coming up for Catherine next month and I know that she'll probably spend it doing nothing around Pullman again being depressed and hanging out leaving paper flowers at CJ's grave or making friends that are no good for her. You own a great big company in California. What are the chances that maybe she and a friend could come down there for the summer and work for you?"

Jacen thought perhaps he had just lost 150 pounds of stress in that moment. It made sense and it was easy enough to do. Catherine could do one of a hundred jobs at his company. He would show her around and let her pick which department she wanted to work in and then they would set a schedule.

"I think it's a great idea. I will talk to Vickie about it and let her set it up with Catherine."

David smiled and then painfully picked up the guitar again. He had wondered when this young man had entered their lives what he had wanted from them. What he had to gain from just showing up. Over time though, Jacen had grown on even the skeptic in the Stewart clan.

"Thanks, man. I just can't watch her waste away here, you know? I thought after a while she would start to get better, but she's just not." He shrugged his shoulders and shook his head.

Jacen opened up some files that Meghan had sent him and began leafing through them. Then he rolled his eyes and pushed the nurses call button. When she arrived, he put on his demanding face.

"I can't give you any more pain meds, Mr. Owen, you just gave yourself a dose. Is there anything else you need?"

"I need to see my cardiologist, Dr. Alyster, his number should be on standby. I know that he's available somewhere here in the hospital."

"Are you having heart problems?"

Jacen was growing impatient. It had been a long time since he had been in a hospital and this hospital had not dealt with the likes of Jacen Owen had not invested anything into this hospital so this nurse didn't necessarily have to take any of his tantrums seriously either.

"That's for me to discuss with my cardiologist. Page him." He demanded. The nurse came around and checked his vitals first and listened to his heart. Before leaving the room to grant his request. It was more than 40 minutes before Vickie and Kyle entered the room. David had nodded off to sleep again by then.

"I hear you're being difficult again." Kyle said as he came around the bed to listen to Jacen's heart. Jacen rolled his eyes and pushed him away.

"I just need a favor." He said. It was Kyle's turn to roll his eyes and he crossed his arms over his chest.

"What can I do for his highness now."

"Can you call Meghan for me and tell her to open the house and hire some staff for the kitchen, and the rooms."

Kyle looked puzzled. Jacen had closed up his parents mansion on the beach shortly after his father died. Not because he didn't have the money to care for it, but simply because he didn't like the memories of the place. He never sold it and he still payed for the grounds to be kept neat and the pool to be cleaned, but he hadn't entered it in eight years.

"May I ask what this is about? Are you moving back in?"

Jace looked up at him and smiled the biggest smile Kyle had seen on his face in a long time and then Jace looked at Vickie.

"I'm going to have some company this summer I hope."

SCENE XIV: SAN DIEGO, CALIFORNIA

The streets were crowded as they worked their way down a busy boulevard. The stretch limousine eased it's way as people careened their necks and peered at them trying to get a look inside the deeply tinted windows. Kyle had gone home a week after the surgery after he had been sure everything had gone smoothly. Jacen had returned home a week after that after he had convinced Vickie to take two weeks off for a summer vacation and allow Catherine to do a summer internship with his company. Catherine was surprisingly eager to make the trip if for nothing else to leave town for a little while. He had offered to allow her to bring a friend and her parents had felt that was a safe idea, but much to their surprise, Catherine had declined.

J.R had opted not to come along. He was not a fan of big cities or big crowds. He trusted his wife to care for their daughter while they were together and he hoped that Catherine would hate it and come home with her mother. That failing, he would check in daily until his youngest was home again and he would pray. She was sixteen now and growing up and he would have to learn to trust them all a little.

Lynn, who had been the first recipient of the Carmen Stewart Scholarship award two years ago, had completed her sophomore year of college studying child development and child psychology. When she was given a personal invitation for a summer internship at the companies child development center by Jacen himself , she jumped at the chance. A chance to work first hand at a growing development center that focused on children's needs and learning skills and a chance to possibly see and get to know Jacen better couldn't be all bad either, right?

Jacen had sent a company car to pick the three of them up at the air port with a driver and an assistant. A lovely woman by the name of Meghan met them all at the gate when they deplaned with the driver who, with a courteous hand shake and a smile, loaded all of their luggage onto a cart from the baggage claim merry go round and out to waiting limousine. As they made their way out of the airport, Meghan explained that Jacen would be meeting them at the estate and that he hoped that their flight had not been too bad.

Meghan and Vickie had met over the phone briefly regarding negotiations and check exchanges for the charities that Jacen had set up through the companies. It was nice to put a face with the pleasant voice on the other end of the phone so many miles away Vickie thought.

Megan looked at each of them in turn and sized them up individually.

Lynn. The winner of the first scholarship award. She seemed reserved, plain, and conservative.

"How is school going for you, Lynn?" Meghan asked. Lynn smiled sweetly and her deep brown eyes glistened. She laced her hands together as she thought of her answers before she spoke.

"It's always a challenge, but I'm enjoying it. I know if I work hard it will be worth it in the end."

Meghan's eyes wandered over to Vickie who was watching with amusement her daughter's fascination with the world outside that Catherine hadn't experienced before. She wondered as she thought about her own young children how this woman had been able to cope with losing one and then nearly sacrificing another. Still, here she was, smiling even with a sadness behind her wise eyes. The things a mother does to keep going at the expense of her own pain one can never measure,

Meghan realized. Could she cope, if it had been her? She hoped she would never have to know.

Catherine, the sister. Meghan wondered where she was at in her stage of recovering from all these things. Had she been too young to be badly scarred by what had happened to her sister? She seemed quiet even in her wonder. Meghan was curious how she would fit into the company this summer. Jacen had indicated that she would get the opportunity to search throughout the whole company until she found something that she liked and that suited her and that is what she would do. Her salary would be determined and based upon what she chose and how well she did at that job. Jacen could be a task master when he wanted to be, but would she prove to be a spoiled brat and would he send her packing or would she rise to the challenge? Meghan wanted to give her the benefit of the doubt, because she trusted Jacen and so she let this all fall where ever it might and she would help where she could.

Catherine looked up at the larger than usual tinted sun roof above them and smiled. Megan pushed a button and Cath gasped as it began to slowly open up. Meghan smiled at her as she said,

"Go ahead, you can stand up and look out side. We won't be going under any bridges or streetlight from here on to our destination. It's really o.k. Go ahead."

Slowly, Catherine stood to her feet and peeked her head and her torso up out of the sun roof. She closed her eyes and felt with everything that was inside and out the sun on her face and the wind blowing her long, blond hair back behind her. She reached her arms out in front of her to feel the wind in-between each of her fingers and then snatched them back again to her chest as she laughed.

The car began to slow to a crawl as the driver put on the right turn signal and they began to turn down a long private drive towards the beach. Meghan encouraged them all to stand and look out of the sun roof and view the estate grounds as they made the long drive up to the house. To the right of them was a lush golf course with 15 holes. To their left was a beautiful rose garden with every color of rose they could have imagined. Meghan informed them that behind the house was an olympic size pool and spa as well as tennis courts should they wish to us them. There was also an indoor pool and sauna and a rec room stocked with pool tables, fuse ball, etc. should the weather take a bad turn. Catherine laughed a little as she looked up at the remarkable blue sky. Meghan smiled at her.

"What's funny?"

Cath looked her over and snorted,

"Have ya' been to Washington? Ever?"

"Catherine! Don't be rude!" Vickie chided her daughter, and then to Meghan,

"Excuse her. I truly did not raise her to be so offensive."

Meghan smiled, as always. She decided right then and there that she liked them all. She could see how Jacen had fallen so hopelessly for this family. They were always genuine, every one of them.

They pulled up to the house. It wasn't a house so much as a sprawling mansion. From the front it was whitewashed stone with large marble pillars at the entrance. The front doors were side by side huge deep, thick red cherry oak.

"It's the Fortress of Solitude." Catherine claimed in awe as the limousine came to a stop in front of the house and she climbed out of the back passenger door. She was suppose to wait for the driver to let her out, but she never had before, so why should protocol and proper pretension stop her now? Meghan waited until everyone else was out before she got out with the help of the driver.

While they all waited patiently for their bags to be unloaded from the back of the limo, The large front doors swung open, as if by remote control and Jacen emerged. He looked very small in comparison to large entry way. He was dressed more businesslike than Lynn, Vickie and Catherine were used to seeing him, however, he was as Meghan saw him daily.

He greeted them all with hugs, even Meghan, whom he had grown more fond of with her growing support of his pursuit to change his life and establish an extended family.

"Welcome to California! Sorry I was unable to meet you at the airport. I had a few meetings that needed to be taken care of today so that we would have the rest of your vacation free of company distractions. I gather Meghan and Jerome," He said nodding towards the driver who bowed humbly, "were able to get you taken care of."

"They have been more than exceptional. Are they doing this extra for us, or is this on company time?" Vickie asked.

Jacen scrunched up his face and put his hands inside his jacket pockets.

"Why do you ask? Are you afraid I don't pay them well enough?" He was smiling because he had just given everyone a pay increase due to another large increase in the overall revenues.

"Well," Vickie began, "I was only wondering because I felt that if they had gone out of their way to take such great care of us when they still have other responsibilities, it would be nice if you said thank you buy offering them a nice gift certificate to a restaurant of their choice or perhaps a coupon for a day off at a later date, something like that. It's just a suggestion. You are the boss, of course." She finished. It was put to him as a suggestion, however he knew that it was smart and more than fair.

"If I agree, can it be because I said so and not because you did?" He said still smiling.

Meghan stepped in then.

"Please, Vickie, that's not necessary. I volunteered. I needed to meet you face to face so I was happy to be a part of this. No further Thanks is needed."

Jacen held up his hands in surrender.

"Jerome, please go home and ask your wife if she would rather have a nice night out with dinner on the town, or a three day weekend at a spa for two. Get back to me as soon as you can. Meghan, you are getting a three day weekend at a spa for two like it or not. Just make arrangements for the kids and let me know when you want to go and I'll take care of the rest."

Vickie smiled as she watched the satisfaction spread across his face. He was very pleased with himself. His smile was so big that it got lost on either side in dimples. Meghan began to protest but he would hear none of it. She turned to Vickie and smiled a thank you. Then, She climbed into the front seat of the limousine and Jerome, after closing her door behind her, got into the drivers seat and slowly drove away from the house.

Jacen waited until the car disappeared and then turned toward the house once again. His countenance became more somber as he began giving them the tour of his parents home.

As they walked into the foyer, to their right was a massive circular sitting area with an open fire pit in the middle. The ceiling above that area was all skylight and solar paneling so the direct sunlight coming in lit up the room and the plants and cacti that were living there seemed to be glorified in it. Then directly in front of them was an open stair case that went to what looked like a little bridge.

Jace took them first, past the stair case into the kitchen and showed them that the refrigerator had been fully stocked. There was a cook available to them should they wish to have anything prepared, but they could feel free to cook themselves if they wished and they should expect to have several meals out on the town with him.

They then moved down a long, wide hall that had stained glass on one side and large open windows that overlooked the ocean on the other.

At the end of the hall they came to a series of rooms. Each room was enormous with it's own walk in closet. Each room also had a bathroom with a complete bathtub, shower, toilet, sink and vanity. One room was very plain with pale pink walls that Jacen explained was one of the many guest rooms that they had used throughout the years. Lynn laid claim to that room and set her suit case down.

The next room was a pale blue with an ocean view out of one window and mural of a humpback whale on another. Catherine decided that this would be her room for the summer. "I like that I can hear the ocean from in here." She said. Jacen smiled. He would tell her later that this had been his room when he had lived here and that he had painted the whale because it had given him peace for a while.

144

Vickie planned on just taking any one of the number of spacious rooms that were left. She had no intentions of being picky. She had never imagined there houses that existed that were like this one let alone ever expected to be a guest in one. However, as she began to move towards the next room along the hall, Jacen pressed a button on a monitor that was on the wall just inside the room and waited for it to beep.

"Yes, Mr. Owen, Sir?"

"Hi, Pete, We're down at the South end bedrooms. I have a guest who will be staying in the master suite. Can you or one of the other staff please come and gather her things. We'll wait right here."

"Right away."

Jacen smiled that sly smile of his at Vickie and she blushed. If only she or J.R had been blessed with the genetic disposition for dimples so that they could have passed them along to their children, but no such luck. For all the special qualities and good looks that the Stewart's might have, there wasn't a dimple among them, but Jacen, that kid had them in spades.

A moment later, A young man in kaki pants and a Hawaiian shirt met up with them and smiled. He held his hand out to shake so Vickie took it and smiled back.

"The name's Pete. I and my staff will be taking care of the house here for you so if you need anything; pillows, new sheets, an alarm clock, dinner, or just how to work the remote control for one of the televisions, please call us day or night. No time is a bad time."

Vickie liked him already, but she felt a little out of sorts. She had never been waited on outside of a restaurant so she didn't know what to say or how to take all this in.

"Thank you, but you may regret those words when my 17 year old daughter calls you at 2am for something crazy."

Pete smiled. He couldn't have been more than 25 years old or so himself, but she did notice the wedding ring on his finger so she didn't feel too worried.

"We all live on the grounds so I welcome the company and it will be interesting to have a teenager around to keep us on our toes." He said with a wink. He picked up her suit case and began walking away. Jace followed and Vickie, after one more confused look back at the spacious guest room they were leaving behind, followed them.

They climbed the open staircase and then crossed the open bridge way to room that was bigger than all three of the large bedrooms that Vickie had seen downstairs. As she walked in, she was facing the most magnificent ocean view she could possibly have imagined. The large california king size bed was along the far wall with a chase lounge along the opposite wall and the rest of the room was glassed in with a patio outside and patio furniture that was covered in plastic.

"Pete, can you uncover the patio furniture, for Mrs. Stewart, please."

"Right away. I'll get that done now. Please let me know if you need anything else, Mrs. Stewart."

Vickie did not hear him. She was gaping at the walk in closet that was the size of her and J.R's bedroom back home. Just in front of the patio was a jacuzzi tub with marble tile that was set down into the floor so you could step down into it.

She walked over past the bed and into a separate room where there was a vanity and two sinks. Just beyond that was a shower that had a detachable head and a ledge for sitting as well as a completely separate room just for the toilet.

"So, what do you think?"

Vickie turned to Jacen and didn't know if she should hug him or cry. It was all a little overwhelming at that moment. She wished right then that CJ were there. She would know what was the right thing to say.

"I think this is your room. I would be happy to stay downstairs with the girls."

Jacen shook his head.

"Um, no. I don't live here. I live in a penthouse 2 miles up the beach. I want you to have this room because it was my parent's room and as far as I'm concerned, you are more a parent to me than they have ever been. This room is where you belong. Enjoy it. You deserve this."

He was surprised to see that her face did not seem pleased. He thought that she would be happy. After three years though, Jacen still had a lot to learn about gifts and giving and the heart of the matter. Vickie looked around the room. It had amenities that she had never seen or experienced, but it was lacking so many things that her own home had in clutter masses. There weren't any pictures of his parents together in this room. Where was the loving couple? Where was the proof of where all of there material possessions had come from? Where were the portraits of the family? Albums of vacations and of a child chasing the family pet around this spacious property?

"So," She began, a little disappointed, "You won't be staying here with us." It wasn't presented as a question. More like confirming a fact. Jacen turned towards the ocean view. He couldn't bear to look at her at that moment. He had never cared before wether he disappointed someone or not. Not until now. How she felt about him mattered in a way no one else's feelings did and it was strange and confusing.

"You are the first people to enter this house besides the staff that keep it running since I was 15. After my father died, I emancipated myself, with the agreement that I would not touch my trust fund until I was 21, then I walked away from everything that reminded me of him, her and them."

Vickie watched the bright California sun beaming into his dark brown eyes and saw the lingering pain, anger and resentment that was at home inside there.

"No," She began, "You didn't. You kept the house. You held on to your pain and misery because it made you feel powerful. The problem with anger and bitterness is that it festers and twitches and even after a long time, after you think you've gotten better and healed, you still go back to the place where it started from, and it still haunts you. You don't stay here because this place still reminds you of all of things that you believe you missed out on in those relationships but that doesn't mean you don't still live here."

Jacen walked over to the sliding glass doors and stepped out onto the patio. He watched as Catherine and Lynn lounged by the pool, laughing and whispering as the staff brought them towels and drinks. Vickie reached out and gently touched his shoulder. He hung his head down and placed his hands in his pockets once again. He knew she was right. If there was one thing Vickie had, it was a radar for reading people's inner demon's. He could hide them even from himself, but they were always evident to her.

"Jacen, you can't begin the process of complete healing or forgiveness until you allow God to use the past to teach you something in the present. Now it's time to heal the broken spirit in you, but you have to be willing."

Jacen's head snapped up.

"That's what CJ said."

The words were out before he could snatch them back. He had never told anyone up to this point about his conversations with CJ. No one other than Kyle and that was before he had even known who she was. At that time she was just a mysterious girl who had visited him on his death bed

He turned to Vickie and expected to see confusion or distrust on her face, but all he saw was patience. She was a mother waiting for her child to talk. She had waited years for David to communicate, she would wait many more years to talk to CJ again. She would listen now to Jacen.

Jacen guided her to a lounge chair and then took up his own seat across from her. He took her hands in his own.

"Vickie, this isn't going to make any sense, but I want you to try and keep an open mind."

"I will." Always the understanding woman.

Jacen took a deep breath and began his story about how when he had first seen CJ on the beach in a dream two weeks before the transplant, and then a few more times in the week before in various states of injury and illness. He told her of all the messages that CJ had given him. He had not understood all that they had meant but she had made such an impact on him in such a short amount of time that he had felt compelled to find out more. That was why the visit rather than the letter after the transplant.

When he was finished, he let go of Vickie's hands and went back to the balcony ledge and leaned on it. He couldn't look at her. He was afraid of what he would see in her eyes. Would she be angry? Would she believe that he saw her daughter on her death bed from two states away?

"CJ had a gift for talking that we teased her about constantly. However, for what it was worth, sometimes she was talking because what she had to say needed to be heard. Wether people believe in God or spiritual gifts or not, I believe she had one for knowing what people needed to know about their deepest self. I'm glad you had a chance to meet her. The question is, are you making the most of the messages she had for you?"

Jacen smiled and rolled his eyes as he turned back towards her. She was still sitting in the lounge chair, patients still her virtue. He walked over to her and held out a hand to help her stand.

"So you don't think that I'm crazy?" Vickie smiled.

"You're probably as certifiable as the rest of us. We've all had one experience or another with CJ since her death I think. Some of us have talked about it, some of us have chalked it up to coincidence or something else. Some won't talk about it at all. The important thing to remember is that we all need to heal and we need each other to do that."

"Ok." Jacen agreed as they worked their way back out of the master suit and down the staircase.

"So," Said Vickie as they walked out the back of the house towards the pool to meet Lynn and Catherine who had stripped to bathing suits and were in the water now.

"Have you now changed your mind about staying here with us?"

Jacen looked around at the massive estate. The house, sprawling grounds with the pool, the boat dock down along the beach, the peach tree orchard on the south side of the property. He could feel nothing but loss, pain and anger standing there. He watched as Catherine and Lynn splashed each other, laughing and teasing. It was a scene he had never witnessed in that pool before. It was refreshing in a way for him and yet it was too foreign to process in that moment. He shook his head.

"Not yet, Vickie. Baby steps. That's all I can do."

The limousine pulled up in front of the estate at promptly 7:22am, same as everyday as both girls grabbed their purses and headed out the door to be greeted by their driver. The company, they had discovered, employed an entourage of drivers so they met new people daily and only the same ones occasionally. It had been a week since Vickie had returned to Washington and three weeks since they had arrived in sunny California.

As they filed into the back of the vehicle, the driver secured the door and strode around to the drivers seat, Lynn smiled at once again beginning another day with bright sunshine and beauty. She had only been here a little while but she could get used to this life. Waking up to breakfast being served and the sun shining into her bedroom. Looking out at a peach orchard and the ocean close by.

Going to work everyday and being greeted by 20 or so laughing children who loved her as much as she loved them. Yes, this was a wonderful life, she thought.

She looked over at Cath as the car began to pull away from the house and down the long drive. Cath sat across from her with her hands drawn together in her lap and her classic Stewart blue eyes focused out the car window. Her gaze seemed to be seeing something far away. She had braces now, but Lynn rarely saw them. Cath wasn't one to be angry or even to frown much anymore. She didn't seem to smile or talk much either. Her hair was long and thick like CJ's had been, but blond and straight rather than mousy brown with spiral curls, Lynn observed. From a profile though, they were stunningly similar. Same petite nose with freckles sprinkled across from cheek to cheek, same firm bone structure along the jaw, and most importantly, same piercing deep ocean blue eyes.   Everyone else in the family had a lighter shade, but Catherine and CJ's eyes had come in a deeper, darker shade of blue and it had always felt to Lynn that it was only fair that Cath should at least have that of her sisters. Beyond that, there was nothing alike about them. Cath was neither bubbly nor giving in personality, but tragedy changes people. She loved Cath like a sister, but she didn't understand her now any better than CJ had then. To look at Catherine now made Lynn's heart ache for her long gone best friend.

Soon the limousine stopped and the driver came around and opened the door and held a hand out to Lynn. Lynn smiled at the young driver but declined graciously.

"May I have just a minute please?" The driver bowed courteously.

"Of course." And he stepped out of hearing range, yet left the door slightly ajar so he could hear her say when she was ready.

Lynn turned to Catherine and reached across the gap between them and took one of her hands. Cath startled for an instant and then a look of concern crossed her face.

"Catherine. Are you o.k? I know that I was CJ's friend and I've just hung around because I didn't have anywhere else to go, but I still care about you and we don't talk, but I need you to know that we can if you want."

Catherine smiled a little. There were the braces! She looked down at their joined hands and then pulled back a little. Little Catherine, always distancing herself just enough to be friendly and yet independent.

"I'm o.k. Thanks. I like it here. I'm not looking forward to going back home and one more year of school after having this experience, that's all."

Lynn was floored. She was sure that was the most sharing Catherine had done in a long time. She smiled and gave Catherine a quick hug before getting out of the car to go into the child care center. It was going to be a great day, she thought as she watched the car pull away again taking Catherine off to the main building where she would work for the day.

Catherine watched as Lynn waved her off and then turned to go into the child care center before she faced forward and pushed the button to roll down the window next to her. As the breeze blew in she closed her eyes and allowed the feel of the southern California sun to reach in and touch her skin. It was only a 2 minute drive from the daycare center to the main company building, but in that small amount of time she felt like the warmth filled her from her head to her nail polished toes. She was experiencing what CJ had always wanted and it was making her feel enormously guilty. The question was, could her pleasure eventually outweigh her pain?

The limousine dropped her off in front of the main building at 8:05am. Jace, who had been watching out of his office window with anticipation let out a long breath. His drivers were under strict instructions to have Lynn at her destination by 7:50am and Catherine to hers by 8am. Catherine was required to check in with Meghan before choosing where she wanted to work for the day. She had been so fascinated by the many aspects of the company that Jacen had decided that she could spend as much time at any location in the company that she wished, she was just required to check in three times a day, when she got there, at lunch and when she was ready to leave so that they could keep track of her hours and pay her appropriately.

Vickie and Jacen would stay in daily contact so that everyone who needed to be on board with Catherine's activities would be and yet still give Catherine some say in what and how she wanted to learn and earn her summer money.

He waited about 15 minutes before pushing the button on his intercom that was labelled "M".

"Yes, Sir."

Jacen sighed and then laughed a little.

"Do we have to do this every morning?"

Meghan laughed back. She was enjoying the changes that she had seen Jacen make over the past few years. He was a young man still in his mid twenties and yet he had grown up in the shadow of great power and responsibilities and with those responsibilities came more struggles and loneliness than any one his age should have had. It was nice to see him starting to laugh and joke and enjoying his life a little.

"As long as they think I respect you, they will behave." She teased him. She could almost feel the smile on his face from the other side the large door between them.

"How was she this morning?"

Meghan shrugged before answering. This family that Jacen had integrated himself into had instantly grown on her as well and she found herself carrying and interested in the goings on and whereabouts of these people as well.

"Same as everyday. Quiet, mater-of-fact. Good morning, Miss Meghan, I'd like to spend the day in the lab again. Please tell Jace I'll call at lunch. And then she was off to the lab." There was a long pause between them.

"Do you think she's o.k?" He asked after a while.

Meghan's eyes followed the place beside her desk where a small 17 year old girl had just been a few minutes before and thought about it. It had been 5 years now since Jacen's transplant and a lot had changed in that time. Jacen came and went, he seemed to have met and made a new family for himself and still managed to bring any other medical supplies company that competed with them to their knees by enlisting his new surrogate mother's financial advice. He never forgot to reward them all as things went well with bonus' and large pay raises. He had found a softer side somewhere, and she wondered if it was the whole family, the woman just down the road at the child care center that he checked on daily, or the little girl in the lab.

"I don't know, Jacen. She's the sister, right?"

Jacen rubbed his forehead and sighed.

"yep."

Meghan crossed her arms and shrugged her shoulders, her head set for her phone giving her freedom to move about.

"What is the statute of limitations on grief? When do you get over losing your sister tragically? I think it's o.k that she's a little moody. Besides, I have news for you Jacen. When it comes to 17 year old girls, we're all a little moody!"

Jacen smiled and she could tell. She was happy he had a new family, but she couldn't imagine that they knew him better than she did at any rate.

"Have a great day, Sir." He laughed again.

"Ok, Lady!" He retaliated and they both hung up.

Meanwhile, Catherine made her way to the laboratory and found a lab coat that had been set aside for her the day before. This would be her second day here in this department and she couldn't be more excited! The day before, she had been given the opportunity to feed the lab rats whose names she had memorized already, there were 12 of them. She had also been given a tour of the chemical compound facilities next door where they test everything from lotions and makeup to new prescription medications that are on their way to the federal drug administration for further testing after they pass inspection here in California. Catherine checked in with Davies, the laboratory supervisor.

"Good morning, Catherine! You came back! That's a good sign! Boss, said that you were going to free float through the company and they you may not stick to any one place so it's good to see we made a good impression. Where would you like to start?"

"May I feed the rats this morning? Unless they've already been fed. Then in that case, I could just do whatever."

"I think that rats are very hungry and will be glad to see you."

"I have one little question about the rats." Catherine wanted to ask, but she was afraid she wouldn't like the answer.

"You want to know if we test our products on them?" Davies guessed. Davies was a tall balding red headed man with thick glasses and a kind easy smile. His office was wallpapered with pictures of his four kids and his plump but sweet looking wife of 20 years.

Catherine only nodded yes in response. If his answer was yes, she was ready to leave the lab and march down to Jacen's office in protest instantly. Davies smiled and patted her shoulder.

"Relax, Catherine. All the rats that we have were rescued from facilities that we have taken over. We took a vote and decided that we had the capacity to house them here. We also felt it was good to research what kind of studies may have been previously done on them and perhaps reverse any adverse effects where we can. Feel better?"

Catherine smiled. She did feel better. Her grandfather had been a rancher for many years and she had watched both the births and the deaths of cattle. She had been awed and disgusted by both, each seeming violent or beautiful in their own right. She was still on the fence about hunting. Her father had taught her to hunt, but he had taught her it was for survival only not for sport. She wasn't sure she could do it even in self defense truth be told.

She took Elmo out of his cage and held him gently with one hand while she transferred him to a holding cage so she could clean out his home and put food in his tray and fresh water in his bottle. One by one she cared for each of the rats. By the time she had finished it was nearly noon. Catherine removed her gloves and washed her hands. Then she pulled a piece of paper out of her pocket and unfolded it. Scribbled onto in was a name and a four digit extension. Jacen 7712. She walked over to the closest phone on the wall, picked it up to call and check in for lunch.

"Don't bother, I'm not there."

Catherine dropped the phone, whirled around and grabbed her chest.

"You, jackass! You scared the crap out of me!" She hissed at him although she was smiling. Jacen stood in the doorway with his hands in his pockets laughing.

"I'm sorry, Cath, but that was really funny and don't make me call your mom and tell her what a potty mouth you've become since coming to California. She'll think I've corrupted you."

Catherine rolled her eyes as far back into her head as she could.

"Oh, please! If only my parents had a clue!"

Jacen raised his eye brows in surprise. Was the ever private Catherine Stewart joking with him?

"Truth be told, Jacen, I'm sure I'm the middle child in this family."

"Do tell." He encouraged her. He came in to the room and sat down on a stool next the counter holding one of the many massive private rat hotels. Each rat was contained in it's own enormous cage, but three times a day their cages were opened and they were all linked by tunnels that came to a common area where their socialization skills could be observed.

"Well, it's simple really. I've never been as difficult as David, but I'm certainly not the angel that CJ was. So, I'm in the middle."

Catherine watched as David opened up the cage closest to him and gently picked up the rat and placed it in the large wheel with a piece of food to encourage it to play. It took a few minutes for the rat to cooperate but with a bit of patience, Jace finally had the rat running on the wheel. He was smiling and she was a little impressed. He turned back to her and became more business like again.

"If I promise to pay you for the whole day, do you want to play hooky for the afternoon? I have a few places I'd like to show you. I'll even feed you american food."

Catherine smiled again. Since she and Lynn had been here, Jacen had been trying to educate them in the different cultural opportunities available to them in China Town and the real authentic Mexican flavors in local restaurants. Lynn was lapping it all up and was becoming one with the land, but Catherine was not so quick to comply. Perhaps she was picky, or her digestive system was uncultured, but she had been forced to turn down more meals lately than not. She held out her hand to shake on the deal. Jace agreed and before they headed out he reached for the phone and dialed an extension.

"Ok, let's go." He said. It was a ten minute walk to the buildings main entrance doors. However, as Cath began heading one direction back towards Meghan's desk where she had come in at that morning, Jace whistled to her as he headed down a different hallway. They walked together for about three minutes across a beautiful sky bridge that overlooked most of the property where she could see all the other corporate side buildings and she stopped for a moment when she saw the child care center in the far northwest corner. She wondered if Lynn was out there on the playground with all the children. It was impossible to know since they all looked like tiny little specs of sand from that distance.

"Our car is waiting." Jace whispered in her ear so they hurried along and came to a door at the end of the sky bridge that entered into one of the adjacent buildings. From there they took an elevator down 8 floors and out of that building to a town car and a driver that was waiting for them. Jacen smiled at the driver and asked for the keys before turning to Catherine.

"You can ride in front." He told her. In all the time so far that she had known him, she had never seen him drive before. She didn't even know he knew how. She climbed into the front seat and he got into the driver's seat. He rolled down the window to address the driver who was still standing patiently near the car.

"You can get in, Aaron. I'll give you a ride back."

Aaron held up a hand to protest politely.

"Oh, Sir, I appreciate that, but you have an agenda and I'll be happy to call the service to come and get me. It will only take them a moment."

Jacen rolled his eyes.

"You're on my way out. I'm the boss, get in." Aaron smiled. Aaron had been with the company for a few years now and he liked Mr. Owen. He felt that he was fair and kind. He had heard rumors that he could be demanding and harsh, but in the three years that he had worked for the company, he had not had these experiences with Jacen Owen and so he opened the back door of the car and climbed in.

"Aaron, I'd like you to meet Miss Catherine Stewart. Catherine, this is Aaron Simms. One of the esteemed caretakers of my illustrious collection of vehicles."

Catherine turned in her seat and offered her hand. Aaron shook and smiled.

"Nice to meet you. Are you a new hire?"

Catherine smiled and squinted her eyes at Jacen who made a passing glance her way before pulling the car forward toward the main building where Aaron needed to go. He wasn't sure how much about Catherine or Lynn he wanted his general staff to know about personally. He felt a lot of things about the situation from both sides. He knew his staff well and trusted them, but very few outsiders had ever been let in. Family had become paramount in his life and the less any one in the company knew about them the happier he would be. People can change some, but he was still a little bit of the same old Jacen he had always been and what was his was still his and his alone.

"I'm just here for a summer job, then it's back home to finish high school and figure out the rest of my life." Aaron smiled at her.

"Wow, I would have sworn that you were on a college internship or something."

"Nope. High school and then she'll go home to her boyfriend." Jacen replied quickly feeling as if things were getting too friendly.

If a dagger could have pierced his heart faster than the look of scorn and shock Cath shot him, he would have wished for the dagger. Jacen pulled up in front of the entrance to the garage to let Aaron out.

"Thanks, Sir."

"No, thank You. I owe you one. I promise to bring it back safe and sound."

"Nice to meet you, Catherine."

Jacen could still feel the stinging glare of Catherine's eyes staring him down as Aaron entered the building and they pulled the car away.

"What's wrong?" Jacen asked defensively.

"How did you know about my boyfriend? No one knows. Or at least their not suppose to. And since the only one one you really talk to much is Mom, she must know and she's one of the last people I want to know!"

Jacen smiled a little. It wasn't even really a smile. It was more like a devilish smirk. They drove out into traffic and headed down towards the beach.

"I was just making stuff up to keep him from getting friendly. See, Cath, I try to keep business and personal as separate as I possibly can. Aaron is business and you're personal. I encourage you to have fun while you're here, maybe even enjoy a little wild life, but not with any one I might have to fire because they crossed a line with you that they can't uncross. You get me?"

Catherine ran an irritated hand through her hair as Jacen opened the top of the car and her hair began to blow wildly about her neck and face.

"Yeah, I get you."

"So," Jace said as he turned a corner and slowed the car as they approached a parking lot.

"Tell me about this boy friend."

The car came to a stop and Catherine unlatched her seat belt and popped open the car door.

"No." She said and began walking towards the beach. Jace got out of the car and peeled his layers off until he was wearing only a pair of shorts. He had his tan had back now for a few years but his hair was still dark and his eyes still brooding. He was running again on the beach daily and swimming so his lean body was toned but his massive scars were still visible.

He had been surfing again for a few years now as well. He had not tried since the kidney donation, but he hadn't been told he couldn't. It had been a couple of months now and he was feeling great. He rented a board and then met Catherine down near the water. She seemed a little surprised.

"You don't think it's too soon?" She asked and reached out for his left flank. It was strange feeling her thin fingers tracing where his kidney had once been. He looked at her eyes and for just a moment he saw CJ. He blinked again and was back with Catherine. He looked down at the sand and shrugged. It had been five years since he had seen CJ on this very beach for the first time in his dreams and he had only been two years older than Catherine was now. He sighed.

"We'll find out!" He ran out into the water, board in his hands and made a running leap belly first onto the board once he had reached a deep enough. Catherine waited a few minutes and watched, taking shallow breaths as he paddled farther and farther out into the great ocean. When he felt like a good wave was coming on, he stood up and she was surprised at his amazing balance as he rode the great wave into shore and met her on the sand. She clapped approvingly and cheered.

"That was awesome!" She exclaimed. He shook his wet hair at her and she giggled and backed away. He was laughing and panting.

"Are you o.k?" She asked. He nodded, but sat down to take a break on the board.

"Yeah, I'm fine. It's fun. Want to try? We can get you a wet suit and a board. I can teach you." Catherine thought about it for a whole 2 seconds before she jumped at the chance.

Six hours later, with Catherine exhausted and limping, but Jace feeling accomplished at having taught someone a skill, for Catherine did ride in a few waves towards the end there, they pulled into Jacen's Penthouse for a quick showers and change of clothes before picking up Lynn and heading for dinner.

Jacen escorted Catherine into one the guest rooms and showed her where to find everything.

"What size are you?"

"Why?" Catherine asked defensively. Jacen rolled his eyes.

"Well, since I live here by myself I'm a little limited on my girl supplies but I can have something delivered quickly. So size please."

"3. But, um. I'm sorry to be picky, but just what will you have delivered?"

"How about jeans and a couple of shirts to choose from The CUBE?"

Catherine's eyes got really big and she hugged Jace. It was rare that she got to have nice clothes from a nice place.

"How long should I wait?" She called as Jace headed down the hall towards somewhere else in his massive house.

"It will be on your bed before your done with your shower." He called back.

She sat down on the edge of the bed.

"No way." she said in disbelief shaking her head.

" I heard that!" he yelled from some strange far off place. She smiled and headed towards the bathroom that was attached to the guest room.

As promised, after her long jacuzzi bath, waiting in the bedroom were a pile of jeans, causal pants, hoody sweatshirts, causal tops, tennis shoes or heels as well as bras and underwear in every size and style. Catherine's eyes were as big as plates when she saw the assortment of clothing and wanted to try them all, but in the end she chose a pair of pale jeans, a casual pale blue top with overly long sleeves that covered her hands and her own comfortable sandals. She pulled her hair back away from her face and knotted it up in a scrunchy high on her head with a few disobedient strands peaking their way out.

She stood at the window for a few minutes and enjoyed the breathtaking view of the ocean and smiled for a while. It was beyond her how anyone could live this life and find sadness in it. She was sad a lot she knew, but Jacen, he was sad too, she figured. The letters that he sent were somewhat superficial. California this and day to day that, but she always sensed there was something sad and lonely deeper. He was brooding and angry like David she thought. She still had yet to answer one of his letters, but she kept them all and read them often. There were things he needed to say, but perhaps he wasn't ready, she figured. It hadn't occurred to her that she wasn't ready to listen.

She took a deep breath and then turned to the bedroom door and the rest of the penthouse. It was time to explore she decided. It had been more than an hour since she had last seen Jacen, but she wasn't in any hurry. Since it was still summer, it would be daylight and warm until long after 9pm and they had lately made it a practice not to eat dinner until after 8. It was just now close to 7:30. Catherine had heard Jacen check in with Lynn when they had arrived and she wouldn't be expecting them for quite some time so Cath wandered down the long dark hallway towards what she figured would lead her to either a kitchen or a living room, library, or somewhere interesting. Before long she found herself in an atrium with fresh, well kept plants two chaise lounges and an enormous book shelf filled with books.

Catherine, who was not a big fan of reading per say, was fascinated by the arrangement of the books on the case. She crouched down and began leafing through the stack of books along the bottom shelf first. There, she found a massive collection of well preserved Dr. Seuss and other children's favorites.

As she moved along, she found other reading moving towards more young adult classics such as C.S. Lewis' Chronicles of Narnia. She had to admit she had read all of those and had enjoyed them. Then she noticed that some of the reading became more mature even though she was only on the fourth shelf of about ten.

Some books by Charles Dickens, then The Graped of Wrath, moving onto the The Scarlet Letter. Even Mary Shelly's Frankenstein was mixed in with a book of poetry collections from Robert Frost. Interesting, Catherine thought. CJ had liked Robert Frost she remembered. It seemed less depressing to think about now then it used to, but it was still present.

Just an afterthought and she shrugged it off as she pulled the book of poetry off the shelf to look through it to try and figure out what CJ had found so fascinating about a man who's life had been so hard and depressing. As the worn book of poems slid out off the shelf into her hands, another slipped off with it and fell crashing to the floor. The notebook like binder split a little and the pages began to slip out a bit. Cath gasped and knelt down to carefully gather the well used book up and try to right it again, but as she was piecing it all back together, there was something very familiar about it.

She set aside the Robert Frost book and began carefully leafing through the fragile pages of the book that had fallen on the floor and piece by piece, date by date, she re-acquainted herself with her sister's delicate handwriting. Some of pages had faded over time, but most of it was still very clear and easy to read. There were smear marks where someone had shed tears through out and as Catherine fought back her own tears, she wondered if they had been CJ's or Jacen's.

She read all her sister's deepest thoughts about her friends, her insecurities about everything from her track and field performances to how she felt about the way her voice carried on stage. She worried about her family. She worried about David and Sarah. She was thankful for Mom and Dad. And then there was Catherine. Catherine was smart and stubborn and pigheaded. She said pigheaded! She said she loved Cath and she just wished she understood that she only loves her too much and that's why all the pushing. She wrote about her walks and her long talks with Gramps. She wrote about family dinner. Catherine rolled her eyes as she closed the cover and wiped her running nose with her sleeve.

CJ had been unbelievably boring! She thought. She had waited all these years to read her journal for that!

Jacen came around the corner. Before he could enter the room, Catherine was up on her feet, and squaring him from across the room, fists curled, eyes blazing fury. He was a little confused by the rage he saw fuming from her swollen eyes until he saw what she had curled up in her fist. He saw that she had found CJ's journal and could only imagine what she was thinking in that moment.

"Cath, let me explain." He started.

In an act of madness that would a moment later lead to regret, Catherine hurled the journal at the door frame missing by a few feet where it hit the wall and being as it was barely holding it's binder together as it was, the book cascaded to the floor in a confetti of CJ's thoughts all over the room. Before Jacen could enter the room to help gather the journal and put things back in order, Catherine rushed forward and slammed the door closed sending a shattering echo throughout the penthouse.

Jacen braced his head against the closed door that separated them and listened to Catherine crying quietly on the other side. He pleaded with her for what felt like eternity leaping through Dante's Inferno (one of his favorite books on that shelf) , though it was only a few moments, then he said nothing. He wasn't sure exactly what his crime was, and he was unclear why it mattered to him at all, but his new heart ached.

He went into the den and asked his housekeeper to call Lynn and cancel dinner, but to assure her that everything was fine. He then returned to his place as watchman on the other side of the large glass door and waited for Catherine to come out, or look at him, or anything.

"ahem, excuse me Sir,"

Jacen sat up and rubbed his eyes. He checked his watch. It had only been three hours since Catherine had locked him out of the library and he must have dozed off. He looked in on her.

She was sitting on the Chaise lounge wrapped in a blanket, long, blond hair cascading over her tear streaked face, holding a piece of the journal in her arms. She had also fallen asleep. He turned his attention to his housekeeper.

"I'm sorry, I didn't mean to fall asleep. I need to get her back to the estate. Can you arrange to get her there?"

"Sir, there's a phone call for you from Washington State. She says it's an emergency."

SCENE XV: WASHINGTON STATE-ALBION

The flight home was unusually quiet Lynn thought as they began their descent in the private jet towards Sea Tac airport in Seattle, Washington. From there, they would all board Alaska Airlines first class seating for a forty-five minute hop into Spokane where Catherine's parents were already waiting for them.

Jacen and Meghan were busying themselves with paperwork but it had not escaped Lynn's notice that he kept a careful eye on the pensive, overly moody girl in the corner widow seat who had been offered a soda that she accepted and then had watched the ice melt in it without drinking any. Something had transpired between the two of them, that much Lynn had surmised, but what and how serious she couldn't know for sure. Her imagination ran the gamut from everything ranging between he had taken advantage of her and she had refused which seemed unlikely. Who would refuse him? Just because she hadn't seen a devoted following of the female persuasion at his heels only made her feel like there was a better chance she could take her sweet time getting to know him herself. To, Cath had made an aggressive pass at him and he had turned her down and Catherine probably wasn't used to not getting her way. The thought of this made Lynn snort a little. She loved this family more than anything, but Catherine had a lot to live up to if she was ever going be as ready to face the world before her as CJ was at her age.

The changing of planes went smoothly. Catherine found herself seated next to Meghan in first class and she felt both anxiety and relief. This made her feel confused. Jacen and Lynn were seated across from them. Both Catherine and Jacen were on the aisle. As they began to take off, Meghan reached over and touched Catherine's hand. Catherine looked over and Meghan smiled at her sweetly.

"You seem to be not your usual self today, Catherine. Everything alright?"

Catherine shrugged. How would she know what was usual for her after only knowing her for three weeks? Catherine wondered. Daily phone exchanges with her mother and passings in the morning or at lunch did not, in her mind, make this woman an expert on her. Catherine smiled back weakly anyway.

"If you had known my grandfather, you would understand."

Meghan patted Catherine's hand again and shook her head sympathetically.

"Again, I am deeply sorry." Somehow, a few moments later, Catherine found herself drifting off into a light sleep.

For the first time since she was twelve, she saw CJ. The last time she had laid her eyes on her sister, CJ's body had been broken, her beautiful long hair gone, her eyes closed forever and her doctors talking about shipping her organs off to those who needed them because she didn't anymore. Now, in this moment, CJ stood before her, in full theater attire, full make up, long, flowing hair, teeth straight as a movie star's.

"Where did you come from? Where have you been?" Catherine demanded. She was afraid to touch her. Afraid she wasn't real. CJ, as always, made the first move. The older sister reached out for her younger sister and wrapped her arms around her.

"I died Cath, but I have always been with you. You couldn't find me because you've been so angry and so sad. I sent you messages, but you. You're so stubborn and difficult sometimes."

Coming from anyone else it would have sounded judgmental and perhaps had she still been twelve she could not have heard it any other way, but now, they were words of love, wisdom and truth. Somewhere in the back of her consciousness, Catherine knew none of this could be real, but for this moment, she could touch her sister, smell her, feel her in a way that she never had.

After reading her journal and finally understanding CJ from the heart of her, Catherine felt a sense of closeness with CJ that had been missing before. For all that she had felt was mean and bossy before, she finally realized was simply a misguided need to keep her safe and protected.

CJ went on,

"It's time for you to become who you're meant to be, Cath."

Tears began to form in Catherine's eyes and spill over.

"I needed you."

CJ cocked her head to one side. Signature move when in came to Cath.

"You need to let Mom be Mom, Dad be Dad, Nan be Nan, David be David, and Jacen be Jacen. Don't shut them out any more. They are your life lines."

Catherine frowned.

"I could use less of some of those than others, thank you very much." She said sarcastically. Now it was CJ who frowned.

"You need them ALL, Catherine. And they all need you. Every one of them. They say it takes a village to raise a family. I'm pretty sure it starts with one family to heal the village from a single tragedy. Go heal, Cath. If you will get better, you can make some one else better, too."

Slowly, Catherine began to open her eyes to the feeling of a dry drabbing on her cheek. She looked to her left to see Jacen reaching across the wide aisle to gently wipe a tear away from her cheek. When she moved slowly away from him, he backed away and replaced the linen back in his jacket pocket.

"I'm sorry."

crossed her ams in her lap still thinking about CJ as the plane began it's descent into Spokane.

Catherine had not remembered seeing so many people gathered together at her grandparents ranch house at a single time ever. CJ's funeral had brought the whole family together as well as local friends, but now, there were people here from Montana, Oregon, Idaho, and California that had known and admired her grandfather. She had met people from

166

his crew while he was a Naval aviator, distant cousins from Scotland and Germany that she didn't know she had, as well as local politicians who had admired him for his work in the community.

She worked tirelessly with the rest of the family to make sure that everyone had everything that they needed from cups to tissues. People were being attentive to her grandmother with delicate tenderness and dedication. Every time she took a moment to try and check in with Audrey, there were more well wishers who stepped in first so Catherine shrunk back into the shadows where she felt she belonged for the time being.

"Seems like old times, doesn't it."

David stood on the porch next to Catherine and patted her shoulder. Catherine pulled her shoulders up to touch her ears and sighed heavily. Then the tears came in. It was like the flood gates had opened wide and before she could stop them, they were streaming down her face. David turned her to face him, feeling concerned.

"God, I miss her, David! Every day I just can't get past this. I know it's suppose to get better and as I watch every one else move on and forget her, I find myself needing to hold on tighter to what I can remember about her. I don't want her to be gone anymore."

David sighed and wrapped his arms around his baby sister and let her sob into his shirt.

"No one has forgotten her, Cath. Least of all me. I carry her with me everywhere I go. The parts of her I still see are the parts that help me heal."

Catherine sniffled and pulled back.

"That's what she said! Well, sort of."

"Who?" David asked.

"CJ"

David hugged her again and smiled.

"So, you've been seeing CJ, have you?" Catherine wrinkled up her nose and sniffled again.

"Well, maybe. Sort of." She snorted.

"It's about time. Welcome to the party."

Vickie cleared the table and then reset it again for the family dinner. She watched Catherine sweeping through the living room picking up the last few pieces of left over remnants of mourners. A few tissues scattered here and there. A funeral program or two. As she watched her youngest daughter tuck a stray hair behind her ear, she wondered what had transpired in the last three weeks that had been missing for so long. Somewhere along the way, Catherine had reconciled something. She was a deeper more grown part of herself somehow.

Vickie also noticed though, that Jacen had excused himself immediately following the services saying only that he would call later that day to check on Audrey. She figured she would wait for the right time to ask Catherine if everything was alright between them.

Just then, as if sensing her mother's probing questions, Catherine looked over at her. Much to Vickie's surprise, Catherine made her way over to the table and sat down.

"Is everything alright?" Vickie tried to sound casual. With all of the business and anxiety of the funeral and trying to keep Audrey from becoming too overwhelmed, she and Catherine had hardly had a chance to pass in the hallway let alone catch up.

"I read CJ's journal." Catherine blurted out. She had wanted to talk about it in a lets have lunch kind of setting. She didn't want to end up being defensive, but she felt her mother should know what had happened.

"Oh, that's great, Cath!" Vickie reached over the table and squeezed her daughters shaking hands.

"I gave it to Jacen at a time when he was feeling very lost and bitter. I felt that CJ could communicate a sense of whole and community with the way she was devoted to each us in those pages. He had needed that during those dark days when he first came to this family. He says the journal still comforts him when he is separate from us."

Catherine looked down at their joined hands and felt a familiar mix of rage and regret welling up inside of her. She was furious with her mother for deciding whom should be given the precious journal before all parties had been consulted, and she was still angry that Jacen had kept it instead of returning it after reading it a few times through.

The regret came from having destroyed the one thing that connected them all to the one person who kept them grounded to each other and from being hot headed again and jumping to conclusions. Someday she would realize that they grounded each other despite what had happened to CJ. She would also realize someday, that some of her regret came from having misjudged the one person at that time who truly understood her.

Catherine pulled her hands back, walked away from her mother and out the sliding glass doors. Vickie watched her go and wondered if these things were a sign that God had finally begun to chip away at her daughter's frozen heart.

SCENE XVI: PULLMAN HIGH SCHOOL

The school year started again on a rainy August day that year. Catherine waited on the steps of the high school for Joey who was usually seen darting up the steps five minutes after the starting bell making them both tardy. Mr. McMann leaned on the balcony next to her. After all of these years he had seen many students come and go from this establishment, but CJ and her family had always been with him the longest and made the deepest impact. It was not lost on him that Catherine would be the last in a long line of Stewart's to walk these halls. The bell rang just then and yet Catherine held her watch.

"Waiting for Joey?" Simon asked. Catherine's eyes scanned the parking lot as she nodded. Mr. McMann handed her a paper hall pass. He carried a few in his pockets just in case.

"Just a few more minutes, Miss Stewart and then I need you in first period. It's the first day of your last year. Make it count."

She looked up at him then. For the first time she noticed that he had some grey hair. Catherine smiled at Mr. McMann and stood to her feet.

"Let's just say Joey missed the boat on this one, shall we?" She said and handed the hall pass back to the principle. He smiled back and walked her towards the building doors.

"Sometime I'd like to hear about your summer in California at the big corporation." Catherine rolled her eyes and she made her way to class.

"I'll sum it up with it ended quickly." She said as she made her way up the first landing towards what would be a creative writing class. Mr. McMann stopped walking with her at the bottom of the steps and sighed.

"Yeah, I'm sorry about your grandfather, Catherine. He was a kind and gentle man."

He watched Catherine walk into class as the second bell went off and shook his head. One kid should not have to deal with so much pain and loss in her lifetime let alone before graduating from high school he thought as he turned back and walked into the front office.

Lunch time was buzzing with activity for the first day of school. Tables filled up quickly with everyone in their respective groups. Football players took up two to three tables near the windows because they were closer the football field. Theater buffs grabbed their food and then would slink down in the carpeted landing away from the lunch room altogether. The cheerleaders found themselves sitting close to the food, but that would change as new friendships were established and relationships with the football players were made. It was the way it was and they way it had always been. Simon missed the days when he would watch CJ float amongst them all and fit anywhere.

He saw Catherine sitting amongst her small group of friends. They were all smiling and laughing, yet she still seamed somehow distant, or absent. He wondered if she would make it through the whole year or if she would fade into the background here and eventually drop out. That would make him sad and he would work harder on her than anyone else to prevent that but perhaps he would understand it better coming from her than any other student. He went back to his office and to his secretary.

"Set up weekly counseling sessions with Mrs. Ohera for Catherine Stewart please." He requested.

Judy looked up startled. Catherine was a descent student, actually better than both of her siblings had been. She was absent more than her sister, present more than her brother but received better grades than both of them. She had been working with Simon for several years now though, and he had always made good and sound decisions when it came to these kids. He always had their best interests at the heart of any decisions he made so she picked up the phone and called into Mrs. Ohera office and scheduled the weekly appointments.

Catherine sat amongst her friends nibbling on a few french fries and sipping on a diet coke. Joey, with one arm draped around her waist was laughing and eating her fries as well as his own as he talked with their friends. The lunch room volume increased as more and more students gathered.

"Hey," He said finally addressing her. Catherine looked up from her book and slapped his hand away from her fries. He waited until she was distracted and took more anyway.

"How come you didn't wait for me this morning?" He asked. She sighed and moved his hand away from her back. Although they had started dating at the end of the school year last year and things had moved fast, the three weeks she had spent away in California had been a nice break from everything in this life. Coming to back to anything familiar even Joey was less than acceptable so she had been distant.

"I did. You were late." He shrugged.

"I'm always late." Then, "What are you reading?"

Catherine looked at the front of the book she had checked out from the school's library that morning. It was book of poetry. A collection of Robert Frost's greatest work. Joey grabbed it out of her hands and began flipping through it. He began to mockingly quote some of the lines from A Boy's Will while everyone at the table laughed. Everyone except Catherine.

"You're not going to get smart or brainy on me are you?"

Catherine snatched the book back, grabbed the rest of her things and stood to her feet to walk away. She got as far as the front doors before Joey caught up with her. He touched her hand gently to persuade her to stop.

"Cath, I'm sorry. I didn't mean to upset you. I never know what to say anymore. You're getting so sensitive."

Catherine pushed him away, pursed her lips together, pushed the door open and moved outside. She took about ten steps before she spun around and headed back in with a fury that was signature for Catherine and nearly knocked Joey in the face with the door who had still been watching her walk away. She flew at him with a finger in his face.

"Just so you don't forget, Joey, I am and have always been very, very smart." Then she was gone.

Simon stood at the office door and watched the exchange between Joey and Catherine and although a part of him knew he should intercede and send them both back to class, he let her go. Joey was no where near her status. It wasn't about money, Joey's family had that in bucket loads. He just wasn't good enough for her plain and simple. Simon thought of his own daughter who was now married and trying to start a family of her own. Sometimes it takes a village he thought.

When Catherine got home she found on the table sitting amongst the mail, another letter from Jacen. They still came twice a month and she still had yet to answer one. For a few weeks after she had returned home she hadn't even read them she had still been so angry with him for hiding the journal from her. It fed her fury to tell herself that he knew she was there and he knew she didn't know about it therefore he was lying to her. It was backwards thinking by far but her anger gave her comfort since she wasn't seeing CJ anymore and somewhere in the deepest part of her she knew that she had been wrong. Slowly, though, over time, she began to miss the feeling of importance that the letters gave her. As far as she knew, Jacen wasn't writing to anyone else. He called her mother every other week or so and she knew that they sent e-mails periodically, but the carefully handwritten and thought out letters were hers alone. She sat at the table and opened the letter and began to read.

"Dear Catherine,

I understand that school will be starting for you again soon. Last year! I wouldn't know anything about that since my education came from tutors and private mentors. I think I would have enjoyed having friends to talk to throughout the day as I was learning. That's nice for you. Enjoy it and appreciate it while you have it. Any plans for college? If you do, I would like to help with the cost. I know that your family has spent a lot on other things like funeral expenses this last few years so if you want to go to school, I can help. Don't turn me down because you're still mad, it's just money it doesn't have to be personal. If you want to take some time off and get away, you're always welcome here.

I hope you know that...."

Catherine put the letter down as the tears began to sting her eyes. She stood, headed for the front door and walked out making her way down the street, across the field and up the hill to the cemetery.

SCENE XVII: SANDIEGO, CALIFORNIA

"It's our anniversary today, Jacen. Six years since we were joined together."

Jacen sat up and rubbed the sleep from his eyes. It was always amazing to him how much time could go by and yet she never changed and he could always recall every detail about her so vividly when he needed to. The subconscious was funny that way. It protected you from the things that could hurt or destroy you, but it saved all of the most vital and important information that you held most dear even if you thought you didn't need or want it anymore.

"I know what day it is." He replied frankly. She smiled a little smile. It was a knowing smile as if they had danced this dance before.

"Still smarky are you?"

"Only with you." He pulled back the covers and put underwear on and a pair of sweatpants before making his way over to the window where he stood and watched the waves crashing in. It was still dark outside but his eyes were adjusting. CJ stayed where she had been in the bed, still dressed as he had first seen her for the very first time in jeans and a sweater, her long hair cascading down as she drew her knees up and wrapped her arms around them.

"Why are you here? Why now?" He asked. He was a little tired of these moments in his life where he would be ready to move on and make significant strides forward and then there she would be, pulling him back again. Reawakening feelings he thought he had long buried because of what could never be.

"You don't exist. I have done everything that you asked of me. I went to your family and I did more than just meet them, I became a part of them. I tried to help them all. I even came full circle and donated an organ back to David."

He continued still looking away from her. It was too painful to see her there. It was too hard to know how temporary she was. That she only stood in a single time and space and for all his wealth and power, he could not control any of this. He dare not get too close.

"I do exist, Jacen, I just don't live here anymore. You aren't done being the hope for another yet. I don't think that all of your walls have fallen down yet either."

Enraged because he was tired of fighting the good fight about things that he had never understood for the girl he had loved with all of his new heart but could never have, he flew at her and grabbed her by the arms. He clutched her so tightly, that had she been able to feel, she might have been afraid from the pain. Yet she pushed past his death grip touched his face and brought his eyes into focus with hers. Once again as before, he felt himself swimming in the depths of the blueness there and he saw and felt all that he needed to find. His sense of calmness, his center.

"Why are you really angry?" She asked. He collapsed against her shoulder. It was amazing to him that she wasn't really there, and yet she smelled like jasmine anyway.

He waited a few minutes and breathed in the essence of her before he rolled onto his back and he spoke again.

"I'm angry because I have loved you for six years and I lost you. You can't know how much it sucks to always take three steps forward and two steps back with you. I get better, I think that I'm moving on, I've even started dating again and then you show up and I'm right back where I started. The saddest part of the whole situation, CJ, is that you and I have never truly met face to face. I will never know if you and I could have had a fighting chance at anything real. That is what is killing me every time you come by for a visit and leave me these messages. I love you still and I can't have you. I'm dating a girl now who probably will never live up to the standard I hold because of you. Tell me what to do."

CJ rubbed her eyes and then ran a hand through her hair.

"Oh, Jacen. If only my friends could see me now!" Then she laughed.

"I was never the pretty girl with the hot guy on her arm. Never! Now, to be alive and have a chance with you, that would be an honor. If I could love you back, and give you everything that you need, I would be a lucky girl. What I need you to understand is that I stay for HER. She is out there, Jacen. She's still waiting for you to make the right move. Love will find you again. She's the one who will push me out for good."

Then CJ screwed up her face and shook her head as she looked over towards the bathroom door connected to the master suite. She pointed towards it and snorted.

"Her?" She whispered.

"You can do better."

Jacen laughed. CJ may not be able to love him but she was being very judgmental and protective of their communal heart.

"She's a supermodel who owns a restaurant." He defended the woman who was in the shower. This time CJ laughed.

"Explain again how that makes her selfless, happy, or important."

Jacen was struggling now. Again she was here. The woman who was all the things he wished for: smart, selfless, important, and if even for just this misty moment, present.

He took her in his arms again, just like he had a year earlier when he had donated his kidney, slid one hand through her thick, long hair, the other hand he buried beneath the folds of her sweater. When their lips met this time it was with such a fever that Jacen felt as if he were lit on fire. CJ reciprocated with equal passion wrapping her arms tightly around him. If Jacen could have had that time with her forever, he would have kept it that way just the two of them holding each other, touching, breathing each other in for eternity.

"Jacen,"

"Jacen."

Jacen's eyes popped open to the sun coming into his room. He looked around him and the day seemed to have been upon him hours before and CJ was gone again. All that remained were the same bed, the same guy, and Shannon the supermodel beside him. Shannon's hand was resting on his bare chest, caressing him as she was smiling and babbling about all of the things that she thought that they should fill their day with. Jacen looked away from her and sighed heavily. Maybe CJ was right. Shannon, for all of her beauty and success, could not spend her time giving back. For the few months that he had been getting to know her he had not once been asked what he wanted to do or where he wanted to go. Neither had he noticed her donating her time or money to anything or anyone.

In the time that he had spent with the Stewart's he had learned to give back what he had received. That with new life came new responsibilities. He had been proud to be a part of charities built in CJ's name and for her sake. He was a better tipper because of David and he understood small children because of Sara, Rea, and Christine.

"I need you to go now. I'll call you later."

Shannon sat up and pulled the sheets defensively around her. Jason got up and began dressing quickly.

"Have I done something wrong?" She asked. Shannon had never been asked to leave a relationship first let alone the bed before so she was feeling a little taken back and confused.

"No." His answer was short, abrupt, but not reassuring.

"I need to make a phone call. It's important."

Shannon got to her feet with the sheet still around her. Gathering her clothing that she had neatly draped over the sofa in the corner she headed for the bathroom once again.

"Can I call you later?" She asked. Jacen made his way to the door before turning and facing her.

"I'll call you to reschedule the day." He told her before leaving the room.

Vickie was typing rapidly on her computer at work when Angie burst into her office and startled her. After all of these years, Vickie should have been used to these bombardments from Angie by now, but she only did them when something truly important was, did, or could happen so Vickie had to stay on her toes.

"Line one is a call from California." Angie told her. Vickie's eyebrows went up in concern. She and Jacen had regular e-mail conversations and monthly meetings about the status of each of the charities. He called them all at home every other Sunday night. What could be so urgent that he would call her at work in the middle of the week? One way to find out she supposed.

"This is Vickie." She said picking up the phone.

"Hello, Vickie."

"Hello, Jacen. Is everything alright?"

"I saw CJ."

Vickie paused for a moment before she answered. It wasn't a matter of belief or disbelief it was simply a matter of why had she come again and what was the message, had he gotten the right one and what would he do with it. Jacen had seen her before just prior to her death, and they had all felt her in some way since then, so in what capacity he was seeing her, well....

"How are you doing?"

It was Jacen's turn to pause.

"I don't know what to say. She doesn't think that Shannon is right for me."

177

"Is that what she said?" Vickie found it hard to believe that her dead daughter would or could have an opinion about who Jacen should be dating now or ever.

"Not in so many words. I explained that Shannon was beautiful and successful and CJ wanted to know how that made her selfless or happy among other things. It made me think that she was right."

Vickie smiled. He had definitely been talking to CJ. She was pleased at the way she had seen Jacen transform over the years from and angry kid to a thoughtful and thought provoking young man.

"Or perhaps you can help Shannon become all of those things. This is a new relationship Jacen. If you want out, that's o.k, but if you're having a good time, there's room for that too." Now there was more pausing from both of them.

"Jacen?"

He sighed. He could not thank fate enough for bringing Vickie Stewart into his life. Everything from her was calm always. He suddenly felt a sense of peace wash over him.

"Thank you, Vickie, really. I think I understand now what I need to do."

Vickie smiled.

"Ok, Jacen. Keep in touch. Just because you're a grown man with a multimillion dollar corporation at your finger tips doesn't mean you shouldn't check in with your mother." She slapped a hand over her mouth instantly and her eyes nearly bugged out of her head. The words were out before she could wish them back. As if he he could sense her regret on the other line, Jacen gave a little chuckle.

"I am so sorry, Jacen. I shouldn't have said that."

"Why not? You've been more of a mother to me than I could have ever dreamed my own mother was. I missed her every day growing up, but I didn't have a friends mom to compare her to. You have exceeded all my mom expectations, Vickie, so if you consider me as one your own, then I have been blessed."

Vickie relaxed as she said goodbye and hung up the phone.

Jacen set his phone down on the receiver and then picked it up to dial again.

"Owen Medical Supplies and Pharmaceuticals, Jacen Owen's office, Meghan speaking, how can I help you?"

" Good Morning Meghan."

"Good Morning, Jacen."

"Were we able to get that item repaired and sent off?"

"Yes, we did. It went out three days ago. It should reach it's destination tomorrow. Would you like me to call tomorrow and make sure it got there alright?"

"No thank you Meghan. I'll take care of it."

He said good bye to Meghan, replaced the phone in the receiver for the last time and gathered his things to go out and find Shannon.

SCENE XVIII: PULLMAN WASHINGTON

David checked his watch again and began pacing while Sara redressed both girls in their pajamas. A moment later there was a knock on their door. David answered the door and was relieved to see Catherine carrying a book bag and out of breath pushing her way past him and into their apartment.

"Sorry, but there is no parking anywhere near here!" She exclaimed as she plopped down on the worn couch and began taking homework out of her bag and searching for a pen.

"Sara, we gotta go."

David called back towards the bedrooms at the back of the apartments. Sara came rushing out with her purse in hand.

"Thanks for doing this Cath." Sara said as they made their way to the door.

"Oh, it's my pleasure. Any chance to spend time with the girls is good for me."

"The number to where we'll be in on the refrigerator so call if you have any problems or questions or whatever." Sara headed back into the girl's room for one last goodbye. David shifted his feet impatiently at the door way, but still he waited for her.

"I love that she has you wrapped around her finger, David." David shot Catherine a warning glance and then smiled. Sara came back and they headed out the door.

Catherine latched the lock behind them and then went to check on her nieces who were tucked into bed listening to music with the lights dimmed. Catherine entered the room quietly and found it a bit odd and out of character for her brother to have his children listening to Stevie Nicks. Too mellow for David and not exactly the baby einstein she would have expected from Sara.

"Is this your favorite music?" She asked as she crouched down between their beds. Rea giggled at the prospect of Auntie Cath babysitting and being in their room while Christine simply leaned over, kissed Catherine on the cheek and then shimmied back under her blankets.

"Daddy says that Auntie CJ listened to this music a lot so I like it too." Rea volunteered. Catherine smiled and nodded her head. She kissed each girl in turn and then reached for a fairytale classics book off the shelf to read to them.

"Which story do you like the best?" She asked. Both girls smiled at the prospect of getting a story.

"All of them!" Rea shouted as she bounced up and down on her knees. Catherine laughed and grabbed Rea swinging her around and then resting her back gently on her bed.

"Ok, o.k! Settle down and lets get started then."

Catherine sank down again between their beds and began to read story after story of Peters and pirates, princesses and peas. After what seamed like a very long while, both girls had drifted off to sleep.

Catherine stood quietly and replaced the book in it's rightful place amongst the others on the shelf and made her way to the door.

As the music quietly played on in the background, she thought again of CJ, her mom, dad, David, Nan, Gramps, Sara, and how intertwined they all were at their very core. She realized then what CJ had meant when she had said that it takes one family to heal a village. Her counseling sessions with Mrs. Ohera had proven to be a good thing in the long run. She had been able to gain perspective by speaking to an impartial party. Someone without prejudice had been able to show her who the real victims in the story of her life were and who the real heros had been as well.

She was still learning and she had a ways to go, but CJ was right again. Healing would come and she would learn to help where she could when the time was right. Armed with these thoughts, Catherine left the girls room, found the telephone and dialed a number. She listened while it rang for a while before someone finally picked up.

"Hello?"

"Hi, Dad?"

"Hey, Kid! Aren't you suppose to be at David's babysitting tonight? Is everything alright?"

Catherine smiled. J.R the ever protective father. He was learning to let go a little here and grab on a little more there. She had been too young to have known him during his darkest days. They were two of a kind so they had shouting matches and battles of wills to rival the best bull fights in Mexico, but she knew he would stand by her disagreements or not and she found security there.

"I'm good, Dad. Is Mom home? I need to talk."

"Sure. I'll grab her." Then in the distance as she heard the phone being placed on the counter, "Hey, Vic, it's Number 3, she wants to talk to you." Pause, " I don't know! Probably something girly I don't want to know about!" Then static noises on the phone again as it is picked up.

"She's coming Kiddo."

"Thanks, Dad, Oh, and hey,"

"Yeah?"

"I love you. You know that right?"

J.R. Chucked on the other end of the line.

"I love you too, kid, but if you keep this up I'm going to get suspicious." He teased. She smiled.

"O.k, I got it." She heard somewhere in the background and then,

"Catherine, are you o.k?"

Catherine sat down on the couch and settled in for the long awaited heart to heart with her mother.

"I'm good, Mom, listen, I just thought that you should know how much I love and admire you."

It was almost like playing the game of telephone with two cans on strings seven miles long, the distance between them, as Catherine waited for her mother to respond.

"Thank you, but where is this coming from? Did something happen?"

It shouldn't have surprised her that this was coming as a shock to Vickie. Catherine had gone to great lengths for many years to put distance and silence between them so for her to bridge the gap now without provocation would seem absurd and foreign to the mother who had waited so long for just such an invitation.

"Just a minute, Mom, I need to think."

For the first time in a very long time, Catherine prayed. She prayed for guidance. She asked for wisdom and steadiness. What she didn't know, however, was that on the other end of the phone line, someone else with more love, more faith, more wisdom and more practice was also praying. Peace that passes understanding fell over Catherine in that moment. It passed from mother to daughter and back again.

"Mom, I can never begin to know what you suffered in losing CJ. I watched you take care of Dad, fix David and Sara, include Jacen who took her heart. I know that you had room for my pain, but I thought if I gave that to you as well, you would never have time for your own grief and in my own warped way I thought we had to suffer.

I know now that we make choices. What happened is only a part, what we choose to do with what happened molds us. I chose to become angry and distant, you chose to become helpful and embrace the best parts of her memory."

Tears began to form in both of their eyes and spill over.

"And now?" Vickie asked giving Catherine this moment to grow.

"Now," Catherine continued, wiping her sleeve across her nose in place of a tissue.

"I wish to embrace the best parts of CJ also. I want to help others who can't get past what happened move on by remembering where she was going rather than where she left us. I want to believe that at 18 she had finished all that God had asked of her and it was enough. I have to believe that He was satisfied. I have to believe that she would have believed that, right?"

Vickie held the phone to her chest and sobbed a moment in triumph before choosing to respond. Her daughter was on the eve of turning 18 and at last she had reconciled with her loss. Her grief had come full circle and she could finally begin to feel whole again.

"I won't kid you, Cath and tell you there won't be dark days ahead. Her birthday will be hard for you, The day she died will be a day you will mourn always. There's nothing wrong with that. Or, again, you can chose those days to celebrate. She is always with us. In the music she loved that we hear, or a catch phrase she used to say that we remember.

I see her every time I look into your eyes that match her eye color, or David's head tilts. I love those things, though, I don't resent them and neither should you. I feel blessed that Jacen came into our lives and brought a flesh and blood piece of her back with him."

Catherine groaned and leaned back against the back of the couch. This was not lost on Vickie.

"What's the matter, Cath?"

"I think in some small way I punished Jacen too. I just wanted CJ back. Jacen wasn't good enough. Not even close so I found ways to pick at him. We started to get along, but when I found CJ's journal it was just another means to an end."

Vickie. Always the voice of reason and sound mindedness. Always the mother.

"You and Jacen will figure things out." Catherine shrugged.

"I guess. Hey Mom?"

"Yes, Cath."

"thanks for everything. You are greater than you know."

Vickie smiled. It was good to hear, but what she heard underneath was the healing heart of her daughter. A corner had been turned.

"Mom, just one more question."

"Shoot."

"If David is number one, and I'm number three, who's number two?"

"CJ. Why?"

"I just didn't know if Jacen replaced her."

"No. Everyone has their number in order of appearance. David, CJ, Cath, Jace. One, two, three, four. O.K?"

"Ok."

When Catherine hung up the phone she felt liberated in way she hadn't since she was twelve.

———

Jacen flipped through his mail half heartedly. Bills, bills, more bills, and then...a letter. No name, but he recognized the return address. He sat down on his couch and tore open the envelope. Shannon came around the corner from the kitchen,

"Who's that from?" She asked sitting next to him and leaning over his shoulder. "Shh!" Jacen said, pushing her away as he unfolded the letter and began to read.

"Dear Jacen," It began,

"Although I've never written before I felt it was about time and I have a few things that I think need to be said..."

Jacen wasn't sure he wanted to read the rest. He continued anyway. "I owe you an apology. Truth be told, I probably owe you a thousand. I'm sorry for the way that I have treated you. I think that I was always jealous of you for getting to have a living part of CJ beating inside of you. I think that if it's alright with you, I'd like to start over. I'd like to try and be friends so that I can feel close to that part of CJ rather than make you and therefore her a stranger. I'm also sorry about the journal. I was selfish and immature to think that CJ's thoughts should be meant for myself or my family only. After all, you are as much a part of this family as anyone else. As always, I look forward to your letters,

Sincerely, Catherine."

Catherine sat on the airplane excited for the first time to be headed into her future. As the plane began to climb higher and higher, she looked out the window and watched as the greater Seattle area got smaller and smaller. After a while, she reached into her bag and took out the precious book. She had read it before but the binding was new and re-enforced. The pages had been laminated.

"I haven't seen a book quite like that before, who wrote it?"

Catherine looked up from the book at the person sitting next to her. She appeared to be a middle aged woman sitting with a cross-stitch pattern that she had just started working on. Catherine smiled and proudly showed her the burgundy cover.

"My sister wrote it. It's her journal."

"Wow!" The woman exclaimed as Catherine allowed the woman to look the book over.

"It's been published?"

"Not exactly." Catherine corrected her.

"You see..." And Catherine went on to explain how CJ had died tragically, how her heart had gone to another, how her diary had been destroyed and how it had been restored. She expressed how all of these experiences had led her to this moment where she was now on her way to school to study medicine.

"Do you know what kind of doctor you want to be?"

Catherine beamed at the question. She knew exactly what kind of doctor she wanted to be. After all the CJ, David and Jacen had been through, she knew it was time to give back.

"I'm going to be a surgeon."

SCENE XVIIII: SANDIEGO CALIFORNIA

"Are we having lunch today?"

Shannon. Jacen wadded up a piece of paper on his desk and threw it at the garbage can in the corner of the room. He blew out a small breath and rubbed his eye brows. He and Shannon had been dating off and on for over two years now and while he'd like to think that he had become a better Jacen, she was still the same Shannon.

"I can't today. I have other things to take care of."

"O.k. Don't forget we have the gala tomorrow in Vegas."

Jacen rolled his eyes. In the last two years he had been to more social parties and made more public appearances than he had in all of his life. His name had been plastered all over more tabloids and society magazines than he cared to be a part of.

"I'll be there, don't worry."

"I'm counting on it. See you soon."

"Bye."

Jacen hung up the phone and walked out into the font of the building to Meghan's desk. He waited patiently for her finish her own phone call before addressing him.

"Good morning, Jacen. To what do I owe the honor."

"Just wondering what is on the agenda today."

Meghan opened her date book on the computer and skimmed through the week.

"Well, Sir, Today is Thursday so you've got the board meeting at 9am. Your weekly lunch at the estate after you have a very important audience with a group of 4th graders."

"Ah, yes!" He said, smiling and slapping the top of her desk pretending that he had forgotten that he had volunteered to meet her daughter Samantha's 4th grade class and present information on what it's like to be young and in the hospital.

"Are you sure you don't mind?" She asked again. Jacen had always been such a private person and she knew he resented all the new publicity.

"I am honored. I adore Sam. I enjoy all your kids, Meghan. I do."

"So, do you have any plans for little people of your own?" Ten years ago she couldn't have asked him that without worrying he'd chop her head off in front of the entire company, but she felt like family now. So much so, that when she had branched out and invited J.R and Vickie down for Thanksgiving last year, they had come.

Jacen shrugged.

"Maybe. What's the hurry? I'm only 28. At least for four more hours!

Jacen walked through the foyer of the large house on the main estate and was amazed at how well preserved everything stayed after all of these years. The staff honored their well paid positions and the students had remained respectful of his family belongings as requested. As he made his way through the living area and kitchen towards the glass doors that led out to the patio by the pool he began to hear voices. He smiled as he recognized each intonation.

The deep bass of Dean, a Senior at UCLA studying biology among other things. Then came the squeaky, high pitches of Becky, a sociology major. He didn't hear Lyle, a good ol' boy from Georgia who had come here to finish graduate school for Veterinary Medicine but Jacen was sure he was lurking around somewhere. That was the thing about grad students, he thought, they didn't have quite as many classes, but more paperwork, so although Lyle talked less, he hung around more and that somehow didn't sit quite right with Jace. He himself had never pursued an education beyond high school graduation so he wasn't in a position to judge, but as he came around the kitchen corner and just as he had suspected, saw Lyle buried in paperwork and books with headphones in his ears, long red hair hanging in his face and an energy drink beside him, while the others were taking the usual Thursday lunch break, Jace wondered what drove a man like that. He stopped anyway and tried to get Lyle's attention. After a few attempts, Lyle finally looked up and took the headphones out of his ears.

"Sorry, Man, didn't see you there. Is everything alright with the house?" Lyle asked, addressing the man he regarded as their landlord. Jacen smiled.

"Every thing's fine, Lyle. I'm just here for my usual weekly lunch. Will you be joining us?" Jacen asked knowing the answer before the words were out of his mouth. Lyle began putting the headphones back in his ears and bending back to his books even as he answered.

"No, Man. I have to finish this paper by next week or I loose this class for next semester."

Jacen began heading outside before Lyle had finished his sentence. Outside, Dean and Becky were lounging by the pool, but both rose and came with drinks and hugs when they saw him coming. He knew they both had a little crush on him.

Becky was a 20 year old sophomore from Nevada with short brown hair and dark green eyes. She was suppose to be some kind of a genius with a super high IQ and a photographic memory, but Jacen found her to be extremely immature compared to her other roommates. Dean was an openly gay 21 year old who was so beautiful to the eyes of any man or woman that he supplemented his education with some modeling and acting on the side. Jacen was flattered by the flirting for even he had to admit that Dean was a magnificent man to look at, but since he was of a different persuasion, he and Dean had agreed to remain friends.

The three gathered together at the lounge table beside the pool. Jacen removed his jacket and tie, rolled up his sleeves, and called for a drink.

"What's new with you guys?" He asked and listened as they talked about school, social lives, and the house. This was always the best day of Jacen's week. The time that he got to spend here away from the business of his everyday life and delve into theirs was a great escape for him, but today something was missing.

"Where's...?" He was about to ask when the glass door opened and she came through followed by Meghan carrying a cardboard box. Dean and Jacen both jumped to their feet to race to help, but she shewed them both away as she smiled the biggest smile he had ever seen on her face. She set the box down in front of Jacen, opened it and removed a large, beautifully decorated cake with a number 2 candle and a number 9 candle on it. She lit the candles and looked at him still smiling. Jacen stood and when he did he was mere inches from her. Her face, her beautiful smile, her long, beautiful hair, her ocean deep eyes, and he was seeing her as if for the very first time after all of these years.

"Make a wish." She said. It was barely a whisper. He heard it clearer than he had heard anything before. He couldn't move, couldn't breathe.

Only twice before in his life had he ever felt so compelled to grab onto someone and never let go and those times he had only been dreaming.

Finally, she had waited long enough for him to make his move and she rolled her eyes at him, moved in front of him and blew out his candles herself. Dean clapped, Becky whistled, and Meghan frowned at him while the cake was removed from the table as lunch was being served. Jacen lowered his eyes as he sat back down again. She sat next to him. They listened to all of the chatter going on around them and after a few minutes, she reached out and took his hand in her own. Her hand, although it had been working very hard lately, was still soft, almost as if it was the quite part of her. Jacen felt forced to look up at her again.

"Were you surprised?" She asked. Jacen smiled. It was at that moment that he realized that he had been surprised. Not just by the birthday cake or the party, but by his new found revelation.

"I was very surprised. You pulled it off beautifully and Meghan didn't say a word." He said winking at his secretary who smiled back knowingly.

"You're welcome." Meghan said with a smile.

They ate lunch and laughed and everyone had a great time as they always did on Thursday afternoons. Then they sliced the cake and each person enjoyed a piece, still laughing and telling their favorite stories. As the afternoon turned into evening, Meghan said goodbye to return to her family. Jacen thanked her again and promised to see her the following day at the office. Dean agreed to escort Meghan safely to her car while Becky made her way back over to the swimming pool.

Sitting alone at last, Jacen turned and filled her glass with more red wine then leaned back in his seat to look at her. She was wearing a straight, white skirt that was long enough to cover her bare feet and a fitted tank that was very feminine despite her tom boy personality. Her hair was longer now than he had ever seen it and she had began to cut into layers which made her appear more mature than her 22 years. Always thin, always tan, but still the childlike freckles and still the blue eyes that he had always found a home in.

"Catherine, are we friends?" He asked. She sipped her wine, smiled at him and then laughed a little before answering.

"God, I hope so! I mean, after all of these years, you and I haven't got very many other friends to speak of do we? Besides, I don't want to owe some other benefactor I'm unfamiliar with for my giant student loan for the rest of my life! Why do you ask?"

Jacen shrugged.

"Here on the eve of my 29th birthday, I guess I just wonder where I stand with my life is all."

Catherine leaned forward, reached for his hand again, and gave him a comforting, confident smile.

"Jace, what are you really getting at? You can't possibly be insecure about our relationship. We are family and if you know nothing else, I know you know that. Is it Shannon? Is she giving you the cold shoulder lately?"

Jacen rolled his eyes and sighed.

"Exactly the opposite! She's clinging more than ever." Catherine shrugged.

"Does that bother you?"

Jacen stood then and began to walk towards the orchard. He turned and beckoned Catherine to follow. As they walked, the sounds of the ocean crashing on the shore came in and the sounds of Catherine's roommates began to fade.

"You and Shannon have been together a long time. Why?"

Jacen laughed recalling the conversation he had with Vickie on the phone all those years ago the last time he had seen CJ.

"I thought that I could change her. I knew she was shallow but she filled a place I thought I needed filled and now I think she wants something I can't give her.

Catherine stopped walking and turned toward the water. She crossed her arms in front of her as if she were pondering all these things. Jacen moved in front of her and watched the gentle breeze blow at her hair and watched her eyes narrow before she spoke again.

"I think that if you love someone, there are things that you are willing to change about yourself if you need to in order to co-exist together. It's called compromise, Jacen. You can't change people just to make them fit. If Sharron doesn't love you enough to compromise or let you be the way you are then be done with her. It's OK if she wants to be in the spot light and it's OK if you don't. If she won't see that, why are you trying so hard? If you aren't ready to spend you're life with her yet, then she's not the one. God, Jacen, for the smartest guy I know you're thick! I can't stand the way she uses you for your money and your status. You're better than that, and even without the money and the status, you're a pretty awesome guy. If all you had was your art and your surfing, We'd get by, you and I." She wiped a tear from her eye and walked away leaving Jacen standing in the wind dumbfounded.

Jacen left the estate and headed back to the penthouse feeling a mix of confusion and confidence. He went straight for the telephone and sat down to dial the number at the hotel in Las Vegas where he was suppose to be meeting Sharron the following evening. While he waited for them to answer, he looked up and over at the glass door that led into the library. The very library where Catherine had first discovered her sisters journal. Their first confrontation. The very thing that had torn between them had brought her back here. His mind brought back the picture of her collapsing on the floor in front of him in anger and exhaustion and spending the night there with him watching and waiting on the other side for passage and forgiveness. Here, now, on the phone alone, he realized how important Catherine had always been.

As he waited to make his phone connection, he began to recall all of his conversations with CJ and it all began to make sense. Every "she" and "her" began to fall into place. CJ's messages finally began to find clarity for him. Catherine had been the heart of the matter all along. It was Catherine that he was meant to help heal and she was meant to heal him as well and together they would teach the other how to forgive.

"Yes, I need to speak to room 123 please." He said when he got an answer on the other end of the line. He waited again for another answer.

"Hello?"

"Sharron. I need to talk to you."

"Hey, Babe! What time are you coming tomorrow?"

Jacen sighed.

"I'm not coming tomorrow."

"What do you mean? What's wrong?"

"When you get back we'll talk but I'm not coming to Vegas. I'll explain when you get back."   Jacen felt as if time stopped in that moment and yet he also felt a huge amount of release as if he had lost 110 pounds all in an instant. Finally she spoke again.

"Have I done something wrong?"

"No. I just need a change and so do you. I don't want to be disrespectful to you by leaving it this way, Sharron, so we'll talk more when you get back. I just wasn't coming tomorrow and I thought you should know why."

"Is there someone else?"

What could he say? Jacen had never lied to anyone. He had even made it a point in his life to be bold and sometimes brutally blunt. He had cared deeply for Sharron for a long time, but Catherine mattered so much more. Would he betray the one by revealing the other?

"Yes." He said simply, honestly. The pause that followed was longer, quieter.

"I see." Was all she said before she hung up. Jacen flinched at the force of the click. Jacen picked up the phone again and dialed another number.

"Hello?"

"Mom?"

"Jacen! Happy Birthday! Good to hear from you, but if you're calling this late, is everything o.k?"

Jacen smiled. Vickie the caring.

"Yeah. I broke up with Sharron and Catherine's mad at me, but I think it's a good day."

He waited for Vickie to size all of the information up and absorb it. After a moment, Vickie spoke again.

"So, Catherine finally made it clear to you that she didn't think Sharron was good enough and in this revelation she let it slip that you matter more to her than you used to and she's mad at you because she let her guard down and she's afraid you don't feel the same."

Jacen thought it was uncanny the way that Vickie could see clearly all of the things that he was feeling as well as know her daughter despite Catherine's distance.

"Here's my big question, Mom. What if I find that I do feel the same? Would that concern you? What if I've realized that I am in love with Catherine?"

He had expected Vickie to pause a long time the way that Sharron had. However, Vickie who loved them both, spoke with confidence and clarity.

"I hope that you do. It would mean that God has finally brought this family full circle and all that we have lost has not been in vain. It would bring together the best in both of you."

"So I'm not crazy?" Vickie laughed.

"We're all a little loony in this family and that's why you fit in! Take care of your heart and hers, Jace. I wish only happiness for you both. May this finally bring the healing that you both have needed all this time. However, expect a little bit of a hard time from her father and brother. It will all be in fun, but they will torture you. Just thought I should warn you."

Jacen smiled.

"Thanks, Mom. I'll call later, if and when Cath starts talking to me again."

"Oh, Jace, hang up the phone and call her. She's ready. You'll never guess which hot tempered daughter I was talking to before you called."

Catherine sat up and rubbed her eyes. She had taken three days off from the hospital during spring break this week and she was looking forward to the much needed rest. She thought that she had heard something lurking in her room so she slowly reached into her night stand drawer beside her bed to grab the can of pepper spray Jacen had given her when she had first moved in four years earlier.   "Shh" a voice sitting on the couch in the corner of her room said.

"I didn't mean to wake you."

Catherine leaned forward and swung her legs over the side of bed. She was wearing her Super girl pajamas but she was feeling a little violated and vulnerable at that moment.

"Jacen?"

The figure came forward a little and she could see Jacen's silhouette in the moon light. His dark spiky hair glittered and his dark eyes were pools of blackness.

"I always find it odd that you came back to this house and this room. You always give away the master suite." Even in the moonlight Catherine could see the whale painting and the shelf next to it where she always kept her family pictures.

"This is where you were before me. It makes me feel a little closer to you. I love the painting. Why are you here? It's the middle of the night, is something wrong?"

Jacen Shrugged, but made no effort to leave.

"I can go if you want."

Catherine stood and walked over to open the sliding glass door to let in the breeze. It was still warm out and the warmth felt good on her bare arms and yet knowing Jacen was here, in her room with her now gave her goose bumps. She felt like she was fifteen again and she was sneaking a boy in through the downstairs window. Jacen stood and fell in behind her.

"I think Sharron should know where you are." She said not looking at him. She could feel his breath on her skin behind her but she didn't dare turn and be that close to him she thought. It was getting too hard now. When she was younger, it was a battle between them of who had lost the most and she wanted to be angrier than he, but somewhere, in all these years as she had grown to accept that they had lost equally she had grown to care more for him that she had wanted to and she was afraid now that he would leave her here in this place for his model girlfriend who didn't deserve him. Not that she knew she did, but for all that they had suffered and understood about one another, perhaps they just belonged together.

"I broke up with Sharron. It's over." A sigh of relief. She hoped he hadn't caught it. He did.

"How are you?"

He reached out and put a tentative arm gently around her shoulder and drew her body in so that her back was touching his chest and his chin rested on the top of her head. She stiffened but only for a moment before she relaxed and leaned into him. It was as if they were designed to be a perfect fit. "I feel relief" He told her.

"You were right."

She laughed.

"About which part."

"All of it."

They stood there for a long time before his other arm came around and rested on her waist. She placed a hand on each of his arms and they swayed together there looking out the window waiting for the sun to come up. Finally Catherine turned and looked up into Jacen's face as if really seeing him for the first time. As many times as he had looked deeply into her eyes, she was finally able to look into his and see his soul. She saw all of the things that she had forgotten belonged there.

CJ's heart, his missing family, his longing for love. All of the things that she herself had needed. In the darkness there she saw that they were two halves of the same whole.

"How long have you known?" He asked. It had all seemed so sudden to him this afternoon, and yet, here he was, looking at her, as he always had since she was thirteen, the same girl, the same pool of eyes, and it was as if he were finally coming home again.

She slid her hands up to cup his face and drew him closer to her. She touched his lips with her own so softly and sweetly he felt as if a butterfly had brushed by him. Even when a moment later her kiss became deeper and more urgent, it was still light as feather, soft as a whisper.

"Probably a year or so now. You?"

"Today. But you did point out I was thick."

Jacen guided her back deeper into the room closed the glass door and drew the blinds. When he turned again, Catherine had already shed her clothing and began undressing him. As he was clumsily helping her with his pants and shoes, she froze and looked into his eyes again pleading with him.

"Are you sure about this?"

He gazed down at her. In the moonlight, her silhouette showed perfect curves in all the right places, but Jacen's focus was on her face and her eyes. Always her eyes. Jacen laid her gently on the bed he hadn't slept in since he was fifteen and stroked her hair. He kissed her again with a gentleness and tenderness that could only come from having loved her since time had began. His fingers interlaced with hers as their bodies melted together to become one. He poured into her over and over and she cried out, but never in pain, only in release. They both shed tears, but no longer of loss, only of finally recognizing that this was home and the other was the cornerstone. The sun came up and was high in the sky before they collapsed together in exhaustion.

"My god, Woman, I think I'm going to have to call out for the day. I can't go to work like this!"

He said tucking her body close to his. She rolled over so she was facing him and peeked at his naked body under the covers then looked up at him and giggled.

"Sure you can. You're the boss!" She teased. They both laughed and then Jacen reached up to move a stray strand of blond hair away from her eyes while she traced his scars with her delicate fingers.

"How could I have been so lost all this time?" He wondered aloud.

"Blind leading the blind. We're better now, though, right? Eyes open?" She asked. He kissed her button, freckled nose.

"I've never seen more clearly, Cath."

Jacen kissed Cath one more time before making his way into the bathroom and turned on the shower. Catherine reached over and picked up the phone.

"Owen Medical Supplies and Pharmaceuticals, Jacen Owen's office, how may I help you?"

"Good morning Meghan."

"Good morning, Catherine. How are you today?"

"Never better! I was just calling to let you know that Jacen may be coming in very late today if at all. I'm sorry."

"Don't be. Is he with you? You don't have to tell me. It's really none of my business, it's just that there was an angry message from Sharron this morning on his voice mail, and I have wanted this for you both for so long."

Catherine sighed.

"Yes, Meghan. He's here with me. Thank you. I'll let him tell you more when he's ready."

"Well, have a great day both of you. Congratulations." Catherine hung up and joined Jacen in the shower.

"You called in. You don't have to go to work today."

"Thanks!" Jacen said as he shampooed her hair.

The next few days were filled with making love and eating in. Jacen had never known that a relationship didn't have to be about a public forum or devoted fans while Catherine was finally able to explore expanding boundaries.

They even found that disagreeing was refreshing because it allowed them to be individuals and find ways to compromise.

The last night of Catherine's time off, they built a bon fire on the beach and brought down food, drinks and desert.

"So, Dr. Stewart, how much longer do you have for school?"

Jacen asked. He was very proud of how hard she had worked all these years here. She had exceeded his expectations. When she had arrived at 18, he hadn't known if she had the chops to keep up with the grueling schedule that medical school demanded, but she had buckled down from the beginning with a full load and when she had asked, he had hired tutors and she had even worked every year through summer school to complete some of her programs earlier.

"Well," She began, "I will take my MCAT in the fall, and if I pass,"

"You'll pass." Jacen reassured her. Cath rolled her eyes. Every doctor everywhere had to pass their boards to become an MD, but every doctor everywhere lost sleep for months before the exam. She continued.

"If I pass, I will go on to grad school in the fall and complete three to four years of surgical internship."

"How can I help?" Jacen asked running his fingers through her silky long hair. She smiled.

"You help by keeping me from throwing any more books at the wall." She teased.

"How is the journal holding up?"

Catherine fell back in the sand and laughed harder as she recalled the memory of how she had once destroyed the book and yet he had found a way to push back and restore it. Then Jace pulled himself and Cath up.

"I'll race you back to the house and we can read through it together. Won't that be fun? Besides, there might just be new surprises in it you haven't seen before."

Jacen grabbed a bucket and filled it with ocean water to douse the fire.

"I'm intrigued." she said as he made sure the flames were completely out.

"When should we start our big race?" He asked. Catherine started running at a full sprint kicking sand up at him.

"Go!" She called back to him over her shoulder. The race was on! Although Catherine had been born with asthma, she was CJ and David's sister. She was genetically built for speed and when she took off at a dead run with a head start, Jacen didn't stand a chance at catching up with her even with all his daily running and surfing. When they reached the patio with Dean and Becky cheering, they collapsed against each other laughing.

"You cheated!" Jacen accused.

"Of course I did. I'm not CJ!"

Jacen grabbed her by her arms first and then, once he had his breath under control he held her face in his hands and kissed her deeply for a long time.

"I know who you are, Catherine."

Was all that he said before guiding her by the hand into the house through the kitchen.

"Having a nice time?"

Jacen looked up from Catherine and the others as they made their way through the kitchen to see a shadow standing near the foyer. His gut churned and Jacen moved Catherine behind him instinctively.

"Sharron, why are you here?"

Sharron moved out of the shadows and closer towards the kitchen, into the light where they could see her a little better. Her face was pulled tight and her lips were a thin line of anger.

"I could ask you the same thing." She replied dryly.

"I live here." He answered.

"No." She corrected.

"You live in a penthouse two miles away. This is your parents house that you lease to UCLA students one of whom you had introduced to me as your sister. I have recently learned that she's not related to you at all. She's the sister of the dead girl you got the heart from."

"What's your point Sharron?" Jacen tightened his grip on Catherine behind him. Dean and Becky had moved back out on the patio and called the police just in case.

"THE POINT IS...." Sharron began, her tone sharp and biting,

"That you have ruined our relationship and my reputation apparently for a mediocre small town girl with nothing."

"O.k." Jacen said. Catherine poked him with a finger biting back her own anger.

"O.k?" Sharron mumbled the aggression becoming more and more apparent.

"O.k I left you for someone who doesn't need or want my money or status. She loves me for my baggage and because we share this broken and used heart. She came to me expecting nothing from me and for that I'm going to give her everything that I have."

The shot that rang out cracked the air, shattered the glass behind Catherine's head and sent an echo of screams that rippled from Catherine to Dean to Becky and back again.

Jacen fell in Catherine's arms. Catherine look up to see Sharron raise her arm again to fire another shot when out of the west corner of the room a football flew threw the air and pinged her in the side of the head, causing her to stumble back, grab her head with both hands dropping the gun. Lyle kicked the weapon away and pinned Sharron down.

"Cops are coming up the drive." He said as he held Sharron in place. Becky was weeping uncontrollably while Dean tried to assess the situation as best he could. Catherine fell back against the cabinets and heaved Jacen up against her looking into his eyes.

"Jace, baby, please talk to me. Are you alright?" Jacen coughed up a little bit of blood and Catherine sobbed. She laid him down gently and tried to examine him. She tore his shirt off and tried to clear away the blood to figure out where it was coming from but there was too much and she became desperate.

"Becky, I need a hot wet towel NOW!" She yelled to her roommate who was still screaming.

"O.k, O.k," Becky said running hot water at the sink and grabbing a large towel from the bathroom.

The police arrived then, took Sharron into custody and began asking questions. Once paramedics had arrived and the blood had been cleared away, It was clear that the bullet had entered the left side of the chest.

"NO!"

Catherine collapsed in a heap on the kitchen floor next to Jacen who had lost so much blood, he was unconscious. As the paramedics were loading him on the gurney and moving him towards the ambulance, Catherine stumbled along with him lacing her fingers with his.

One of the paramedics looked over at her left shoulder, noticed that it was oozing blood and stopped her.

"Miss, your shoulder, it's bleeding. We need to check that out."

Catherine pushed past him in an effort to stay with Jacen. The paramedic tried to restrain her. He called for help. Dean stood by her.

"Cath, you're bleeding pretty bad, let them check you."

"No, I need to stay with him!" She protested. The paramedic held her gaze firmly.

"We'll all go the same place, Miss. He needs to go now. We'll check you out and get you there right behind him."

As he peeled back her shirt sleeve, her shoulder began to bleed freely. Dean frank passed out. The paramedic rolled his eyes as he unravelled a piece of gauze to press firmly against her shoulder to suppress the bleeding. Catherine flinched from the pain.

After a moment or two he peeled away the gauze to reveal a small hole in shoulder the size of a bullet. He checked the posterior shoulder and didn't see an exit wound. He pressed the gauze again firmly and yelled to both police and more paramedics.

"Hey! I think I found our bullet! Check on this guy and make sure he didn't hit his head when he passed out." He said referring to Dean who was out cold on the kitchen floor face down in Jacen's blood.

"We need to get her to surgery to get that bullet out."

Catherine was vaguely aware of being headed towards the front door and out to another waiting ambulance. Jacen had been on his way to the hospital for about ten minutes now and was pulling into the ambulance bay she guessed. This was where her mind was as they moved her gurney towards a waiting ambulance to follow.

Then she saw her. She was still standing outside the police car in hand cuffs giving statements not to the police at this point, but to the press?

"Stop. Stop!" She shouted to the EMT's as they were moving down the walkway. She watched as this woman who's only agenda during her relationship with Jacen was to achieve power and status was still trying to manipulate the system into thinking that she was somehow a victim in this scenario. Catherine's eyes narrowed with rage and as the fury built within and she began to unstrap herself and she jumped off the still moving gurney and stumbled towards Sharron. One slow, small step at a time and then faster and faster until she was almost upon her.

"You, might have killed him, you low life Bitch!" Catherine yelled at her lunging for her. A police officer grabbed her before she could reach Sharron.

"I'm better than both of you and I hope he does die!" Sharron shot back.

Catherine smiled and began to relax when she realized that Sharron just buried herself. Her eyes glazed over as she watched them place a handcuffed Sharron in the back of a police cruiser.

"You don't look better to me right now."

Then Catherine passed out.

———

The unbelievable pain shooting through Catherine's arm woke her and she screamed aloud. Kyle reached over and pressed the button that would send pain relief instantaneously. It took her a good fifteen minutes before she felt roused enough to look around the room. Vickie, J.R., Audrey, Kyle, David, Becky, Dean, even Lyle were there waiting for her to wake and let them know she was o.k. It was good to have so much support. She had always been the supporter.

"Jacen. When are they going to release him? He was hurt the worse. When can he go home?"

It was amazing the way all the faces in a room could go from happy to somber in a second. Catherine had been working in a hospital doing her clinical long enough to know what their faces meant. She could read the signs. She had been seeing that look since she was twelve.

"What happened?" She asked Kyle. He shrugged and then sat on the side of the bed and took her hand in his own.

"She shot him in the heart and he died almost instantly. I'm sorry, Catherine. I'm sorry to all of you. I know that it's not just Jacen that you lost but that was the last piece of CJ you had."

Just then a police officer entered the room.

"Excuse me folks, My name is Detective Carmichael, and I couldn't help overhearing. Could you please explain? Is this a double homicide?"

So they explained. They told the story of the remarkable eighteen year old girl, loved by many who lost her life, but in doing so donated her heart to a young man who thought he didn't need or want anybody. Through that experience, that young man gained a whole family, and they regained the heart of their dead daughter, sister and friend.

"She will pay, folks. We have the gun, the bullets, and all the witnesses. It's a done deal." Catherine's tears spilled over and fell down her cheeks as did everyone else's.

"It's not enough." Catherine told the officer.

"If you can't bring either of them back. It's not enough."

SCENE XX: SANDIEGO CALIFORNIA:UCLA MEDICAL CENTER

Vickie had been in more hospitals than she knew what to do with. Perhaps she was in the wrong line of business. Perhaps she should be seeking a career in the medical profession. She could give tours. The elevators were usually in the same places, as were the ICU, the CCU, ER,etc..

It had been a while since she had visited the NICU though and never had she been to this one at UCLA Medical Center she thought. Hope I can find it, she wondered. The hospital seemed to be well marked and she hadn't had to ask anyone for help so far.

She made her way to the labor and delivery area first and stopped at the nurses station.

"I'm here to visit Dr. Catherine Owen, please."

The nurse smiled and led her down the corridor to her daughters delivery room. She loved to say "doctor" in front of Catherine's name now and she did it as often as she could. Catherine had passed her MCAT's last summer which officially had made her an MD. She still had other boards she would have to pass to be certified in to be a surgeon and more schooling but a doctor was doctor damn it!

Catherine had taken Jacen's name also. After every one had left and Catherine had been given time to absorb all that had happened, Meghan had called Vickie to inform her that Jacen had bought Cath a ring. He had hidden it inside CJ's journal and had intended to propose that night when both of their worlds went black. She felt that Catherine should still have the ring since Jacen also changed his will and left everything, the company, stocks, all of it to her, knowing that if anything happened to him, she would ask her mother and her mother in turn would work with the board of trusties to continue to build the company and not destroy it. Vickie and Meghan together had gone and retrieved the ring and presented it to Catherine at the time that seemed appropriate. When they felt that she was ready to receive it. Thankfully Jacen had left a letter with it expressing the depth of his everlasting love for her. With the ring, the letter and her anger still intact, Catherine had gone to the judge presiding over Jacen's case and asked if they could be married. It was unprecedented but with Kyle agreeing to stand in for Jacen, and the Judge, having reviewed the case, and a tender heart, for he himself had lost a daughter to violence, agreed. Jacen and Catherine were married four months after his death.

Now it had been eight and a half months and Vickie was here again in the same hospital where Jacen had both received CJ's heart and that same heart had stopped beating again. She had to stop outside of Catherine's room and weep a little. She wept for a daughter lost, for grandchildren born, for relationships severed and for relationships healed. She also wept for a son lost. The door opened and Catherine stood there waiting for her.

"Mom?" Catherine, still in her hospital gown and robe even though she'd been there a whole two days already, gathered her mother in her arms and hugged her close.

"I know, Mom. It's o.k." She said. Peace. Peace that passes from daughter to mother.

"Do you want to see them?"

Vickie wiped the tears from her eyes and nodded her head.

"Yeah? o.k.!"

Catherine guided her mother down the hall to the NICU where they could see all the little babies from a window. Catherine put on a protective yellow paper gown and then dressed Vickie in the same so that they could go in to the unit. Once inside the doors, Catherine guided her mother to the far corner of the room where two small bassinets lie side by side.

Inside each was swaddled a tiny little bundle of a baby one in pink and one in blue. One bassinet was labeled "baby boy Owen" and the other, "Baby Girl Owen". Catherine was beaming as she rested her head on her own mother's shoulders while they looked down at the new members of the Stewart family together.

"Mom," Catherine said as she picked up each of the babies and laid one in each of her mothers arms.

"I'd like you meet Carmen Joselin, and Jacen David Owen."

Vickie eased herself down onto a rocking chair behind her and kissed each baby in turn.

"hello, C.J., hello, J.D." They both had their father's dark hair.

"I think they look a little like their dad!" Vickie said. She looked at Catherine who looked wistfully out the widow to the world outside.

"Dimples and all." She said looking back again at her children.

As the day wore on, Vickie and Catherine returned to Catherine's delivery room so Catherine could get some more rest. Vickie helped her daughter to bed and then settled in to the rocking chair by the window.

"So what's the plan, Cath?" Catherine laid the bed back to a more comfortable position and settled in. She sighed heavily.

"I'll hire a nanny and finish school. I'll testify at Sharron's trial and every parol hearing to make sure she never sees the light of day. As a family we'll make sure that my children always know who their father was, what a big heart he had, where it came from, and that he loved each and every one of us for always." As an afterthought she said, "I wish he could know, Mom."

"Know what, Cath?"

"Neither of the kids were born with his congenital heart defect. They are whole and perfect."

Vickie smiled. She was at peace. Peace comes in the knowing that you have done all that can to love, honor and protect what you can, and let God have the rest.

ENCORE:

"Sharron Malone parole hearing case: 233214"

The room was small and there were only a few parties allowed in the chambers. This would not be the circus that the original trial had been seven years earlier. At the front of the room were a panel of six people, all of whom sat at a table across from Sharron and her lawyer. Seven years in prison now had stripped Sharron of her class, her status, money and fame. Oh, she was infamous for sure. Still, there was a striking beauty about her as she sat waiting to be addressed.

"Miss Malone. On September 4th 2001, you shot Jacen Owen in his home in front of witnesses, do you deny this?" The first member of the panel addressed her. Admit and repent her lawyer had told her.

"It was not his home exactly, but yes, this is true, the gun I was holding did go off and he was killed."

Her lawyer kicked her under the table. She had done what he asked hadn't she? Truths

"Do you feel as if you're time has rehabilitated you?" Another panel member asked. They did not look pleased so far. Sharron began then to pour on the charm. She talked of all of things that she had done in the last seven years to improve the health and welfare of her fellow inmates. How hard she had worked to find fault and forgiveness for her crimes. The panel discussed amongst themselves briefly and then asked for witnesses to testify.

At that moment, the door at the back of the room swung open and three people came strolling in. A tall thin man in a grey suit with his long brown hair pulled back in a tight pony tail, A greying man, well manicured in a dark suit, and leading them both, a woman in a pantsuit with her blond hair pulled high and tight in a neat bun and a pair of sharp looking glasses on the tip of her nose. She was carrying a folder that she kept tucked close to her chest. They came in and sat down at the table next to Sharron, not glancing over.

"Mr. Stewart, and Dr's Alyster and Owen we presume?" the panel addressed them.

"We are all here, thank you for hearing us today." They answered.

"Then let us begin. We have already heard from Miss Malone so Dr. Owen, if you are ready, please..."

Catherine stood then, opened her folder and approached both the parol panel and the defense table her with her case.

"What are these?" Demanded Sharron's lawyer when Cath presented photos.

"These," Cath said firmly, "Are the faces of the children that Jacen will never see because in her jealous rage she stripped that from them. These are the babies that can never know the man who donated money and time to others. Who's face they bare a striking likeness too."

The panel passed around the pictures of CJ and JD at various ages. Some were taken of them laughing by the pool with their father's dimples. Cath had photoshopped the pictures to superimpose Jacen in with them so they could see the resemblance. Some of the pictures were with her taking them to the Albion Cemetery where they went often to pay their respects to all of their loved ones. There were pictures from the earlier years of everyone with Jacen laughing and loving.

Catherine turned to Sharron.

"What you took wasn't yours."

Sharron smirked. She couldn't help it.

"Doesn't look like it's much yours anymore either, does it?" she whispered hoping the panel couldn't hear her. In seven years, she had not changed.

"God dammit, Sharron!" Her lawyer hissed under his breath.

Catherine rushed to the panel and took a picture of the children and flung it at Sharron who had not known about them until now. Catherine, per her own lawyers advice, had kept the pregnancy a secret and out of the press during the original trial.

"I got the best parts, Woman. Never forget that."

She said moving herself mere inches from Sharron's still perfect nose. Sharron, who was handcuffed to the table leg and flanked by an officer couldn't escape her.

"Enough!" The panel shouted. "Dr. Owen, please return to your seat. We have made our decision." Catherine sat again between David and Kyle and griped each of their hands under the table in turn.

"Sharron Malone, for the crime of Murder in the first degree which you have committed against Jacen Owen, you will remain incarcerated. It has been made evident to us during these proceeding that you have been sufficiently rehabilitated. We will not need to deliberated further. Parol had been denied. We will revisit this again at the time of 7 to 10 years or at such a time as a judge should deem otherwise justified. You are all dismissed."

As Catherine, Kyle and David were leaving, Catherine took one of the pictures of her children and pressed it into Sharron's palm tightly.

"The very best parts." She repeated again before leaving the room with her brother holding onto her hand.

Cath, David and Kyle left the courtroom with Sharron shouting at her lawyer in the background. Outside, Kyle squeezed Catherine.

"I'll see you around. Tell that old Fart, Perkins that I said hello. And bring those kids by to see me once in a while."

"I will. Thank you, Kyle. Jacen would have been grateful."

After he left, David and Cath continued their walk. It was only a mile back to the penthouse. Catherine had never sold it. She kept it and the staff and used it as a guest house for when family came to visit. She still lived at the main house in spite of what had happened there. In time, after she had finished being angry and then sad, it began to bring her comfort. As her belly had begun to expand and she began to feel the moving and life beginning anew inside of her, she believed that she should stay where she and Jacen had began.

"So, what now, Cath?" David asked. She shrugged.

"Now, I'm still waiting for the court order to exhume Jacen's parents bodies and move them back home."

"why, Cath? I thought he hated his father. What difference does it make now?"

Catherine stopped walking along the boardwalk and looked out over the water.

"It's about family and forgiveness, David. You will be buried there, I might live here and raise my children here, but I want to be buried there. It all comes full circle. Life, love, loss. Jacen's family belongs with him, with us." They began walking again.

"Speaking of buried things. Cath, I was digging around a little and I discovered this."

David pulled a faded piece of paper out of his pocket and handed it to Catherine. She unfolded it and squinted at it. The writing was small, sloppy and transparent, but she recognized it.

"Where did you find this?" David laughed.

"You didn't bury it deep enough. Soil shifts a little over time. That's why when they bury people they put them down so deep."

Catherine read the letter she had written while CJ was in the ICU all those years ago and then when her mother had given it back to her, she had buried it beside CJ's grave.

"Dear CJ,

I know that when you wake up you will have a lot of things you will want to say and do and people to see before me. I just wanted you to know that I have realized that I love you more than I ever thought I possibly could and I wish you could just open your eyes and see me thinking and feeling these things right now. Please wake up and help me understand what is happening. I need you, miss you and love you. Love, Catherine."

Catherine looked up at David and blinked back tears.

"Thank you." she whispered.

David hugged her. He had been hugging Cath her whole life. He imagined he always would. Parents would leave at some point in ones life, a spouse one chose a quarter way though one's life, but a sibling was the only true life partner a person ever has.

"Let's go get the kids and go home for a while. Even the best surgeon needs a vacation." Catherine looked back towards the courthouse one last time.

"I'll call Meghan and make the arrangements." She said. It was time to go home again and she was ready. She had been working long hard hours lately and hadn't seen her parents in nearly two years. It was time to go back and be less the Dr and more the mother and daughter she wished to be.

"I'll call Mom." David said.

"Don't bother." Catherine retorted.

"I'm sure she knows we're coming. If I know Meghan, she was on the phone the minute we left that building, because I know Kyle called her."

Vickie was home in Washington making arrangements for her son, daughter and grandchildren to return home again. She began making the usual phone calls and assembling all of the usual family members for the reunion. They would all be together again as it should be. Family filling a room, eating, drinking, crying, laughing and loving for always.

ACKNOWLEDGEMENTS:

I imagine that the question that I am going to be asked the most is what is fact and what is fiction? So, I would just like to say that this is fiction in whole. The story was inspired by a single significant event in my life that led me to several what if's. What if the girl in the accident doesn't make it? Had she done enough in eighteen years? How does the family cope? As individuals? As a whole? Can they help others cope?

Based on the inspiring people in my life, this how I imagine a story like that might unfold. Oh, and there has to be an imaginary billionaire who gets the girl and lots and lots of heartache and trauma that's not real or what's the point, right? I mean, my real life isn't that exciting!

Thank you always to my mother who when I asked how I put such a phenomenal woman to paper she replied simply, "just fold and flatten.". You have always inspired me achieve great things. You believed I could when they said I never would. If I am ever half the woman you are, then I will have accomplished great things.

Thanks Dad for overcoming and being my buddy. You are greater than you know.

Chris, I admire you daily for all that are and all that you pretend you're not. I know who you really are.

J.B., You have become one of my greatest friends. Who'd a thunk?

Nan and Gramps. I aspire to have what you had always. I hope you are proud.

Aunt Carol, Uncle Bob, Aunt Bonnie, Uncle Ron, You were there when it happened at you ought to know. You have your place in my heart always.

Cory, Alex and Sam: Always patient and understanding through this process. Thank you. I love you.

Debbie: Thanks for all the books!

To those of you who might find familiar places and memories here in these pages, enjoy your walk through. I wrote it with you in mind as well. Although none of the people are real nor the events, the places do exist.

Sincerely, Cara Maddy

Breinigsville, PA USA
21 September 2009
224468BV00001B/22/P